27/10

DYING FOR JUSTICE

Books by L.J. Sellers

The Detective Jackson Series
The Sex Club
Secrets to Die For
Thrilled to Death
Passions of the Dead
Dying for Justice
Liars, Cheaters & Thieves
Rules of Crime

~~

The Lethal Effect
(Previously published as *The Suicide Effect*)
The Baby Thief
The Gauntlet Assassin

DYING FOR JUSTICE

A DETECTIVE JACKSON MYSTERY

L.J. SELLERS

THOMAS & MERCER

Published by Thomas & Mercer
P.O. Box 400818
Las Vegas, NV 89140

ISBN-13: 9781612186207
ISBN-10: 1612186203

Library of Congress Control Number: 2012943268

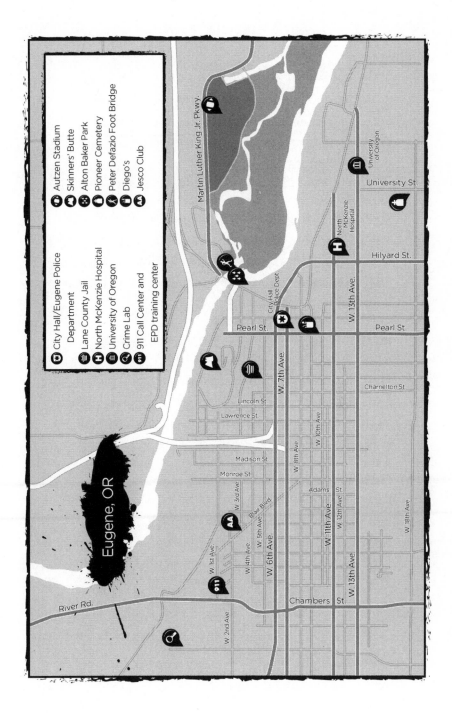

Eugene, OR

Legend

- 🏛 City Hall/Eugene Police Department
- ▥ Lane County Jail
- Ⓗ North McKenzie Hospital
- ▤ University of Oregon
- 🔍 Crime Lab
- 911 911 Call Center and EPD training center

- Ⓐ Autzen Stadium
- ▥ Skinners' Butte
- ⊞ Alton Baker Park
- 🪦 Pioneer Cemetery
- ⚔ Peter Defazio Foot Bridge
- Ⓓ Diego's
- Ⓙ Jesco Club

Martin Luther King Jr. Pkwy.

University of Oregon

University St.

North McKenzie Hospital

Hilyard St.

City Hall Police Dept.

Pearl St.   Pearl St.

W. 13th Ave.

W. 7th Ave.

Charnelton St.

Lincoln St.

Lawrence St.

W. 10th Ave.

W. 8th Ave.

Madison St.

Monroe St.

Adams St.

W. 3rd Ave.

W. 11th Ave.

W. 12th Ave.

W. 18th Ave.

Blair Blvd.

W. 1st Ave.

W. 4th Ave.

W. 5th Ave.

W. 6th Ave.

W. 13th Ave.

911

Chambers St.

River Rd.

W. 2nd Ave.

Cast of Characters

Wade Jackson: veteran detective/violent crimes unit
Kera Kollmorgan: Jackson's girlfriend/nurse
Katie Jackson: Jackson's daughter
Rob Schakowski (Schak): detective/task force member
Lara Evans: detective/task force member
Michael Quince: detective/task force member
Denise Lammers: Jackson's supervisor/sergeant
Sophie Speranza: newspaper reporter
Rich Gunderson: medical examiner/attends crime scenes
Jasmine Parker: evidence technician
Joe Berloni: evidence technician
Rudolph Konrad: pathologist/performs autopsies
Victor Slonecker: district attorney
Jim Trang: assistant district attorney
Clark & Evelyn Jackson: Jackson's parents/homicide victims
Hector Vargas: inmate/confessed to killing Jackson's parents
Gina Stahl: assault victim/two-year coma
George & Sharon Stahl: Gina's parents
Gary Bekker: Gina's ex-husband/police sergeant
Rick Santori: internal affairs detective
Ben Stricklyn: internal affairs detective
Ray Durkin: ex-loan shark turned business owner
Joni Farmer: heroin addict/sexual assault victim
Tricia Cronin: prostitute/ sexual assault victim
Steve and Gloria Hutchins: Gina's neighbors/witnesses

DYING FOR JUSTICE

CHAPTER 1

Sunday, September 5, 8:05 a.m.

Gina opened her eyes, taking in the white blanket and blue-scrub nurse. Her first thought was, *This is a hospital.* Her second thought was, *Someone tried to kill me.* She wanted to speak, but her throat was dry. "Water, please," she managed to say, sounding weak and scratchy.

The nurse jumped, eyes popping open in surprise. She fumbled in her pocket for a cell phone and ran from the room. Gina wanted to call after her, but she had no strength. She'd been half-awake off and on for what seemed like weeks, but this was the first time someone was in the room when she had the clarity and strength to speak. How long had she been in the hospital?

The nurse returned after a few minutes with more medical people—a woman in a white doctor's coat and a man in a suit. The nurse offered Gina some water, and the woman in white said, "I'm Dr. Ellison. Do you know where you are?"

"A hospital?"

"Not exactly." The doctor smiled gently.

A wave of apprehension rolled over Gina.

"This is a long-term-care facility."

Dread seeped into her fragile bones. "How long have I been here?"

The doctor hesitated. "Two years."

Two years? Gina closed her eyes. No. This was just another strange dream. She'd had a lot of unpleasant dreams lately.

"Gina, stay with us."

The voice sounded real. The blanket between her fingers felt soft, textured, and real. The feeding tube in her belly ached with real pain. Gina opened her eyes again. "Two years?" She remembered being forty-four. That would make her forty-six now.

"I know this is difficult to process, but the important thing is that you survived. And now you're awake." The doctor kept smiling.

A terrifying memory flooded Gina's senses, making her heart pound. The masked man had been in her dreams sometimes, but this was different. Gina practiced the words in her head first, then struggled to say, "He tried to kill me."

The group at her bedside registered a collective look of surprise, followed by disbelief. Again, the doctor was the first to speak. "Your file says you took an overdose of Valium and Demerol. Do you remember that?"

"No." Gina shook her head. Her brain felt fuzzy, as if she were about to drift off, but she desperately wanted to say something. "I was attacked."

The medical people looked at each other, puzzled. The man in the suit said, "There's no record of that in your file."

The nurse gently touched Gina's arm. "Would you like me to call the police?"

Gina would have laughed, but she didn't have the energy. Two years had passed, and the bastard would likely get away with it. Was anything left of her life out there? Despair washed over her, and she fought back tears. "Yes. Call the cops."

"I'll do it now." The nurse left the room.

The man in the suit followed, saying, "Let's keep this low-key."

Gina fought to stay awake. She'd been asleep for so long. Yet a wave of fog rolled over her, and she drifted. Before she went under again, a small piece of her life before this room bubbled to the surface. She'd been compiling evidence against her soon-to-be-ex-husband. *What had happened to the notebook?*

CHAPTER 2

Detective Wade Jackson held the envelope in the tips of his fingers while the pit of his stomach went cold. The postmark was labeled *Oregon State Penitentiary*, the name below it, *Hector Vargas*. How could a man's name make him tremble? Jackson dropped the letter on the table, where it had been buried in a pile of mail since he'd brought it from work yesterday. Vargas was doing a life sentence for the murder of his parents, Clark and Evelyn Jackson. Ten years earlier, they had been shot for the money they'd kept in a small cashbox in their bedroom, their thousand-dollar emergency fund.

Why was Vargas contacting him now? To offer an apology as part of his making-amends program? Jackson didn't want an apology or the burden of forgiveness. He didn't think about Vargas often, but when he did, contempt seemed appropriate. He felt entitled to a single case of hatred.

"Who's the letter from?" Katie said, through a mouthful of scrambled eggs. His fifteen-year-old daughter was dieting again, eating a lot of protein and few carbs, but he knew better than to comment on food and weight issues.

Jackson hesitated. "A man in prison."

"That's creepy." Katie shook her curly brown hair and reached for the salsa. "Why is he writing to you?"

"I don't know yet."

"Open it. I'm curious."

"He murdered my parents."

Her round little face fell. "Oh. That man. This must be really strange for you." Katie had been a toddler when her grandparents died, and she didn't remember them.

"It's strange, all right." Jackson took a sip of strong black coffee. "What are you doing today?" His daughter would start high school the next day, and he worried about her constantly.

"I'm going for a run, then hanging out with Zoe." Katie stood and studied his face, then gestured at the letter. "Just rip it open like you tear off a band-aid. Like you always say, pain is temporary." She kissed his forehead and left the table.

Jackson fingered the envelope again. Another load of emotional bullshit was the last thing he needed right now. Katie didn't need it either. Renee, his ex-wife and Katie's poor excuse of a mother, was drinking again, so Katie wasn't spending time with her. He'd also put their house on the market to get out from under the joint mortgage. It was the only home Katie had ever known, and she was not happy about selling it. Now to top it all off, a cold-blooded killer was forcing him to think about how much he missed his parents. About how vulnerable he'd felt for years after their deaths, because his backup was gone and the fountain of unconditional love permanently shut down.

Jackson mentally slapped himself and tore open the envelope. The note was handwritten in plain printed letters.

Dear Mr. Jackson,

My name is Hector Vargas and you know who I am. But you do not know me. I am not a killer. I was a thief on that day, but not a killer. Now I am sick with cancer, and the prison doctor says I won't live much longer. I want you to know I didn't kill your parents. I want to tell you the whole story. Please come to the prison so I can tell you in person. It's hard for me to write it down. Come soon, please.

—Hector Vargas

Jackson read the letter again, then let it fall. What the hell was this? It had to be some kind of scam. The convict was trying to manipulate him for some gain he didn't understand yet. Vargas had confessed to the murders and entered a plea bargain to avoid the death penalty. His guilt was never in question.

Jackson pushed up from the table and took his coffee out to the back deck. The sky was blue and warm, he had the day off, and he'd planned to take his gorgeous girlfriend on a long trike ride. Life was good, he reminded himself. He sipped his coffee and tried to remember how he'd felt before he'd opened the stack of mail. But his peace of mind had been shattered.

Reluctantly, he went back in the house and called the state prison. After a short, tense conversation, the warden agreed to let him visit that afternoon. Jackson's conversation with Kera Kollmorgan was longer and friendlier, and she made him promise to come over for dinner later, with Katie. Jackson was grateful for his girlfriend's patience with his job. Police work could be a relationship killer.

An hour later, he was cruising along I-5 on his newly built three-wheeled motorcycle, deep in thought.

Jackson waited in a small windowless room containing only a wooden table and three chairs. The metal chair was already bothering his surgery site, and he'd only been sitting for twelve minutes. Still, it was better than waiting in the main visitors' area with the beaten-down wives and surly children. He felt sorry for the kids whose fathers were locked up, but he had less sympathy for the women who clung to a relationship long after the man had proved his worthlessness.

Jackson's law-enforcement status gave him a special pass to visit Hector Vargas, so a deputy had escorted him past the other visitors, through three electronically controlled steel doors, and down a maze of hallways to this little closet room. He would be allowed a private conversation with the inmate, and Jackson was both grateful and worried. He wasn't sure he trusted himself to be alone with the man who'd murdered his parents. Jackson didn't know how he would react. So many years had passed, and he wanted to believe he could remain cool and detached. Just another conversation with another scumbag. He'd been through so much lately—a stunning health diagnosis and surgery, followed by the shooting of a young suspect and nearly quitting his job—so his emotions felt close to the surface.

After another five minutes, an overweight deputy with a nasal wheeze escorted Vargas into the room. The inmate had been a small man even before the cancer consumed most of his muscle, but now Vargas was as emaciated as an anorexic teenage girl. His mustache and knuckle tattoos seemed out of place on his fragile body.

"I'm Deputy Jenkins," the wheezer said, as he pushed Vargas into a chair. "How much time do you need?"

"Thirty minutes at most." Jackson didn't expect to hear anything new or truthful. He was annoyed with himself for making the trip. Yet how could he not come?

"Behave yourself, Vargas," Jenkins said with a nasty laugh.

The door slammed shut and Jackson's pulse quickened. He dreaded the emotions that were about to surface. "I'm going to document our conversation," he announced, setting his digital recorder on the table. Vargas didn't object. "This is Detective Jackson with the Eugene Police Department. I'm in the Oregon State Penitentiary in Salem at the request of an inmate. Please state your name."

"Hector Vargas. I make this statement willingly."

Jackson got right to the point. "You confessed to killing Clark and Evelyn Jackson, then entered a plea bargain. Why should I believe anything you say?"

"I have cancer and I'm dying. I have no reason to lie." Vargas' dark eyes were watery, but they held no deceit. "I didn't kill your parents. They were good to me, and I'm ashamed that I took their money, but I never hurt them. Never!" Vargas' speech had a Mexican accent, and Jackson knew English was not his first language.

"Why did you confess to their murders?" This was the part that made no sense.

Hector hunched forward, his voice intense. "The police kept me in a little room for three days. They screamed and threatened my family. They held a gun to my head. For three days, I had little food and water. They left my hands cuffed and wouldn't let me use the toilet." Fear and bitterness transformed the inmate's face. "I wet myself and became so hungry I was dizzy. If I fell asleep, they would wake me. At the end, I didn't know what I was saying. I just wanted it to stop."

Jackson didn't want to believe it could have happened in his department, but much had changed in the last decade. Ten years earlier, he'd still been a patrol officer, but he'd heard rumors. The sergeant who'd run the violent-crimes division back then was old-school and not exactly respectful of anyone who wasn't white and male. "Why should I believe you?"

Vargas rolled up his sleeve to display two small round purplish scars. "Detective Bekker burned me with a cigarette."

Jackson stayed silent. He was starting to believe Vargas, and rage made his chest tighten. He hated officers who abused their power and made the rest of the department look bad. Even more, he was outraged they had not searched for and caught the real killer. "What was the other detective's name?"

"Santori. He seemed to be following the older cop's lead."

Jackson wrote down the names, but he would never forget them. Rick Santori was now working in internal affairs, and the irony of that was hard to take. Gary Bekker had transferred out of the detective unit a few years back for a promotion to patrol sergeant. Jackson knew both men, but not well enough to say what they were capable of. "Why did you wait so long to tell someone about this? Why didn't your family hire a lawyer?"

"We had no money. My wife and kids moved to New Mexico to stay with her brother. And I knew God was punishing me, so I accepted it." Vargas let out a small noise, like a man trying to hide his pain. "I took your parents' money, and I'm ashamed of that." He hung his head for a moment, then looked up with pleading eyes. "My family was hungry, and we were about to be evicted. I was desperate and I knew the money was just sitting there. I planned to put it back when I could."

He paused, but Jackson didn't offer any empathy, so Vargas continued. "When they found the money in my house, they called me a killer and slammed my head into a wall. I was shocked to hear the Jacksons were dead. I told the police I didn't do it, but they wouldn't listen. They said I had killed a cop's parents and I would pay, one way or another."

Guilt fueled Jackson's anger, and he didn't trust himself to speak. Vargas had spent ten years in prison for a crime he didn't commit. For the theft alone, he would have been released in less than a year. Finally, Jackson said, "Tell me about the day my parents died. I want to know everything."

Relief washed over Vargas' face as he sensed that Jackson believed him. "I came to the house to finish building the little rock wall in the front yard. I had done a lot of jobs for your parents and they liked my work. No one was there when I arrived, but I thought they would be home soon so I got started." Vargas winced in pain and held his stomach.

Jackson waited him out. He still had twinges of pain from his own surgery that spring, but cancer was in a class by itself. "Do they give you medication for the pain?"

"Some," Vargas said through clenched teeth. In a moment, he continued his story. "I had to use the bathroom, so I went around to the back of the house. Your mother always left the back door open for me when I was working so I could use the toilet by the laundry room. I checked to see if it was open and it was. She knew I would be there that afternoon."

Jackson's heart ached with the memory of his mother's kindness. For people who worked hard and lived honestly, she would do almost anything. His father had been kind as well, but a little more cautious. Jackson could imagine him disagreeing with his wife's decision to leave the back door open for Vargas. "You went into the house?"

"I did. I regret that." Another flash of guilt, or maybe just cancer pain. "When I left the bathroom, I heard a radio playing in the back of the house. I thought maybe someone was home, so I called out. No one answered, so I went down the hall. Their bedroom door was open, and the room looked messy, like someone had been searching for something. It was odd. I had never seen your parents' house look like that. Everything was always perfect."

Oh yes, Jackson thought. *Clean as a whistle.* He'd had his ears twisted as a young boy for wearing muddy shoes in the house.

"I saw the closet was open and the locked gray box was sitting there. I knew it had money, so I grabbed it and left. I went out the back, like I came in, then I got in my truck and drove home. I broke the box with a sledgehammer and found a thousand dollars in it." Vargas moved his cuffed hands from his lap to the small table. "It was enough money to take my family and leave Eugene. I called my cousin in Redding and told him we were coming. My wife wasn't happy with me, but she wanted to leave Eugene too. We weren't doing that well here. We packed everything and waited for the kids to come home from school, but the police got there first. I was stunned when they said your parents were dead. I never saw them that day."

Jackson thought parts of his story didn't add up. "You said the cashbox was just sitting on the closet shelf in plain sight?"

"It was on the floor, but yes, in plain sight."

Why would his parents get their cashbox out and leave the house with the back door unlocked? And why had their bedroom looked messy? "You searched the room, looking for the money, didn't you?"

"No."

"How did you know the box had money in it?"

Vargas shrugged. "I knew your parents. They were old and careful, and they always had cash."

Old and careful. He had thought of them that way too when he was a kid. Yet they were also sweet. His father had been stern at times, but he'd hugged his boys every night before bed for as long as they put up with it. Jackson tried to fill the hole in his heart with details from the case. He had to think like an investigator, not a grieving son. His parents had been found dead in the living room. Both shot with an unregistered gun that had never been located. A coffee table had been knocked on its side, and his father's body had bruises that were consistent with a fight.

"Did you tell any of your friends or relatives that my parents kept money in their house?"

"No." Vargas was emphatic. "I didn't think about the money until that day when I saw the cashbox."

"Did any of your acquaintances own a handgun?"

"I hardly knew anyone in Eugene. We'd only been there for a year. Their deaths had nothing to do with me, I swear." Vargas made the sign of the cross on his chest. "I will soon meet God, and I'm trying to make everything right. I'm telling you this now so you can find the real killer."

Jackson believed him. "Did you see or hear anything that seemed out of place that day?"

"Not really."

"You said you came to finish a brick wall. Did you work the day before?"

"Yes, for about five hours. Why?"

"How did my parents seem that week? Were they worried? Did they argue about anything?" Vargas was probably not the right person to ask, but he had to start somewhere.

"Everything seemed fine." Vargas grimaced and held his stomach again. "I have no idea who would hurt your parents. They were very kind. They had no enemies."

Except the bastard who shot them. Despair washed over Jackson. His chance of finding the killer—or killers—after all this time seemed hopeless. He had no crime scene to analyze, no witnesses to interrogate. Even if the same people still lived next door to his parents' house, what were the odds they would remember anything useful after ten years?

He had to try, but he worried he would make himself crazy in the process. He tended to become obsessive about working a case, even when the dead were strangers to him. "What else can you tell me about that day? Any little detail could help."

"I didn't see Clark and Evelyn. They weren't home and the truck was gone."

"The car was there and the truck was gone?"

"That's right."

Jackson didn't know how it could be connected, but if they had taken the truck, they had expected to buy something big or haul something dirty. He felt jumpy now, anxious to get out of the cramped, windowless room. He stood. "Thank you for telling me this." He wouldn't apologize to Vargas for the way the detectives had treated him. Someone should, but it was not his responsibility. If the handyman hadn't taken the money, he wouldn't be here.

"Thank you for believing me." A strange look passed over Vargas' face. He started to say something, then stopped.

"What is it?"

"Probably nothing."

"Tell me anyway."

"You asked about the day before. Late in the afternoon, right before I left, your brother, Derrick, came to see your parents. He had a duffel bag and a suitcase with him, like he planned to stay for a while."

"Did he say anything to you?" Jackson didn't think the information was relevant. Derrick had moved in and out of his parents' house a few times.

"We didn't talk. He rushed into the house and I left soon after."

"If you think of anything else, please contact me." Jackson pressed the red buzzer to summon the guard.

On the drive home, he rehearsed telling his boss, Sergeant Denise Lammers, that he wanted to work an old case that had been successfully adjudicated. No matter how he presented it, Lammers didn't approve, even in his visualized version.

She wouldn't like that he was personally connected to the case, and she would hate hearing that two Eugene law-enforcement personnel had abused a suspect until he had confessed, even if it had happened a decade ago. Typically, if an officer violated department rules, the case would be turned over to internal affairs. But one of the accused, Santori, was now working in IA, so what was the protocol? The district attorney would also have to be notified, as the one to file new charges...if Jackson found the real perpetrator.

It was screwed up at least six ways.

Two young guys in a sports car passed and gave him a thumbs-up. His three-wheeled motorcycle often affected people that way, and it gave Jackson a jolt of pride every time. The memory of building it from a pile of VW and motorcycle parts helped him clear his mind and enjoy the rush of wind on his face. He didn't get many opportunities to experience the open road.

By the time he reached Eugene, he'd decided to keep the case to himself and work it on his own for a while. He would focus on finding a new suspect and not bring up the abuse of Vargas just yet. They were separate circumstances, and bringing justice to his parents was more important than punishing two cops who'd thought they were doing Jackson a favor at the time, however misguided it was. He would not let the abuse go forever though.

Jackson pulled into his driveway on Harris Street, relieved to be home. Before putting the trike in the garage, he took a moment to gaze at the canopy of trees over the cozy bungalow he'd lived in for fourteen years. The *For Sale* sign in the front yard disturbed him every time he saw it. He didn't really want to move, but his ex-wife owned half of the house, and she was pressuring him for her equity. Other than sell, his only option was to refinance on his own, then take out another loan to buy out the thirty grand she figured she had coming. His banker had said he'd never qualify for both.

After a long talk with Katie, Jackson had put the house on the market, and they'd talked about moving in with Kera—and her entourage—when it sold. He was still trying to come to grips with all the changes in store for him.

While he waited for Katie to come home, Jackson sat at his kitchen table and made a list of things he could do to get the investigation rolling: *1) find the old case file and read through the paperwork, 2) talk to old neighbors, 3) call Derrick.*

The last entry would be the hardest. He hadn't spoken to his brother since the month after their parents' funeral. They'd argued about what to do with the house and personal items. Their parents' will had instructed that the house be sold and the profits split. Derrick, who had just moved back in, wanted to stay in the home and buy out Jackson's half of the inheritance. Jackson knew his brother would probably never pay him, but in the end, he'd given in rather than be an ass about it. Derrick had made only two payments, but he was still living in the house. After an argument about the equity, ten years of silence had followed. Jackson never meant for the rift to go on that long, but somehow it had.

He didn't care about the money, even though he needed it now more than ever. It was the principle. Derrick had caused his parents a lot of grief as a young man. He'd been in one mess after another. Even after he settled down and found steady work, he never quite paid his own way. Jackson resented the burden Derrick had been to his parents when they were alive, and he resented Derrick's presence in their real estate now.

But he had to put all that aside, because he needed Derrick's cooperation. Some of their parents' personal items were likely still in storage in the house, and Jackson wanted to examine everything. He didn't know what he expected to find, but it was a place to start. Someone had come to the house and shot Clark and Evelyn Jackson. Now that robbery was not the motive, there had to be another reason.

The front door flew open, and Katie rushed in, finding him at the kitchen table, his favorite place to think and talk. "Hey, Dad. I discovered a great band today. Have you ever heard of Rebel Jar?"

"They're local, right?"

"Yes, and they're awesome." She dropped her backpack on the floor. "What are you thinking about? You look sad."

"My brother, Derrick."

"Are you going to call him?"

"I plan to stop by and see him."

"Woohoo!" Katie gave him a high five. "About freaking time."

Later, at Kera's house, he rang the doorbell but no one answered. They heard voices and a baby crying.

"Let's just go in," Katie said. "Kera told me to treat her house like my home." His daughter opened the door and called out, "We're here." Jackson followed her in.

Kera was in her bright, spacious kitchen with little Micah, and the baby's mother. Danette held the red-faced baby over her shoulder while Kera tried to rub his gums. "Oh hi," she said, giving Jackson a kiss as he stepped close. "Micah is teething."

"Red licorice works wonders for that," Jackson teased.

Kera gave him an indulgent smile, and Jackson felt happy for the first time that day. Tall and muscular, with long copper hair and wide cheekbones, Kera was a striking woman who made people of both genders stare. He'd met her during a homicide case the year before, and they'd started dating soon after. At that point, she was living alone in the house, still grieving for her son, who'd died in Iraq.

"If we get desperate, we'll try the licorice," Kera responded. "For now, a little of this numbing gel should work."

"What are we having for dinner?" Katie asked, peeking in the oven.

"Chicken enchiladas and corn salad."

"Yum. Can I hold Micah?" Katie held out her arms. Jackson was surprised by how bonded his daughter had become to Kera's grandchild.

"Sure." Danette, who looked much like Kera even though they weren't genetically related, handed Micah to Katie, and the baby squealed with joy. The young mother had dated Kera's son before he shipped out to Iraq, and Kera had taken her in after the baby was born. Jackson loved Kera for her generosity, but Danette's presence had altered the course of their relationship.

During dinner, Kera asked both young women about the classes they'd signed up for. Danette would soon start at Lane Community College to take prerequisites for nursing school. Jackson didn't think she seemed like the nurturing type, but he kept it to himself. He listened to the women talk about school, careers, and clothes—between interruptions for feeding and wiping the baby—and wondered what it would be like to experience this every night. Was he ready to move in here when his house sold?

"You're pretty quiet, Wade," Kera said later, as they cleaned up in the kitchen.

"I keep thinking about my parents and how to investigate their case." He'd called and told her about the letter before visiting the prison.

"Is there a file from the original investigation?"

"I'll find out tomorrow."

The concern on her beautiful face made his heart swell. Jackson reached for Kera, pressing his lips to hers in a lingering kiss. "When are we going to be alone next?"

"I'll have to come to your place. Danette never goes any-where," Kera whispered, and kissed his ear at the same time. Jackson filled with lust and had to step back. The kids could burst in at any moment.

"I think Katie has plans to be out of the house this Friday."

Kera gave him a wicked smile. "I hope I can wait that long."

His daughter stepped in and announced. "Micah won't stop hiccupping. What should I do?"

"Make him laugh," Kera said. "If that doesn't work, bring him to me."

When Katie left, Kera asked, "Have you had any buyers interested in your house?"

"An older couple looked at it last week, but I haven't heard back from them." Jackson loaded dishes as they talked. "My agent thinks I should lower the price."

"Are you going to?"

"It seems too soon."

"It's been on the market all summer."

Jackson was quiet.

"Are you having second thoughts about moving in here?"

He'd had second and third thoughts by now. "I admit, it makes me a little nervous, but nothing has changed. I want to get out of my mortgage with Renee, and I want to wake up every day with you."

"Then let's get your house sold. Maybe you need a new agent."

"We'll drop the price a little first and see what happens."

"Is there anything I can do to help?"

"Just be patient with me. Especially while I investigate my parents' murders."

"I'm worried that you'll lose yourself in this one."

"Me too."

CHAPTER 3

Monday, September 6, 8:30 a.m.

Detective Lara Evans watched the sergeant approach Jackson with an assignment and wondered if the case was a homicide. He always got the prime investigations, but as her mentor he usually chose her to be on his task force. She loved working closely with him.

This morning Jackson looked worried. His dark eyes held new pain, and the little scar in his eyebrow twitched as Lammers talked. Evans loved watching Jackson interact with people. He was good at keeping his face impassive. His strong jaw and lush lips never gave away anything, but she'd learned to read his eyes. As the boss walked away, Jackson seemed relieved.

A moment later, Sergeant Lammers strode up to Evans' desk, her massive body rustling papers along the way. "What are you working on?"

"The Josh Myers case," Evans answered. "I found a witness and arrested David Russo. He's still denying he did the beating, but his hands say differently. I took photos, so I think he'll plead."

"If you're ready, I've got an interesting case for you."

Lammers' smile made Evans nervous. *Interesting* could mean so many things. "What is it?"

"A woman who's been in a coma for two years woke up yesterday and said someone tried to kill her. At the time, everyone thought it was a suicide attempt."

"Two years? Should it go to the cold-case volunteers?"

"It was never investigated as an assault, so we have to treat it like a new case." Lammers handed her a small sheet of notepaper. "The woman's name is Gina Stahl."

Evans stood, ready to get moving. "Sounds like a good change of pace from the testosterone-fueled assaults I usually get stuck with." She would have preferred to be assigned a real homicide, but attempted homicide was close enough. "Where is she?"

"Rosehill Care in Springfield."

"We have jurisdiction?"

"The assault took place in her home in Eugene in August 2008. It's our case."

Evans found the address online, grabbed her jacket and carryall bag, and headed out. She carried the jacket over her shoulder, not planning to wear it until she had to. Even in the shade of the underground parking lot, the temperature was in the nineties. It was one of about five days a year that Eugene, Oregon, could be considered hot. She wouldn't complain though. Anything was better than the cold. Growing up in Alaska, she'd come to hate the dark and cold. At nineteen, she'd left that godforsaken frozen place and her miserable redneck parents and never looked back.

Her city-issued Impala, affectionately called "the Geezer," because only old men (and cops) drove the model, was ten degrees warmer than the parking lot. She cranked up the air-conditioning, not wanting to sweat into her new jacket. Five blocks later, she was on the expressway to Springfield, their adjacent sister city, a sprawled-out blue-collar town with about half the population of Eugene. She'd lived in Springfield when she first moved to the area and worked as a paramedic there. But Eugene—with its downtown university, performing-arts center, and colorful Saturday market—had appealed to her more. Evans chuckled at her hypocrisy. She rarely participated in those activities, but she liked knowing they were there and that she lived in a city rich with art and education.

The Rosehill facility was just off Q Street, not far from the freeway. Long, low, and white, the building shimmered in the heat. Evans reached for the wide front door and found it locked. She saw a sign saying to push the green buzzer and, a second later, heard a click. She looked around for a camera and didn't see one. The locked doors were probably intended to keep dementia patients from wandering away.

Evans stepped inside and immediately recoiled. The cool air stank of feces and rotting flesh. People came to the facility to die. She braced herself and strode to the administration desk, staffed by a bored young woman. "I'm Detective Evans, Eugene Police. I'm here to see Gina Stahl."

The desk clerk perked up. "It's so cool that she woke up. I think they tried some new drug or something." The girl suddenly scowled. "Why do the police want to see her? Is Gina a criminal?"

Evans needed to talk to staff members, but the yappy desk clerk was not on her list. "What room is Gina in?"

"She's in 112, but let me call one of the nurses to go with you."

Evans would have preferred to see the victim alone, but this was no ordinary interview. She waited a long five minutes, and eventually a middle-aged woman in blue scrubs came down the hall. Her hair was pulled back tight and she had dark circles under her eyes, but when the nurse smiled, it transformed her appearance. "I'm Jeri Richmond. I've been Gina's nurse for eight months."

Evans introduced herself, then said, "Can you tell me about Gina's condition?"

"She was in an unconscious state for two years and twenty-three days. Yesterday, she woke up. Her muscles are weak and she'll need months of rehab, but she'll be fine." The nurse gave Evans an odd smile. "I can tell you this information only because I have Gina's permission."

"What caused the coma?"

"She ingested large quantities of Valium and Demerol, sending her brain into a deep sleep. The ER doctors pumped her stomach and kept her from dying. Because there was no injury, Gina continued to show brain function. At first, they thought she would come out of it in a few weeks, but she didn't." The nurse gestured and they started down the hall. "When one of Gina's doctors suggested her parents disconnect the feeding tube, they transferred her here."

"You said she ingested a drug overdose. That sounds like a suicide attempt."

"That's what everyone thought until she woke up and said she'd been attacked."

As they passed open doors, Evans avoided looking into the patients' rooms. "Is Gina coherent?"

"She drifts in and out of consciousness, but if you talk to her for a while, she'll come around. She's surprisingly lucid when she does."

"What made her wake up after all this time?"

"We have a new doctor on staff, and he started giving her Ambien. It's a sleeping pill, but it's had great effects on other coma patients around the country." The nursed smiled. "Gina's parents advocated for it. They've been here nearly every day for two years. They never lost faith."

After passing several more open doors with unpleasant smells and sounds oozing out, they stopped at a closed door. The nurse hesitated. "Now that Gina's back, I feel like I should knock." She rapped on the door but there was no response. "Her parents also paid for daily physical therapy, so she's in pretty good shape and her body will be fully functional again soon."

They stepped into a cream-colored room with sunlight flooding through the window. Evans was happy to see the lush courtyard outside. From the moment she'd entered the building, she'd been fighting the urge to turn and run.

Seeing Gina made her throat tighten. The woman's colorless skin, closed eyes, and total stillness made her look dead. Her long charcoal hair contrasted sharply with the white sheets, but the symmetry of her facial lines transmitted beauty even in repose.

The nurse grabbed a chair from against the wall and pulled it next to the bed. "If you sit here and talk to her, she'll wake up. Dr. Ellison thinks she'll be completely awake by tomorrow."

Evans took a seat, feeling awkward. She hoped the nurse would leave.

"I have to check on another patient, but I'll be back." Jeri hustled out, leaving Evans wondering what the hell she would say.

Evans thought that if she had been in a coma for two years, she'd want to know what she'd missed. She introduced herself and reluctantly launched into a monologue. "The last few years have been a little intense. First, there was the oil spill, but maybe you knew about that. We've also had several mass shootings, and gun control is a hot debate. We need tougher laws, for sure, but I don't plan to give up my weapons." Evans cleared her throat. "We're gearing up to another election, and the rhetoric is getting out of control. I'm still surprised by how conservative big chunks of the country are, even though I grew up with rednecks. I'm not very political, but I always vote, because my parents vote and I figure I owe it to the country to cancel out at least one of their ignorant opinions."

Evans wished she hadn't said that, but it was too late and likely didn't matter. She pressed on. "The economy is recovering but unemployment is still high. Especially here in Oregon. So people are unhappy and state budgets are in a lot of trouble."

The woman's eyes came open and a smile played on her lips. For a moment, Evans thought she might have seen her before. "Gina Stahl? I'm Detective Lara Evans. Sorry if I bored you or offended you with all that stuff."

"You didn't bore me but it's depressing." Gina gestured with a couple of fingers. "Would you raise my bed?"

Evans looked for the button, pleased Gina was lucid. "Do you feel ready to answer questions?"

"Sure."

Evans wanted to ask about the drugs found in her blood the night she went into the big sleep, but there was no point in making Gina defensive. "You were admitted to North McKenzie Hospital on August 3, 2008. Tell me what you remember about that night."

"I was reading, then I went into the kitchen to make some popcorn." Gina's voice was weak, but she sounded sure.

"What time was that?"

"Around nine o'clock. Would you hold the water bottle to my lips? My throat is dry and my hands are still weak."

Evans stood and grabbed the water. She hadn't known what to expect from Gina, and so far, everything had surprised her.

After a few sips, Gina laid her head back and continued. "I heard footsteps in the hall." Her eyes flashed with remembered fear. "I turned, and a man in a ski mask was suddenly there. He grabbed me by the throat, and a moment later I blacked out." Gina swallowed and closed her eyes. "I woke up here, two years later." When her eyes opened again, they radiated pain. "At times, I was partially conscious. It was like morning sleep, right before you wake up. I could hear some things, but I couldn't break out of the dreams."

Evans didn't want to think about what that had been like for two long years. "Describe the man in as much detail as you can."

Gina bit her lip. "It all happened so fast."

"Let's take it one step at a time. Was he taller than you?"

"Yes. Taller and stronger, but not huge."

"Would you say he was under six foot? Under two hundred pounds?"

"Yes."

"What was his skin and hair color?"

Gina closed her eyes again. Evans waited. Jackson had taught her not to prompt.

"I don't know. He wore a ski mask and gloves, but his jacket was brown and his body was familiar." Gina locked eyes with her. "I'm pretty sure it was my ex-husband."

Evans tried not to show her surprise. She was terrible at hiding her reactions, but she was working on it. "What makes you think that?"

"I had filed for divorce, and I was collecting evidence against him."

"What kind of evidence?"

"He had been cheating on me for years."

Oregon was a no-fault-divorce state. Judges rarely granted alimony unless the couple had been together a long time and the woman wasn't capable of supporting herself. There had to be more to this story. "Why did you need evidence of infidelity? Had you filed for alimony?"

"It wasn't about the divorce. He was a predator."

Something in Gina's voice made the hair on the back of Evans' neck stand up. "What kind of predator?"

"A sexual predator. He took advantage of vulnerable women."

"Why do you think that?"

Gina sighed. "I caught him lying, then I saw him with a woman I knew was a prostitute."

"Visiting a prostitute doesn't make him a predator." Evans kept herself from throwing in further commentary.

"He also spent time with drug addicts and women with criminal records."

So the guy liked to slum around for his extracurricular sex. Evans thought Gina might be a little paranoid. "I still don't see why you think he's a predator or why he would want to attack you."

"I'm tired now. Please ask my parents about the notebook when they get here." Gina's eyes were closed.

"What are their names?"

"George and Sharon Stahl." She sounded half-asleep.

Evans needed one more piece of information. "What is your ex-husband's name, and where can I find him?"

"Gary Bekker. He's a cop."

CHAPTER 4

Monday, September 6, 5:15 a.m.

Jackson slammed off the alarm and bolted from bed. He wanted to get to the department early and read the old case file before his workday officially started. He skipped his morning run, showered, and made a half pot of coffee. Travel mug in hand, he went back to the bedroom and strapped on his Sig Sauer, then kissed his sleeping daughter on the forehead. He would have liked to see Katie walk out the door on her first day of high school, but she probably preferred that he didn't, so it was okay, he told himself. She'd been getting herself up and ready for years. Having an alcoholic mother and a workaholic dad had given her an early sense of responsibility.

Just before he headed out, Jackson remembered to take his prednisone. In theory, the drug was shrinking the fibrous growth around his abdominal aorta. In practice, it produced mood swings and ten extra pounds, but he could live with that.

Other people with retroperitoneal fibrosis had chronic pain, and many ended up with colostomy bags. His doctors said he was lucky, and Jackson, still only forty-two, was grateful his kidneys had been spared. Since the surgery to free his ureters from the growth, he'd been practicing gratitude for almost everything.

Just as the sun was coming up, he climbed in his city-issued cruiser and backed out of the driveway.

The Violent Crimes Unit occupied a narrow space crammed with desks, filing cabinets, stacked boxes, and assorted personal items, like the team's bowling trophy and Rob Schakowski's Buzz Lightyear toy. At this early hour, the room was empty. Jackson passed Ed McCray's old desk and realized he hadn't called him since he retired in June. His good friend and longtime partner had taken a bullet in their last big homicide case and McCray's wife had called "enough." Jackson both envied and pitied his friend. To be free of the job and its on-call, sometimes round-the-clock bonds seemed like a gift. Yet without an investigation going, Jackson wouldn't know who he was.

He turned on his computer and glanced at the two case files on his desk. They were all but wrapped up, with the perps in custody and the DA pushing for plea bargains. He hoped Lammers wouldn't assign him anything new until he'd had a chance to dig into his parents' case.

Jackson went in search of the administrative aide. She had the keys to the storage area for adjudicated cases and would have to document what he checked out. If the case had still been open, the file would be in a box in a room at the end of the hall, along with dozens of other boxes just like it. They tried to keep open cases handy to work on whenever they had downtime. They hadn't had any downtime in months.

He found her in the break room, yawning and pouring coffee.

"Hey, Nikki. I need to check out a file from the year 2000. Can you help me?"

"Tell me what you want, and I'll bring it to you a little later."

"I'd like us to go get it now."

She looked surprised but put a lid on her coffee and started for the stairs. In the basement, she unlocked a steel door and clicked on the overhead light. They stepped into a long musty room crammed with filing cabinets.

"What month and what name?" Nikki asked.

"September. The homicide of Evelyn and Clark Jackson."

Nikki's eyes widened. "Your parents?"

"Yes."

"I'm sorry." She touched his arm, yawning again. "Wait here. You're not supposed to actually be in here."

Jackson was glad to stay near the open door. After a good ten minutes, Nikki returned with a large brown pocket folder. "I hope you find what you're looking for."

Back at his desk, Jackson sipped his coffee and stared at the file. Was he ready to rip open the past and relive that horrible day? He'd been on patrol, and they'd called him in to the department. His sergeant had broken the news to him in small chunks. *There's been a shooting and two people are dead. We believe they're related to you. Do your parents live on Emerald Street?*

Glad to be alone, Jackson sucked in a deep breath and pulled out a stack of papers with two manila folders underneath. A standard form lay on top of the pile. He began to read: *September 23, Evelyn and Clark Jackson, found dead of bullet wounds at 2353 Emerald Street. Patrol officers responded to an anonymous tip about a handyman fleeing the house.* The information surprised Jackson. He'd never had access to the case details before. They'd picked up Hector Vargas within hours of the crime, and Jackson had never had reason to question the chain of events. Now Vargas claimed Jackson's parents weren't home when he left their house with the money. If he was telling the truth, the murders hadn't happened at that point. Who had called in the tip about seeing Vargas leave the house? And why? Jackson noted the time listed for the call: 4:25 p.m. Something was not right about the tip.

He opened a Word document and started his own file of notes and questions, then went back to the case paperwork. The manila folder held plastic sheets with encased pictures. Jackson dreaded seeing them. Yet how could he work the case without looking at the crime-scene photos? After ten years, he still wasn't ready. At the funeral, he'd paid his respects and looked in the open caskets. His parents had appeared whole and peaceful, and that's how he wanted to remember them.

He picked up a small notepad similar to the one he carried and read Bekker's personal notes. The abbreviations and sloppy handwriting made it challenging, but Jackson gleaned that the victims had been found in the living room: two shots in the male body, both in the torso, and one bullet through the female's forehead. A coffee table had been overturned, indicating a struggle. Both victims were wearing outer clothing, as if they had just come in or were preparing to leave.

Page two contained a list of the evidence Bekker had bagged and tagged: a cigarette butt from the driveway, a hundred-dollar bill, and a strand of hair from the female's sweater that was visibly lighter than the victim's dark hair. The notation of the money surprised him. Had it come from his parents' cashbox? Jackson hoped the technicians had gathered more physical evidence than what was listed.

He flipped ahead, realizing only five pages had been filled in. Either Bekker hadn't conducted much of an investigation or he wasn't much of a note taker. Bekker had talked to the woman who lived next door, Rose Harmon, and she reported that a handyman had been working at the house that day. She also denied being the person who'd called in about seeing him. Jackson hoped she still lived next door, but he wasn't counting on it. Finding witnesses who remembered any kind of detail would be challenging.

He flipped through until he found copies of the autopsies. The medical jargon in the report made for slow reading, which was why he always attended the autopsies of the cases he worked. The information was easier to process when he was looking at the body and listening to the pathologist. In this case, the gunshot residue indicated his father had been shot at close range. The bullets had gone through his chest, and the technicians had dug both out of the couch. His mother had been killed at a range of five to seven feet, and the bullet had lodged in her brain. Neither had defense wounds on their hands or foreign DNA under their fingernails, but his father's body had an abdominal bruise consistent with a fist punch. Both had died around four o'clock in the afternoon.

A tremor ran through Jackson's chest. He pushed back from his desk and went outside for fresh air. The sun had warmed the morning air, and the streets and sidewalks were filling with cars, bicycles, transients, and oddly dressed young people. He loved Eugene, cultural diversity and all. Sometimes it bothered him that he had never moved away or experienced another part of the country, but his parents had been proud Oregonians who never considered living anywhere else, and he'd grown up feeling that way too. They'd chosen Eugene to raise their family, and so had he. God, he missed them.

Jackson considered a trip to Full City Coffee for a pastry, then thought better of it. Back at his desk, he read the ballistics report: .22 slug, partially flattened, with lands and grooves consistent with a Jennings. All of which meant little, since they had never found the handgun. He read a brief typed confession signed by Hector Vargas. Jackson wondered if they had a taped version, and if so, where it was. Back in 2000, the interrogation room had not yet been wired for video. Santori and Bekker would have felt free to abuse Vargas as they pleased in the windowless space. Other officers had to have known or at least suspected what was going on. Jackson was ashamed of them all.

He felt around in the bottom of the pocket folder, hoping to find a cassette tape, but it wasn't there. He made a mental note to visit the crime lab at some point and look at the physical evidence, which should have been stored.

"Hey, Jackson." Rob Schakowski, another detective and occasional fishing buddy, wandered up looking sleepy. He noted Jackson's two coffee containers. "Why the hell did you come in so early on Monday?" Schak's buzz cut and barrel-shaped torso made him look mean, but Jackson knew better.

"It's a long story. Better grab some coffee."

When Schak returned with a styrofoam cup of crappy house brew, Jackson spoke softly, not wanting anyone else to hear. "Hector Vargas wrote me a letter, asking me to come see him." Jackson paused to see if Schak knew the name.

His partner raised an eyebrow. "What did the bastard want?"

"He said he was innocent and wanted me to know the truth before he died. I visited the prison yesterday." Jackson leaned in and lowered his voice again. "This is strictly confidential. Vargas said Santori and Bekker abused him until he confessed. He has scars from where he claims Bekker burned him with a cigarette."

A chain of reactions played out on Schak's face. He settled on dead serious. "You believe him. You're looking at your parents' file."

"I have to."

"Does Lammers know?"

"Not yet."

"You know I'm on board. I'll do whatever I can, even on my own time."

"I appreciate that. For now, I don't want anyone to know."

"Lammers may want to hand it over to internal affairs." Schak's eyes went wide. "Shit. Santori is IA now."

"It's a sticky one."

"Did you find anything irregular in the file?"

"A few quirks. I hope to question some witnesses today."

"Here comes the boss." Schak scooted over to his own desk.

Sergeant Lammers strode up, making Jackson feel smaller than his six feet and two hundred pounds. She was the same size, only more so. Lammers projected a force field that somehow diminished everyone around her.

"Good morning, Jackson."

He braced himself. "Morning, Sergeant. Did you have a good weekend?"

"Not really. I got two calls yesterday, both very strange cases." She waved a sheet of notebook paper and gave him a closed-mouth smile. "This one is special and has your name all over it."

He waited her out.

"Dispatch informs me a guy called in and said he found a dead body in the laundry room at his apartment complex. I took an unrelated call immediately after. I was on the phone maybe five minutes." Lammers nodded, her short hair and wide face stiff as ever. "Before I could make a move, dispatch called again. The laundry guy had called back and claimed the body was gone. He'd gone out for a smoke to calm his nerves, and when he came back in, the body wasn't there."

"Oh joy." Jackson grabbed the yellow note out of her hand. "My guess is he was never dead."

"Good luck." Lammers headed toward Evans with a second sheet of notepaper.

Jackson was glad to have a reason to get out. With any luck, he'd wrap up the disappearing-corpse case in record time, then make a stop in his old neighborhood

CHAPTER 5

Monday, September 6, 11:25 a.m.

On the way back from her interview with Gina, Evans drove through Glenwood, a ramshackle strip of industrial businesses and low-rent houses between Eugene and Springfield. She cursed at every stupid driver who crossed her path. What a FUBAR this case was. No crime scene to investigate, no fresh witnesses, a victim who couldn't stay awake to answer questions, and—the frosting on this shit cake—the main suspect was a cop.

What the hell was she supposed to do? If Bekker were just a citizen, her first step would be to bring him in for questioning. But he was a patrol sergeant who had once worked as a detective. He'd never been her supervisor, but she'd heard rumors that he was a jackass. As a cop, Bekker knew how the system worked and would not willingly answer questions. Tipping him off that he was under suspicion would likely backfire as well. Evans wanted to hand the case back to Sergeant Lammers and say *I can't handle this*. But she wouldn't admit that out loud even if she were tortured. Being thirty-two and female, she was already considered the weak link in the unit.

Evans understood that she had to craft a plan and handle the case carefully. At some point, she would have to tell Lammers that her suspect was a Eugene police sergeant, but not yet. Lammers might take the case away from her, and Evans couldn't let that happen either.

She stopped at Carl's Jr., then wolfed down a cheeseburger as she drove to headquarters. She would have to run five miles after work to still weigh 129 in the morning, but that was okay. She did her best thinking while running and for now, her full belly eased her tension. Evans decided to give herself twenty-four hours to work the case and find out what she could—before she told Lammers anything. It was possible Gina had not really been attacked. She could have taken an overdose of medication, then blamed her ex just for revenge. Gina claimed the attacker had grabbed her neck. Had the ER doctors examined Gina's body for bruises? Would her medical chart from that night still exist somewhere?

Evans pulled into the underground parking lot and shut off her car. Even with the air-conditioning on, she'd managed to work up a sweat. Would anyone notice? She headed upstairs, thinking about Gina's insinuations. She'd called Bekker a predator and implied he used his authority as a cop to intimidate women into having sex with him. *Could it be true?*

"Hey, Evans. How did the coma interview go?" Lammers lurked near her desk as she entered the violent-crimes area.

"It was fine until she fell asleep. I'm going back later to try again." Evans dropped her shoulder bag on the floor and headed for the bathroom, hoping Lammers would go away.

"Is she credible?" the sergeant called after her.

"Yes." Evans hurried down the hall and into the women's restroom. She glanced in the mirror and frowned. Her short hair—now light copper brown from L'Oréal—had gone limp, and her face had a moist sheen. It didn't matter, she told herself. She was on the job, and being pretty just got in the way. She wiped her armpits with a wet paper towel and hurried back to her desk.

Evans keyed Gary Bekker into the employee database to get a look at his career path. He'd worked as a vice detective for six years, and before that, he'd trained as a detective in the violent-crimes division for a year, just as she was doing now. Evans studied his photograph, assuming it was probably a few years old. Military-short, receding light-brown hair, cold blue eyes, and a wide jaw that made up for his disappearing chin. She'd seen him in passing, but he'd been promoted to patrol sergeant around the time she'd transferred into the Violent Crimes Unit. They had never worked in the same department at the same time.

Only a limited amount of information was available to her, but she now knew Bekker's address and phone number. She needed a look at his employment records to see if he had any registered complaints or department citations. Would Lammers have access to that file and would she share the information?

Evans wasn't ready to take that step. Who in the department would have known Bekker when he was a vice detective? That had to be when Bekker had contact with hookers and drug addicts. Jackson, of course, would know him, but Jackson had only worked vice for a short while. She thought of Ed McCray, who had just retired after thirty years in the department. He'd been a detective for half of it, including a stint in vice. Evans felt guilty for even thinking of pumping McCray for information. His timely retirement a few months ago had kept her from losing her job to a cost-cutting staff reduction. She owed McCray a favor, not the other way around. Still, she had to call him and find out what she could.

First, she had to read the file for the original incident. Evans opened the database for patrol reports and keyed in *Gina Stahl*. A file dated August 3, 2008, appeared on the screen. Evans scanned the details: Officer Keith Markham had responded to a 911 call about an unconscious woman at the Riverside Terrace. Gina's neighbor had come over to visit and found her unconscious. The neighbor had described Gina as *overdosed*. Markham had labeled the incident as an *attempted suicide*.

Evans printed the report and wondered if Markham was still working patrol. She wanted to ask him a few questions but she had to be careful. If Markham knew who Gina was, he might go straight to Bekker and tell him that the incident was being investigated.

Evans froze in front of the printer. Did Bekker know his ex-wife had come out of her coma? If he'd tried to kill her two years ago, would he try again now?

At her desk, she called Rosehill and asked to speak to Jeri Richmond, Gina's nurse.

"I'm sorry, but she's too busy to come to the phone."

"This is important police business. Go get her."

After a long wait, Jeri came on the line. "Yes?"

"This is Detective Evans. I need to know who was notified of Gina's awakening."

"Just her parents."

"Is it possible anyone called her ex-husband?"

"No."

"I'd like the facility to take extra steps to protect Gina. She claims to be the victim of attempted homicide."

"We're doing what we can." The nurse sounded more impatient with each response.

"What does that mean?"

"Someone checks on her every fifteen minutes. And the front doors are locked, so no one gets in without being screened."

"Thank you." Evans hung up. She would have liked to ask Lammers for a patrol officer to guard Gina, but she knew what the answer would be. Their budget had been stripped to the bare bones, and officers had been laid off. She would have to work quickly and arrest Bekker before he learned of his ex-wife's recovery.

Evans called McCray, hoping to get a feel for whether Bekker had any real friends in the department who would protect him. If he was a predator, he was an asshole and had probably alienated a few people. Still, he was a cop, and the brotherhood always closed ranks.

McCray didn't answer, so she left him a message, asking to meet for coffee to talk about an old case. Next, she found Gina's parents in the citizen database and gave them a call. A female voice offered a soft hello.

Evans introduced herself. "Are you Sharon Stahl?"

"Yes. Did you say Laura?"

"Actually, it's Lara, but it doesn't matter. I'm calling about your daughter, Gina. I'm investigating her assault and I'd like to talk to you and your husband as soon as possible."

"It's about time." The mother's voice broke, and she paused to compose herself. "I'm sorry. That wasn't directed at you."

"It's okay. Can I stop by your house now?"

"Of course. But we'll be leaving soon to see Gina at the care center again."

The Stahls lived in an attractive mobile home in a seniors-only park in West Eugene. Ducks wandered across the well-groomed front yard as Evans got out of her car. She blinked in the bright sun and headed up the driveway. Sharon Stahl opened the door, and Evans thought, *She doesn't look seventy-seven.* The woman was tall and lean and still had a straight spine. Both her knees were covered with large gauze bandages.

"I just had my knees replaced," she said with a chuckle. "I wore 'em out power walking through my sixties."

Evans offered her hand, and Sharon affectionately squeezed it between both of hers. "Come in. Would you like something cold to drink? Ice tea or lemonade?"

"Just ice water please." Evans was already over her calorie quota for the day.

The home was spacious and immaculately clean. It was the first time Evans had been inside a mobile home that didn't disgust her. Compared to the shit-pile trailer she'd grown up in, this home was so upscale it was shameful for the two dwellings to share a name.

After a minute, George Stahl ambled into the room, looking a little less preserved than his wife. He had rounded shoulders, a small potbelly, and a lot of neck sag. The couple sat together on the forest-green couch and held hands. The gesture surprised Evans.

"Our Gina woke up," Sharon said, beaming. "We always believed she would. When she spoke to me yesterday, I thought my heart would burst."

"That must have been amazing." Evans could not imagine the feeling. She had no children, no real emotional connection to anyone...except Jackson. "What did the doctors say when she was admitted? Did they think she would recover?"

"They were conflicted. One said she would never wake up and wanted us to remove her feeding tube after three weeks. But Dr. Bremer said she had brain activity and suggested we put her into a long-term-care facility and talk to her every day. So we did."

"We did more than that," George said, a little gruff.

"Yes, and it was all worth it. Our Gina is back."

Evans hated to spoil the mood, but she had to get to the heart of her visit. "Gina said her ex-husband tried to kill her, which is why I'm here. First, I'd like to know about her history. She had Valium and Demerol in her bloodstream when she was admitted. Did Gina have prescriptions for either drug?"

"She had one for Valium," Sharon said quickly. "But she only took it on occasion. Gina had filed for divorce and was under a lot of stress."

"What about the Demerol. Was it hers?"

"I don't think so. Where would she get Demerol?"

"The neighbor who called 911 reported the incident as an overdose."

"I'm sure that's what it looked like," Sharon said. "But we're convinced Gary gave Gina the drugs to make it seem like she committed suicide."

"Was Gina depressed?"

"She was going through a divorce and having a tough time, but she didn't try to kill herself." Sharon raised her voice in defensiveness.

"Did you tell the police you thought her ex-husband tried to kill her?"

"Of course, but it was a waste of time. Gary is a police officer. Another cop gave him an alibi, and the department didn't even investigate."

George spoke up. "I find it hard to believe a cop would lie to cover up an attempted homicide, but nothing else makes sense. Gina had no enemies."

Evans appreciated his vote of confidence, but he was completely naive about the brotherhood. "Who did you talk to when you contacted the police?"

"Detective Rick Santori in internal affairs, but he said there was no case."

"What is the name of the cop who gave Bekker an alibi?"

George shook his head, but Sharon got up, moving slowly to protect her bandaged knees. "I think I still have some notes I made at the time."

"Gina mentioned a notebook. She said to ask you about it."

The old couple looked blank. "What kind of notebook?"

"I'm not sure." Evans stood as well. "Gina said she had been collecting evidence against her ex-husband. Did she tell you about that?"

Sharon's face and mouth tightened. "At first, Gina just thought he was cheating. Then she started to believe Gary was forcing himself on those women by threatening to put them in jail."

Evans fought to control her disgust. "Did she tell you how she came to that conclusion?"

"Gina followed Gary and caught him visiting other women. She finally worked up the nerve and talked to one of them. It was a shameful story."

Evans followed Sharon down a hall lined with pictures of Gina at various ages. "Did you tell internal affairs about the allegations of Gary's sexual abuse?"

"I tried, but the detective cut me off. He said Gina was bitter and making up stuff, like people going through a divorce often do."

Evans didn't know Detective Santori personally, but she thought he sounded like an asshole too. He was IA, so it went with the territory.

They entered a small bedroom that looked more like a storage unit than a living space.

"We packed up Gina's belongings and brought them here. Except most of her furniture. We kept it in a storage unit for a year, then finally decided it was costing too much. We had to close out her shop too."

"What shop?"

"Gina is a fashion designer. She makes the most beautiful clothing." Sharon shoved boxes around until she had the one she wanted. She pulled out a long piece of purple velvet for Evans to see. A leaf pattern had been etched in the fabric.

"It's very pretty." It wasn't Evans' style, but she could see why women would be attracted to it.

"Her clothes made women feel like goddesses. Some of her clients were movie stars."

"Do you think you could find the notebook?"

Sharon sighed, put the fabric back, and dug through a box labeled *Desk Papers*. "If she had a notebook, it's probably in here."

"Was Bekker ever violent with Gina?"

"I don't think so, but he was cruel in other ways." Sharon kept digging, setting aside a stack of unopened mail and a stack of bank statements. "He made her feel bad about putting on a few pounds, and he resented her for not wanting to have a child."

Evans was starting to hate Bekker and wondered how Gina had ever become involved with him.

As if reading her mind, Sharon said, "Gary could be very charming. They met at a Special Olympics fundraiser. I liked him at first too." Sharon found a small, red notebook with spiral binding. "Maybe this is it." Pulling her glasses up to her face from where they'd been hanging on her chest, Sharon read from the first page. "June thirteenth, 2008, seven forty-five p.m. Gary stopped at the Courtyard Apartments, 623 W. 4th, and entered unit five. He stayed until nine. The apartment belongs to Trisha Cronin."

A shimmer of excitement ran up Evans' spine. "May I see that?"

Sharon handed it over, and Evans flipped through a few pages. Each held one or two entries, all meticulously dated and time-stamped, but few other names were mentioned. "I'd like to take this with me."

"I know you'll never prove he tried to kill Gina," Sharon said with a small shrug. "But if you send Gary to jail for this other stuff, it would be better than letting him get away completely."

Evans feared she was right, but she wasn't giving up the attempted-murder case without making every effort. "I intend to conduct a full investigation. Didn't you say you had made notes at the time?"

"Oh yes. They're in my desk."

Sharon retrieved an envelope from an office across the hall and handed it to Evans. "This is everything, and it's not much."

Back in the living room, Evans racked her brain for what else to ask. If she were at the scene where Gina had been assaulted, she'd have a better idea of how to proceed. "Where was Gina living at the time?"

"She had a condo out by Valley River Center. She moved there after she left Gary." Sharon was still doing the talking. Evans suspected George thought it might be a waste of time.

"What's the address? And where did she and Gary live before the separation? I want to talk to the neighbors in both places."

After writing it down, Evans asked, "Will you look through Gina's things for a recorder? You said she interviewed one of the women Bekker visited. Maybe she recorded it."

"Anything I can do to help."

"With Gina's permission, I'd like to go through her mail too. I'll go see her again tomorrow and ask."

"We're bringing her home as soon as she's able."

"When will that be?"

"If her recovery goes well, probably this week. The doctors are amazed by her progress already."

George added, "She'll still be in a wheelchair and need lots of help, but she wants to come home."

Evans handed them both a business card with her work cell-phone number. "Call me if you think of anything."

Sharon gave her hand another squeeze. "Thank you for taking this seriously."

On the drive back to the department, Evans called the front desk and asked for contact information for Officer Keith Markham. Evans dialed the number immediately so she wouldn't lose track of it. After a few rings, Markham picked up and she heard the sound of traffic in the background. "This is Detective Evans. Are you on patrol?"

"Yes, but I'm pulling off the road now. What's the situation?"

Evans looked for a place to pull off as well, so she could take notes. "Do you remember responding to an attempted suicide at the Riverside Terrace two years ago?"

"Yep. Turned out to be Sergeant Bekker's ex-wife."

Shit. He knew who Gina was. "I've been assigned to investigate the incident, and I'd like to ask some questions."

"That's a little unusual. Why now?"

Evans pulled into a parking lot in front of a shuttered business. "New evidence has come up. Did you notice anything out of place in the apartment? Anything that suggested there might have been a struggle?"

"Not at all. The woman was unconscious on her bed and there was an empty pill bottle nearby. The neighbor lady was there and said she thought it might be a suicide attempt. The paramedics arrived soon after and took her out. End of story."

"Did you see any bruises on the woman?"

"Are her parents digging this up again and trying to blame Sergeant Bekker?"

"Something like that. I'm just doing my job." Evans decided the conversation had possibly done more harm than good. "Please keep this conversation confidential."

"Sure. I hope you don't waste too much of your time."

"I won't. Thanks." *Shit.* She hoped he didn't tell Bekker.

Evans hung up and headed home. It was time to work off some stress and calories.

After a five-mile run in the heat, her tank top was soaked with sweat and she felt five pounds lighter. A little dizzy from dehydration, even though she'd taken a water bottle, Evans walked the last few blocks to her duplex on Dakota Street. She hoped to own a house someday, but it would not be this one. Still, after five years of renting, her side felt like home.

Evans took a cool shower and headed out to the back deck with a Coors Light and Gina's notebook. The sun dipped in the western sky and the evening glowed with pink-and-orange light. The smell of fresh-cut grass made her feel relaxed and content for the first time that day. She loved every moment of summer.

Evans turned on the porch light and sat down to read. Gina's handwriting was purposefully neat, with each date and incident carefully documented. Evans flipped to the last entry, noting it was dated August 1, two days before Gina had been hospitalized. The first entry was June 13, so Gina had documented six weeks of her ex-husband's activity. Evans counted the entries: seventeen. Gary Bekker had been a busy man that summer. And these were only the visits Gina had known about, and they were all in the evening. Had Bekker refrained from making booty calls during his department shifts? Or had Gina simply been at work and unable to document them?

Until page five, the entries were simply addresses Bekker had visited, along with his time of arrival and departure. Then Gina had made contact with one of the women and had written a detailed account. Evans read the journal entry with growing disgust.

After Gary drove away, I knocked on the apartment door. A blonde woman of about thirty answered. I told her I was Gary Bekker's soon-to-be-ex-wife and said I was investigating his activities. I made it clear I had no interest in harming her and I asked about the nature of her relationship with Gary. She tried to blow me off at first, but I convinced her that my intention was to expose Gary and help her in the process. Eventually, Trisha Cronin invited me in and told me her story.

She'd met Gary four years ago when he'd arrested her for prostitution and meth possession. He had fondled her freely while transporting her to jail. After Trisha was released three days later, Gary had shown up at her apartment. He'd been blunt. She could suck his dick or he would arrest her again. She had drugs in her bathroom and in her bloodstream and she was facing sixty days in jail for her next drug charge. Trisha argued and pleaded but ended up giving Gary a blow job. That was the first of many. Over the years, she'd had more arrests and dozens of visits from Gary. On his third stop over, he'd raped her. "That's what he does," Trisha said. "He comes over and rapes me. And I never report it because he's a cop and I'm a prostitute and no one would believe me."

The bastard! Evans slammed the notebook on the table, nearly knocking over her beer. A burning rage filled her veins and forced her out of the chair. She paced the narrow deck, sweat dripping from her temples. She hated sexual predators, and those who hid behind badges were the worst. A memory from the summer she turned seventeen played out in her mind. Evans tried to stop it, but she was powerless, just as she had been that day.

A state trooper had pulled her over late one night on her way home from a party. She'd been driving drunk, but it was rural Alaska and the roads were mostly empty. At least that's what she told herself at the time. She never knew the trooper's name. He hauled her out of the car, asked her to walk a straight line, and declared her intoxicated. He said she could give him a blow job or go to jail. Her choice. Young, drunk, and scared, she didn't think she had a choice. A blow job seemed easier than a trip to jail and, later, a possible beating from her father. Reeling with intoxication and disgust, she complied, then vomited on his shoes when it was over. He slapped her and told her to sleep in her car for an hour, then go home and behave herself.

She had quit drinking and driving after that, but the partying and wild behavior escalated until she finally ended up in jail. The wake-up call that changed her life. Evans shook the memory from her thoughts and chugged her beer. She had to stay focused on Gina and not let her own bullshit get in the way. But Bekker was going down, one way or another.

CHAPTER 6

Monday, September 6, 9:45 a.m.

After checking his voice-mail messages and e-mails, Jackson headed for the University of Oregon campus. If a dead body had in fact disappeared, this would be a hell of a case to resolve and he'd regret taking it. His plan was to spend the afternoon tracking down loose threads in his parents' case. He couldn't even ask Lammers about reopening the file unless he had something to substantiate Vargas' story.

He parked in a tow-away zone under the apartment complex on Seventeenth Avenue and hustled up to the second floor. A tall young woman with braces opened the door. Jackson introduced himself. "I'm here to see Nate Adams."

"He's not here, but he told me about seeing 'the body in the laundry room.'" She made air quotes around the last phrase. "Come in. I'm Sandy."

She moved toward a messy desk in the living room. "I have to get my stuff together and go to class, so I don't have much time, but I think I can explain this." She gathered up papers as she talked. "I asked Nate to describe the guy, and when he did, I knew who it was. His name's Eric. I think he's a homeless drug addict. I've seen him sleeping in the laundry room before, so he's probably okay."

"Do you know where I can find him?"

"He hangs out at Jason's. Apartment sixteen." Sandy moved to the door, then waited for Jackson to step out. "I'm sorry my goofy roommate wasted your time. Nate's a good guy, but he's rather excitable."

"Thanks for your help."

It took five minutes for the guy to answer the door. Jackson heard shuffling and muffled voices, so he knocked again. "Jason or Eric! You're not in trouble. Come to the door."

Finally, a gaunt young man in baggy jeans opened the door a few inches and showed his face. His eyes had the soft, out-of-focus gaze of a drug user. "What do you want?"

Jackson could have pushed his way in, but he didn't. He worked violent crimes; druggies were a waste of time. "Tell me your name."

"Eric."

"Were you sleeping in the laundry room last night? Specifically, around ten o'clock?

"Yeah. So?"

"Someone saw you and thought you were dead."

Eric burst out laughing. "As you can see, I'm not."

"Be careful with the heroin or you could end up that way." Jackson had his camera in hand and took a quick picture.

"Hey! Why'd you do that?"

"To prove you're not a corpse. Thanks."

He hurried down the stairs before Eric could deny him permission to use the photo. Some days his job was so bizarre he felt more like a babysitter or counselor than an investigator.

Back in the car, he sat for a moment, working up the courage to drive to his parents' old neighborhood, only blocks from where he lived now. He'd bought a house near his parents shortly after Katie was born so they would be close enough to spend time with their granddaughter. They'd only had a couple of years with her, and Katie didn't remember them. Jackson had driven by the house twice in ten years, just to see if Derrick was taking care of it. He started the Impala and headed toward his neighborhood. He'd called his brother that morning and no one had picked up. Jackson hadn't left a message. Some things needed to be done in person.

As Jackson parked in front of 2353 Emerald, his chest tightened in a familiar squeeze of pain. He hadn't felt it since he'd started taking the prednisone after his surgery. The CAT scan he'd had two weeks ago indicated the fibrotic growth had shrunk a little, so he hoped this new pain was just stress. Jackson reached for his notepad but left his shoulder bag in the car. The crime scene was long gone.

He stepped out and pulled in a deep breath. It was just a house and Derrick was his brother, the kid he'd played soccer with in the backyard. The boy who'd taught him how to catch a snake and fly a kite and every other cool thing he'd done as a child.

Jackson noted the faded paint, the sunbaked lawn, the lack of petunias in the front planter. Evelyn and Clark Jackson would not be happy with the condition of their home.

A gray Lincoln Town Car sat in the driveway, but nobody answered the door. Jackson still had the key his parents had given him twenty years ago, but it was at home in a bowl above his refrigerator. Derrick had likely changed the locks by now anyway. Jackson took out his cell phone and tried calling his brother, but no answer. Jackson headed for the sidewalk, leaving a message as he strode away: "It's Wade. Something important has come up. It's about Mom and Dad's murders. I need to talk to you. I tried calling, and now I'm standing in your front yard. Please call me."

A visual search of the neighborhood indicated that the Graysons probably still lived across the street. The house had been painted recently, but it was still the same robin's egg blue it had been for thirty years. Jackson crossed over, thinking how lucky he'd been to grow up in this quiet tree-lined neighborhood surrounded by parks and ball fields.

Mrs. Grayson answered the door, seeming more weathered, but still sporting the same permed hair and pink sweater. "Wade Jackson! Good grief, I don't believe it." She grabbed his forearm and squeezed. "Come in. Would you like some coffee?"

He had a policy of not drinking from an open container offered him by anyone he questioned, but this was Mrs. Grayson. He'd consumed plenty of raspberry Kool-Aid in this house as a kid, and she hadn't drugged or poisoned him then. "Sounds good. Black, please."

He followed her to the kitchen and sat at the table. He was eager to get right to the point of his visit, but he owed her some small talk. "How have you been?"

"I'm good. I had my hip replaced last year, but my health is still excellent." She knocked on the cupboard over the coffee-maker for luck. After a moment of quiet, she said, "Sam passed away, and I miss him, but I keep busy with volunteer work."

"I'm sorry for your loss." *How could he bring up his parents' deaths now?*

"What's on your mind, Wade? Are you worried about your brother?"

"Is something wrong over there?"

"Not really. He's just been a little wild since his wife left him."

Jackson hadn't known about the split. "What do you mean by wild? I haven't talked to him in years."

"I don't want to sound like an old gossip," she said, handing him the coffee, "but he comes home in the middle of the night and he has a different woman over every week. I think he's drinking a lot too."

Jackson was neither surprised nor concerned. Derrick had always liked to live on the edge. From the time his brother started driving at sixteen to when he married at twenty-five, Derrick had worried their mother sick. Jackson had tried to make up for it by being accountable. "I'm really here to ask about the day my parents were killed. I know it was long ago, but I have a new reason to think they put the wrong man in jail."

"Good grief." She plopped down in a chair. "But they caught that Mexican fella with the money, and he took a plea bargain."

"I visited him in prison, and he claims he was coerced into a confession. He's dying now, and he wanted me to know the real killer got away."

"Do you believe him?"

"I do."

"It's a shame then." She blew on her coffee. "How can I help you?"

"I want you to think about that day and remember everything you can. Did the police question you?"

"I came home from the library and there were cop cars all over the street. A patrol officer questioned me as I got out of my car, but clearly I hadn't been here to see or hear anything."

Jackson tried not to let his disappointment show. "Had you noticed anything different going on with Clark and Evelyn before that day? Unusual visitors? A change in behavior?" His parents had been the most predictable people in the world. His father had worked for the utility company for twenty-five years, and his mother had taught third grade for just as long.

Mrs. Grayson thought for a moment. "Your mother seemed distracted, maybe worried, the last time I talked to her."

"Did you ask her about it?"

"I did. She said everything was fine." Mrs. Grayson gave him a sad smile. "She was stoic, wasn't she?"

Jackson nodded, momentarily unable to speak. His washed down the lump in his throat with coffee. "What about when you left the house that day? Did you notice anything unusual? Strangers on the street? An unfamiliar car?" He realized he probably sounded desperate. The case was such a dead end.

"Can't say that I did." She shook her head. "I noticed the handyman was over at your parents' working on that stone wall, but he had been there for days, and I didn't think anything of it."

"Are any of the other neighbors who lived here at the time still around?"

"The Brickmyers still live right next door in the yellow house. They had just bought it a few months before."

Mr. Grayson shuffled into the kitchen, and Jackson almost dropped his coffee. Hadn't she said her husband passed away?

"Ernie, you remember Wade Jackson, don't you?" Mrs. Grayson got up to pour another cup.

Jackson stood and shook the old man's hand. He was definitely the Mr. Grayson he'd seen at his parents' funeral. *Who the hell was Sam?* As he stood there feeling awkward, he remembered Sam was their cat.

"Wade is here to ask about his parents' murders," Mrs. Grayson added. "He says the handyman didn't do it."

"I heard most of that." Mr. Grayson gripped the table and eased slowly into a chair. "I was home that day." He looked at Jackson. "I saw a car parked in front of the house next to your parents'. The Tylers lived there then, but they weren't home on the weekdays. And they drove a van, so I noticed the other car."

"What was the make?"

"A dark-blue sedan. A Crown Victoria or a Lincoln, maybe."

"Did you notice anything specific about the vehicle? Or get the license number?"

"It looked new and shiny clean, that's what I remember." Mr. Grayson worked his dentures into a better position. "And there was a guy behind the wheel."

"What did he look like?"

"Caucasian, with short, light-colored hair. Could have been blond or gray or light brown. I only saw him briefly when I went out to get the mail."

"How old?"

Mr. Grayson shrugged. "I'm not sure. He wasn't young though. At least forty."

"How was he dressed?"

"He had on a nice jacket, like a businessman. I think that's why I noticed him. He also wore sunglasses."

Why would a middle-aged businessman be parked next to his parents' house? Wearing sunglasses in late September? The information was odd and probably irrelevant, but Jackson jotted it all down in his notepad.

"How long was he there?"

"I'm not sure." Mr. Grayson ran his gnarled hands through what was left of his gray hair. "I heard the shots. Only I didn't realize they were shots at the time. I was pulling weeds in the side yard and I heard loud popping sounds from across the street."

Grayson's voice was creaky and sluggish, and Jackson willed him to live long enough to finish the conversation.

Mr. Grayson sipped his coffee with shaky hands, then continued. "I looked up and didn't see anything, so I went back to pulling weeds. Then I heard the sound again. I glanced across the street, but there was no one around and nothing happening that I could see. I went inside to use the bathroom. When I came out, I heard a car drive away."

Jackson pressed his teeth together and waited him out. He knew there was more to the story.

"I was curious, so I went outside and looked toward Twenty-Fifth Avenue. I saw the blue sedan at the corner, turning left. I went back to pulling weeds. About twenty minutes later, a cop car came screaming down the street and all hell broke loose."

Jackson remembered the anonymous call. "Did either of you call the police and report seeing Hector Vargas, the handyman, leaving their house?"

"No." Mrs. Grayson spoke, but they both shook their heads.

"Did you see him leave?"

"No."

Jackson looked at the old man. "Was Hector Vargas still over there working when you first saw the blue sedan?"

"I'm not sure."

"Did you tell the detectives about the car?"

"Nobody ever asked me. The police picked up the handyman an hour later, and he had your parents' cashbox. Everyone assumed he did it. I never gave the sedan another thought...until now."

Jackson fought to hide his disgust. The detectives assigned to the case hadn't even questioned the neighbors. They'd beaten a confession out of a thief instead. Jackson wondered how much Vargas' ethnicity had sealed his fate.

Mrs. Grayson echoed his thoughts. "I suppose his being a Mexican worked against him." She shook her head. "I'd like to think that couldn't happen now."

The department had become more politically correct in the last decade, but Jackson knew racial profiling still happened. He'd been guilty of it too, in subtle ways. Everyone looked outside their own cultures and beliefs for someone to blame.

Yet what Santori and Bekker had done went way beyond profiling. They had not only failed to do their jobs, they'd abused a suspect and let the man who killed his parents get away.

CHAPTER 7

After questioning the Graysons, Jackson knocked on the door of the other homes in the neighborhood. He found one young college student at home, but she had only been in the house for a year. Derrick was still not answering the door or his phone.

Jackson checked his watch and realized the morning was gone. He drove the mile home, hoping to have lunch with his daughter. He strolled up the sidewalk, savoring the pleasure of his well-kept yard. In the house, he called out to Katie, then remembered she was back in school. Disappointed not to see her, Jackson made a tuna sandwich and a glass of iced coffee from the cold stuff left in the pot. He kept hoping his brother would call back so he could talk to him in person while he was still in the neighborhood. Jackson laughed at his own twisted thought process. Derrick had lived only a mile away for the last ten years and he hadn't seen him or spoken to him. Why should convenience be a consideration now?

He ate his lunch at the table, skimming through the city section of the *Willamette News* and subconsciously looking for Sophie Speranza's byline. He liked to keep tabs on the young reporter's stories, because she often wrote about his cases, whether he approved or not.

He called Katie as he left the house, knowing she wouldn't pick up at school, and left her a message. "I missed having lunch with you today. I hope high school is treating you well so far. See you for dinner." At fifteen, his daughter was spending less time at home and rarely suggested they do things together anymore. Jackson was holding on as tightly as he could without actually putting a GPS device under her skin. He started to call her again to suggest they take the trike out that weekend, then wondered if he would end up working instead. He tended to get like that with homicide cases—and this one involved his parents.

As he drove back to the department, he decided it was time to tell Lammers about his activities. If she didn't give him official time to work the case, he would ask to take vacation days and work it on his own time.

Sergeant Lammers waved him into her office. As she hung up the phone, she stood and hollered, "Come in and tell me what's going on." She meant to sound friendly, but her voice had a built-in bullhorn.

Jackson sat, hoping she would too. He grabbed his cell and muted it. Lammers was known for becoming agitated by the sound of anyone's phone but hers. "I wrapped up the incident near campus. As I suspected, the supposed body was a young homeless addict passed out on the laundry-room floor. I spoke with him in person. There's no case."

"Great use of our time. Love the U of O students." Lammers produced a nasty smile. "I don't have anything new for you, but with this heat, just give it a few hours."

"I have an old case I want to reopen." Jackson braced himself.
"What case and why?"

"The murders of Clark and Evelyn Jackson in 2000. The man who was convicted says he didn't do it. He says he was abused and coerced into a confession."

Lammers scowled. "Why now? Why do you believe this crap?"

"He's dying and he wanted me to know that the real killer is still out there." Jackson set his recorder on the desk. "You should listen to his statement. He's convincing."

"No." She rapped the desk with an open hand. "This is personal for you. I get that. But you're saying that detectives here in this department abused their authority. Do you know what a shit storm this is for me?"

"Do you know what a shit storm this is for me?" Jackson matched her volume. "Not only did Bekker and Santori abuse a suspect, including burning him with a cigarette, they didn't bother to investigate anyone else."

"Bekker and Santori?" She arched her eyebrows, but not in a completely surprised way. "Who does he say burned him?"

"Bekker."

"How do you know they didn't investigate anyone else?"

"I read the case file. I talked to the people who lived across the street from the victims." Jackson was careful not to make it too personal. "Mr. Grayson saw a blue sedan parked outside the house before the murders. He heard the shots but didn't realize they were shots. Then he saw the sedan drive away a few minutes later, but no one ever questioned him at the time."

"Oh crap." Lammers pushed her hands through her cropped hair. He'd never seen her do that before. After a long silence, she said, "We have two issues here. The abuse of a suspect needs to involve internal affairs, so I'll handle that. We can reopen the homicide case, but eventually we'll need the support of the DA. Both incidents are ten years old, and I don't have much hope that either one will be resolved."

"You know I have to try and find my parents' killer."

"Yes. I understand that. I'll give you two weeks." She narrowed her eyes. "Don't discuss the abuse claim with anyone in the department. Just say new evidence has come up."

Jackson sympathized. Santori was now an internal investigator, so involving Ben Stricklyn, the other detective in the IA unit, could be tricky. "I'm more interested in finding the killer than I am in punishing the police work that let him get away."

"Good. Because Santori is a decent man and I don't want to see him prosecuted."

"What about Bekker?"

Her jaw tightened. "Between you and me, there's been talk that Bekker is becoming unstable, so I'll meet with the chief and see how he wants to handle this."

"Thanks. I appreciate your support."

"Don't thank me yet. I won't let this old murder case turn into an endless, pointless pursuit. Are we clear?"

"We are." Jackson took his cue and stood to leave.

"I'm sorry about your parents," Lammers said softly.

"Me too."

Jackson returned to his desk and stared at the file with his parents' name on the label. What the hell had been going on in their lives that would cause someone to kill them? How could he have been so oblivious to it? At the time, he'd had a toddler at home, a stressful patrol job, and a wife who'd started drinking heavily. His plate had been full and his parents seemed so content with their lives. But parents often kept things from their children out of habit, even when their kids were adults. He wondered if his brother Derrick had known what was going on. When they were young kids, his mother had been closer to Derrick because he was her firstborn. When they were teenagers, his father had been closer to Derrick because the two of them shared a passion for watching sports. Jackson had often felt like the odd one out.

Why hadn't Derrick returned his call? Jackson placed another call and left another message. He planned to stop by the house again late that afternoon to see if he could catch Derrick or the other neighbors at home. For now he would visit the crime lab and examine the evidence the technicians had collected. He wanted to believe they had done their jobs well, even if the investigators had not.

It would be easy to drive past the crime lab if you didn't know exactly what you were looking for. The gray-brick structure had no sign, no windows on the first floor, and no distinctive features. Even the entrance was on the side near the parking lot. The lab was also the only building on this section of Garfield Street that wasn't ancient or dilapidated. The location seemed odd, unless you factored in the dirt-cheap cost of the property.

Jackson ran his ID under the scanner and waited for the gate to open to the back parking lot. Once inside, he went in search of Jasmine Parker, the best technician in the department. He found the tall, pencil-thin woman in the small lab, processing fingerprints on the downdraft. He waited for her to glance over. Her ageless, striking face registered no surprise at seeing him. Jackson thought she would be a killer to play poker with.

"Hey, Parker. Have you got some time to look at an old case?"

"Sure. Give me five minutes here. You can wait in my office if you want."

Jackson was happy to wait in the lab. He rarely came up here, so he welcomed the chance to look closely at the tools used to process evidence. He'd once watched as Parker ran a metal safe through the super-glue dryer, but he usually didn't have time for anything but a phone call to find out what they'd discovered on a particular case.

When Parker finished her fingerprints, they walked down the hall to her private office. She took off her white lab coat and released her long black hair from the hairnet. "You said you were working an old case? That's unusual, isn't it?"

"It's my parents' murders."

"I didn't know. I'm sorry. When did they happen?"

"September 23, 2000."

"Why now?"

Jackson told her about the letter and his trip to the prison. When he mentioned the physical abuse, Parker registered disgust, something he'd never seen on her expressionless face.

"I didn't think that kind of thing happened in Eugene."

"It can happen anywhere, especially to people who are vulnerable."

"What now? Do you want to see the evidence?"

"I have to."

"Let's go."

Downstairs, they entered a locked storage room and Parker flipped on the overhead fluorescents. Rows of metal shelves came into view. They were stuffed with clear plastic bags and white tubs like the kind used to transport mail. Jackson was glad he didn't have to search alone.

"I started at the crime lab in February of 2000," Parker said, heading left and checking the dates on the end of the shelves. "I may have worked the case with a senior technician."

Jackson visualized Parker in his parents' living room, searching his mother's outer clothing for trace evidence. He hoped she'd been as thorough back then as she was now.

"Here's 2000." Parker turned down the row and headed toward the back wall. As they reached an area marked *September*, Jackson gave Parker the case number and they both started looking at labels.

It took twenty minutes to find the right box. Jackson recognized his mother's floral blouse though the clear plastic. He could almost smell the summery fabric softener she'd used on her clothes. A separate bag held a familiar white sweater. Dark-brown stains blotted the collar, making Jackson wince.

Other than two sets of clothing, the contents were disappointingly sparse for a crime scene with two bodies.

"Let's take it upstairs." Parker grabbed the plastic crate before Jackson could. It occurred to him that she realized how strange and difficult this process was for him. He hoped to get past the emotional reactions and start thinking analytically.

Upstairs, Parker suggested they use the lab, where they could lay out everything on a large table in the middle of the room. Joe Berloni, a short man with the face and torso of a boxer, was operating the super-glue dryer when they entered. He soon came over to check out what they were doing.

"What case is this?" Joe asked, as Parker unloaded a collection of smaller plastic bags onto the table.

"Double homicide in 2000," Jackson said, not wanting to get the gossip train going.

"New evidence has come up?" Joe was still curious, and Jackson didn't blame him.

"A new witness came forward so I'm looking at everything."

"Let me know if I can help." Joe picked up a bag with three spent bullets.

"The ballistics report says these are .22 slugs," Jackson said. "Anything unusual about them?"

Joe held the bag close to his face. "Unfortunately, no."

If he found a suspect and the suspect owned a gun, they could compare its fired bullets to these, but otherwise, the slugs meant little. Jackson reached for an evidence bag with a strand of hair. It was short and dark blond. Both of his parents had salt-and-pepper hair by the time they were fifty.

Nothing in the file indicated that Vargas' DNA had been found at the scene. Had this trace evidence been processed or compared to known felons? "I want to run a new DNA analysis on all of the trace evidence, with a priority on this hair," Jackson said. "While we're waiting for it to come back, I'd like to check CODIS for a match with the DNA work that was already done. The perpetrator might be in the system now, even if he wasn't then."

"It really isn't necessary to repeat the DNA analysis," Parker said. "But I'll check everything with CODIS again."

"The investigators were sloppy, because they thought they had the right perp. I'd like to start from scratch and make sure everything is done correctly."

Parker blinked. "I can't ask the state lab to prioritize it, so this could take a week."

"That's okay."

Jackson examined the last three evidence bags: a cigarette butt, a small black comb, and photos of muddy shoe prints near the front porch. The cigarette butt had started to degrade, but the DNA in the saliva should still be there. Where was the debris from the carpet? He turned to Parker. "Do you remember if you worked this case? A couple in their mid-fifties shot in their living room in South Eugene?"

Parker nodded. "I rode to the scene with Walters. He was the supervisor then. He collected trace from the bodies while I took fingerprints. After about an hour, the detectives got word that patrol cops had picked up a suspect. They cleared out soon after."

A flash of worry crossed Parker's face. "Eventually, I heard the victims were the parents of a cop, but I didn't know you then and I never made the connection until today."

"Do you remember anything unusual about the case?"

"It was one of my first, so I had little basis for comparison. Looking back, I now see that the investigators spent very little time in the house."

Jackson realized he was making her uncomfortable. "I'm glad to have you working the case with me now."

"I'll go through our files and find every test and analysis we conducted at the time."

"Thanks, Parker. If you think of anything specific from your own memory, I'd like to hear about it right away." Jackson started loading the evidence bags back into the crate. He hadn't expected to discover much, but he was a visual person and needed to see things for himself.

As he headed out, Parker called after him, "There was something unusual. Your moth—" She stopped and corrected herself. "The female victim had a hundred-dollar bill under her body. I heard the ME make a joke about it. When the handyman was caught with the cashbox, I assumed the bill had been dropped in the struggle." Parker stepped toward him. "But if Vargas left before your parents came home, how did the money get under her body?"

"And why isn't that bill in the evidence crate?"

CHAPTER 8

Evans woke before her alarm went off, as she did every work morning, and felt groggy from not sleeping well. The recurring nightmare she'd had through her early twenties had come back with a vengeance. She'd have to buy melatonin on the way home tonight and see if it helped. Seven years had passed since she'd had the rape dream. Goddamn Gary Bekker.

After brewing a tall cup of Italian roast, she sat down at her computer to read the news. Her browser opened to her favorite sites, and she skimmed through, taking in the main points of five or so articles while she drank her coffee. Evans checked her e-mail, disappointed she hadn't heard back from Mason. She'd met him at the climbing gym last week, and they'd had coffee afterward and exchanged e-mails. She'd hoped they would hook up. Celibacy was making her cranky.

At six thirty, she changed into workout clothes, grabbed her iPod, and headed for the spare bedroom. Cranking up some techno music, she began a vigorous kickboxing workout, followed by forty push-ups and an intense round of aikido practice. She couldn't alter the fact that she was five-five and female, but she refused to feel weak and she would never let herself be victimized again.

Two years before, she'd padded the floors and walls with thick mats so she could take falls and practice flying kicks. At the time, she'd been dating a guy who liked to spar and they'd spent a lot of time in the workout room…and the bedroom. Their relationship had been intensely physical. After Zack tore a hamstring during a particularly robust round of sex, they couldn't spar or screw for a while and she realized they had nothing important in common. He seemed almost relieved when she broke it off.

Still wet with sweat, Evans fried a pork chop for breakfast and wolfed it like a starving animal. She craved carbs, but if she ate them after a workout, they made her sleepy. She checked the time, then showered and dressed for work—dark slacks, topped by a sleeveless knit top and matching jacket with handcuffs in the pocket. It was almost a uniform. She tossed a Luna bar in her brown leather shoulder bag and took a quick inventory. She still had aspirin, band-aids, and masking tape, in addition to all her crime-scene tools. What else would she possibly need that day? As she slung the heavy bag over her shoulder, she remembered she needed to replace the blade in the small utility knife she carried at all times.

Finally, Evans strapped on her Sig Sauer, took a moment to enjoy the look and feel of it, and headed to the department.

She sat at her desk, gulping a tall coffee she'd picked up on the way, and decided to call McCray again. She would never nail

Bekker without the help of other police officers who were willing to tell her what they knew. McCray still didn't answer, so she left him a message, offering to buy lunch.

"Evans, you lucky dog." Tom Dragoo, a vice detective, slid up to her desk.

"Lucky? Since when?"

"You got the coma-woman case. I hear she's Sergeant Bekker's ex-wife and crazy as a box of weasels."

"Where did you hear that?" *How the hell did the information get around so fast?*

"Someone heard Lammers give you the assignment. You know how her voice carries."

"Who told you?"

"Never mind. But good luck." Dragoo gave her a wicked grin and slithered away.

Shit. Did Bekker already know she was investigating his ex-wife's complaint? The department was such a gossip mill. She would have to work fast. Evans grabbed her bag and headed out. It was time to talk to Gina again.

In the parking lot, seeing all the patrol cars, Evans had one of those moments when she couldn't believe how her life had turned out. Right out of high school, she'd been arrested for drunk-and-disorderly conduct and had spent two nights in jail. Hearing the doors clang shut behind her had been terrifying, and she'd decided to make radical changes. Two months before, a sheriff had come to her civics class and said, "Out of these twenty students, one of you will end up in prison." It had been a punch in the gut. Evans had known he was talking about her. Yet until she was arrested, she'd continued to party and shoplift just to see if she could get away with it. Life in Fairbanks, Alaska, was that boring.

She'd been sentenced to three months' probation for the drunk-and-disorderly charge. Her parents kicked her out, and she was homeless, sleeping on friends' couches while she waited tables and saved money. When her probation was over, she left Ketchikan with only an overnight suitcase and took the ferry to Seattle. She stayed with a friend of a friend until she could find work. Her first stop was the social-security office, where Leeann Egerton became Lara Evans. She had not seen or talked to her parents since the day they kicked her out. Birthday calls to her brother were all the contact she had with her old life.

When Evans entered Gina's room at the care center, a physical therapist was working with the patient, and her parents hovered nearby. The family greeted her warmly. "We were just getting ready to leave," Sharon said. "But I'm glad you're here. Gina said you could go through her stuff, but she thinks if you have the notebook, there's nothing else that will help you."

The physical therapist manipulated Gina's fingers and said, "Now squeeze."

Gina scrunched her face with effort, and her hand contracted. She beamed with the result, but tears rolled from her eyes. Joy or pain? Evans wondered. Maybe some of both.

After the Stahls left, Evans took a seat and said to the therapist, "Gina and I need to talk. Can you come back later?"

"I'm almost done." The woman didn't even look up. "You can ask questions while I finish."

Evans didn't like the situation, but what else could she do? Driving back and forth to Springfield to talk to Gina for ten minutes at a time was annoying enough. "I need to know more about the day you were assaulted. Did you get any threatening phone calls or unusual encounters?"

"Not that I recall," Gina said, still squeezing, "but my memory is still sketchy. It gets better every day though.

"Go through as much detail as you can. It might help you remember."

"I came home from the shop and made dinner. I thought about going out to follow Gary again, but after talking to Trisha, I decided to contact another one of his victims instead. I was waiting for the weekend." Gina spoke slowly, but her voice was clear. "I spent time on the computer, then read for a while, then went to the kitchen to make popcorn. That's when it happened."

"How did he get in? Was your door locked?"

Gina shook her head. "I usually didn't lock it until I went to bed."

Evans thought that was beyond stupid. She kept her doors and windows locked, even though she possessed two handguns and carried Mace at all times.

"I know," Gina said, reading her face. "But my condo was in an upscale neighborhood with security patrols."

The physical therapist moved around the bed and picked up Gina's other hand.

"What else do you remember about the attacker?"

"What did I tell you already?"

Evans flipped through her notes. "Between five-seven and six feet tall and less than two hundred pounds. Brown jacket and a ski mask. Your ex-husband fits that general size, but does it match anyone else you know? Or knew then?"

Gina gave it some thought. "I'd been married for five years, so I didn't have any male friends. I ran my own clothing business, and almost all my clients were women. At the condo, my neighbors were mostly older couples."

"Had you seen anyone suspicious around the complex? A delivery man who matched that description?"

"I'd seen Gary at my apartment complex. I'm sure it was him."

"I have to look at all the possibilities."

"Squeeze," the therapist directed.

Gina squeezed for all she was worth. "I want to get up again."

"I'll be back with the wheelchair in twenty minutes," the PT responded. She rounded up her gear and left the room.

"Who else would want to harm you?" Evans asked. "Do you have any enemies?"

"No."

"Were you dating?"

A look of sadness came over Gina. "I had just started seeing someone."

"What's his name?"

"He didn't do this."

"What if Bekker went after him too?"

Gina sucked in her breath. "Oh my god. I never thought about that. His name is Stuart Renfro. He's a nurse."

Evans jotted it down. A nurse would have access to Demerol. "Has he been here to see you?" So far, Gina's awakening hadn't made the news, but eventually it would.

"We had only been on two dates. When I stopped answering my phone, I'm sure he moved on."

"Do you have any other family here in town besides your parents?"

"I'm an only child."

"You had a prescription for Valium. The bottle on your nightstand was empty. Did you take it all? Did you try to kill yourself?" Evans watched her carefully. Gina's eyes didn't shift and her hands didn't flutter.

"I took one Valium that day, like usual. I did not try to kill myself."

"What about the Demerol? Was that yours?"

Gina's mouth pulled tight. "I didn't have Demerol in my house. Gary must have brought it with him. He probably injected me with it."

"Where would he get the drug?"

"He's a cop. He's resourceful. He probably took it from one of his victims." Gina's voice weakened, sounding tired.

Something had been nagging Evans, and finally she hit on it. "If Bekker tried to kill you because he knew you'd been following him and documenting his sexual encounters, why didn't he take the notebook?"

"I left it in my car. He probably didn't find it."

"There's nothing in the case notes or in your neighbors' account of that evening to indicate your apartment had been searched."

"Gary wanted it to look like suicide, so he was careful."

Evans was trying to look for other motives and not be too focused on one suspect. "Did you owe anyone money?"

"I was behind on my bills and I owed my divorce lawyer, but I was making payments."

"When was your divorce final?"

"A month after the attack. My parents told me this morning. If I had been awake when the final papers came, I would have thrown a party."

Evans smiled, then looked at her notes. "Did Stuart Renfro have a wife or girlfriend you didn't know about? Someone who might want to harm you?"

"He was divorced too. And we'd only gone out twice. We hadn't even slept together."

Evans had run out of questions. "If you think of anything else, call me. I don't care what time it is."

"Okay," Gina murmured, her eyes closing.

Evans planned to track down Stuart Renfro, but first she had to talk to McCray about Bekker. The bastard ex-husband was such an obvious suspect she hated to waste her time looking for anyone else, but she would cover everything, as Jackson had taught her.

Earpiece in place, she pressed speed dial #5 as she drove back to Eugene. She turned the air conditioner on low and ate a bite of her Luna bar. *Come on, McCray, pick up.*

Finally, he answered. "Evans. This must be important. What's going on?"

"I have a complicated case I need to talk to you about."

"Why me? Jackson's your mentor and I'm retired now, remember?"

"You worked vice, and I need to know about Gary Bekker."

A long silence.

"McCray, are you still with me?"

"I'm here. You just pulled the scab off an old wound, and I need to know why."

"Will you meet me for coffee?"

"I quit coffee, remember?"

"I'll buy you tea or lunch if you like. This is important. Can you meet me at Full City or should I come to you?"

"Give me an hour. I'll be there at eleven thirty."

"Thanks."

McCray was already in the coffee shop when she got there. He wore jeans and a T-shirt and Evans almost didn't recognize him. It was the first time she'd seen him in anything but brown corduroys and button-up shirts. He was still thin and white-haired, but the lines in his face had softened. Nothing like getting away from dead bodies and late nights staring at phone records to lighten a person's stress load.

Evans hurried to the counter where he stood waiting to order. "McCray, I'll buy."

He smiled. "This place takes me back."

"This coffee kept us going on some cases, didn't it?"

They took their beverages to a corner table, and McCray got right to the heart of issue. "Just because I'm retired doesn't mean I'm going to rat out a fellow officer. Why are you asking about Gary Bekker?"

"Did you know his ex-wife has been in a coma for two years?"

"I did. So? She overdosed, likely on purpose."

"She came out of her coma and claimed she was assaulted and drugged. She says her ex-husband did it."

McCray kept his poker face. Only his eyes registered a reaction. "I'm surprised Lammers assigned you the case."

"She doesn't know yet the victim has accused an officer."

"Bekker had an alibi for that evening. After his ex-wife's parents came in and suggested he was involved, a discreet inquiry was made. IA determined Bekker was drinking with a friend that evening."

"Another cop?"

"Yes."

"So it's probably bullshit."

McCray shrugged. "What do you want from me?"

"Gina says her ex-husband is a predator. That he coerced vulnerable women—hookers and drug addicts—into having sex. Gina was following him and writing down his activities. She says it's why he tried to kill her."

McCray's eyes closed for a split second, like a man who'd said a quick prayer. Followed by, "Oh, christ."

"What do you know?"

"There were rumors about him. He was reprimanded twice for using excessive force."

"What rumors? I need to know what I'm getting into here."

"It's way over your head. You need to take it to IA."

"It's my first lead on an important case. I can't just give it away." Evans grabbed McCray's hand. "Please tell me what you know."

He pulled free of her grip. "Another vice cop saw Bekker's car in front of a hooker's house late at night. The detective assumed he was dicking her and not paying. He gossiped and snickered about it, but that was it."

"Which detective?"

"Didn't you say the ex-wife was keeping a journal? Why don't you find it and see what's in there first?"

McCray was trying not to name other officers. Evans wasn't giving up. "Did you trust Bekker when you worked with him? What was your take on the guy?"

Another long silence. "He was an asshole. He pushed buttons with his coworkers and he got physical with suspects. I didn't like working with him. One of the many reasons I transferred out of vice."

"Is he capable of killing his wife?"

McCray grinned. "At times, we're all capable of killing our spouses."

Evans gave him a look.

"If his ex-wife says he attacked her, then what more do you need? Go to the DA and file charges."

"It's not that simple. Her assailant was wearing a ski mask, so she can't positively identify him. And Bekker had an alibi. I've got nothing to take to the DA."

McCray scowled. "So you're going after his sexual transgressions to break down his character?"

Hot anger flashed in her face. "He wasn't just cheating on his wife. He preyed on women who were in trouble and afraid of him and he forced them into sex. He's worse than scum and needs to be locked up."

"If what you say is true, then I agree. I just don't know how to help you."

"Give me the name of the detective who saw Bekker at the prostitute's house."

McCray hesitated but not for long. "Bohnert.

"No shit." John Bohnert now worked in violent crimes, but Evans didn't know him well.

"That's not who gave Bekker an alibi," McCray said. "That was Pete Casaway."

Casaway had retired last year. "Would he lie for Bekker?"

"If he was certain of his innocence, yes." McCray's eyes bore into hers. "If Jackson were in trouble, you would lie for him, wouldn't you?"

She would do almost anything for Jackson, but McCray didn't need to know that. "That depends on the situation."

"What if his ex-wife died of an overdose and her parents said Jackson killed her? Then he came to you and said, 'I was home alone but I need this to go away.' Would you give him an alibi?"

Evans squirmed. "Probably."

"Remember that when you talk to these guys. Bekker is their friend and a cop, and they thought they were doing the right thing."

"Fair enough."

"Don't tell anyone you got their names from me."

"I won't. Thanks for your help."

"Be careful. This could turn against you very quickly."

CHAPTER 9

Evans hurried across Pearl Street toward city hall. The police department still occupied half of the white-brick structure, but not for long. The city had finally purchased a new building on Country Club Road, and the department would move when the remodel was complete. She was excited about having more work space but would miss the energy of being downtown. As she entered the parking lot below the building, sweat broke out under her light-blue jacket. This was the warmest September she'd ever experienced in Eugene.

Evans stood by her car, undecided. To properly investigate the attack on Gina, she needed to visit the apartment complex where Gina had lived at the time and find out if any witnesses were still around. She needed to question Gina's boyfriend at the time and rummage through the letters and files stored in the Stahls' house. All of it seemed like a lot of work that would lead nowhere. On the other hand, building a case against Bekker for sexual assault would likely have better results. She was eager to talk to the prostitute, Trisha, and get her story on file. Before she went to her boss and called Sergeant Bekker a dirty cop and a killer, she needed something solid.

She called Pete Casaway, Bekker's alibi for the night Gina went into a coma, and left a message. She didn't mention Bekker in her message.

Evans made up her mind. Trisha Cronin's address was nearby, so she'd make a quick stop on her way out to Gina's old neighborhood.

Trisha's apartment building was in an area of the Whiteaker neighborhood called *heroin alley* by landlords and law enforcement. The once-white building hadn't been painted or washed in a decade, and the shrubs had died from neglect. *Or maybe from the toxic piss of its residents*, Evans thought, crinkling her nose as she climbed the stairs up to unit five.

She knocked gently, trying not to sound like a cop.

Trisha answered, wearing a bathrobe and looking half-asleep. She was thirty-something, a little doughy, and had once been pretty. Evans struggled for a way to describe her hair color when she started her notes. Fried-dyed-pink-blond?

"Ah shit." Trisha tried to shut the door, but Evans shoved her foot and shoulder into the space.

"I'm not here to harass you. I want to help."

"Bullshit. Cops are never here to help me."

"I want to put Gary Bekker in jail."

The pressure from the door eased. "Why?"

"It seems like a good place for him. Can I come in?"

Trisha weighed her decision for a long moment, then stepped back and opened the door.

Evans entered the dark apartment, surprised by how clean and uncluttered it was. Still, the stink of cat was evident. "Can we sit at the table?" She didn't want cat hair on her clothes.

"I don't have much time," Trisha said. "I have an appointment soon."

Right, an appointment. "I know you talked to Gina Bekker about her ex-husband's sexual abuse. I read her notes. I'd like to hear your story firsthand."

"That was years ago, and nothing ever happened to Gary. But he pretty much leaves me alone now." Trisha rolled her eyes. "I think he got bored with me."

They moved into the small dining room, separated only by a change in flooring. "Would you like some tea?" Trisha asked.

"No thanks."

Evans pulled her recorder from her bag and set it on the table. "Please state your name and the date of this conversation."

"I don't know if I want to go on record. He can still make trouble for me."

"You're not his only victim. If all of you speak up, we can put him away."

The fear in her face gave way to a little hope. "I'm Trisha Cronin, but I don't know the date. I think it's September."

Evans gave her name, the date, and their location, then pulled out her notepad. "When did you first meet Gary Bekker?"

"I think it was 2006, because that was the year my mother died and I was pretty messed up." Trisha pulled her robe tighter, as if she were suddenly cold.

"Tell me what happened."

Trisha related the same story Evans had read in Gina's notebook, only with more detail and more swearing. The visits—rapes, as she called them—continued for a few months after she had talked to Gina, then became less frequent. "I heard he started up with another woman. Her name's Joni, and she's a heroin user who lost her kid to the state for a while."

"Do you know of other women besides Joni? The more victims who speak up, the more likely we'll get a conviction."

"I was at the White Bird Clinic one day and I heard a young girl named Serena talking about a cop who assaulted her when she was drunk. I think she's in jail now on theft charges."

"Do you know her last name?"

Trisha shook her head. "You need to go now. I have an appointment."

Let's not make the john wait. Evans tried to keep her face impassive, surprised by the depth of her disgust with Trisha. Now she understood why the victims had never reported Bekker. Who would sympathize with a prostitute filing a complaint about sexual abuse? Certainly not one of the male detectives who worked the vice unit and had processed their fill of sex crimes. Evans made up her mind to find all of Bekker's victims.

She thanked Trisha and got the hell out. The sun seemed especially bright after the dark apartment, so she pulled on sunglasses. What next? Her little mantra—*What would Jackson do?*—popped into her head and made her smile. Someday, when she was over him, she'd tell Jackson about mentally consulting his guidance the way others called on Jesus.

Work the case you've been assigned. That's what Jackson would tell her. Start with the basics and knock on the neighbors' doors. Relieved that the Geezer had not been violated or stolen, Evans climbed in the car and headed for the Valley River condo where Gina used to live.

She pulled into Riverside Terrace and noted the security camera mounted to the corner of the gate. Would they have footage from two years ago? Not damn likely. The iron gate was open, so the barrier had to be more about aesthetics than security. She wondered if they closed and locked it at night. Evans found the manager's sign, parked nearby, and climbed out.

The row of pristine white condos stretched along the riverbank and, for a moment, Evans was jealous of anyone lucky enough to live there. Then she remembered the river wasn't so pretty in winter, which lasted a lot longer than summer.

She knocked on the manager's door, heard someone respond, and waited a good five minutes. "Sorry about that, I was just finishing my routine." The older woman wore stretchy yoga clothes and looked damn good for her age. "What can I do for you?"

Evans introduced herself. "I'm investigating an assault that happened in this complex two years ago. How long have you been the manager?"

"About six years. I don't recall any assaults."

"It was labeled an attempted suicide at the time. Her name is Gina Stahl, and she came out of her coma recently."

"Oh my god." The woman's hand flew to her mouth. "I thought she died. She's okay?"

"She will be." Evans was pleased the manager had been around long enough to remember Gina. "What's your name?"

"Raylin Jones. Why don't you come in out of the heat?"

Once inside the converted office, Evans asked, "Are any of Gina's old neighbors still here?"

"I'll have to check. What unit was she in?"

"Number sixteen."

Raylin moved to the desk and opened a file on her computer. "Steve and Gloria Hutchins have been in unit seventeen since 2005, so you can talk to them. But that's it. The woman in unit fifteen moved out in 2008. She lost her job in the recession."

"Will you give me the Hutchinses' phone number? In case they're not home."

"Sure, but they're retired, so you'll catch them at home."

Steve and Gloria were both reading in their living room as she passed the big window. *A picture of contentment*, Evans thought. She didn't see it often.

Gloria looked up just as Evans knocked. Through the glass, she watched the older woman hurry over. "Who is it?" she said through the door.

"Detective Evans, Eugene Police."

The door opened a little. "I'd like to see your badge."

Evans moved her jacket aside and showed her.

"What's this about?"

"Gina Bekker, the woman who used to live next to you."

Gloria sucked in her breath. "Did she die?"

"She woke up and claimed she was assaulted."

"Gina came out of her coma?" Steve Hutchins had followed his wife to the door.

"I'd like to ask some questions." Evans pulled out her notepad, hoping they would invite her in. The temperature had hit ninety again and she wearing a goddamn suit jacket.

"Come in." Gloria had an edge of excitement in her voice. "It's so amazing she woke up." She gestured for Evans to sit on the couch across from their reading recliners. Every bit of fabric in the room, including the Hutchinses' clothing, was in a shade of beige or pink. It was all a little sterile and Evans wanted to spill some coffee to make herself feel more comfortable.

"Were you home the evening Gina went to the hospital?"

"I'm the one who found her and called 911." Gloria's eyes danced, and Evans swore she could hear the old woman's heart pound with excitement.

"What made you go next door?"

"It was Sunday night, and sometimes Gina came over and watched reruns of *Desperate Housewives* with us. I went over to tell her we were starting one, but she didn't answer."

"We knew she was home," Steve cut in, "because we'd heard music earlier."

Gloria shot him a look. It was her story. "I knocked harder, and the door came open a little. It wasn't latched, so I pushed it open a little more and called out." Gloria's hands twisted in her lap. "I got a bad feeling. Gina listened to classical music when she was depressed, and she'd been playing Bach earlier. So I went in. We'd become pretty good friends, and I was worried." Gloria caught Evans' eyes, looking for approval. Evans nodded.

"I found her unconscious on her bed. I could tell by her color and stillness something was wrong. Then I saw the empty pill bottle and called 911."

"Did anything in Gina's apartment seem out of place?"

"Nothing except the door not being latched."

Evans made notes as quickly as she could. "Did either of you see anyone hanging around the complex that day or that evening?"

"No," Steve answered. "This is a secure building."

"Did you hear anything unusual from her apartment before you went over?" This question was directed at Gloria.

"No. Just the music earlier."

"Had Gina ever mentioned her ex-husband?"

They snorted in unison. "Oh yes." Gloria nodded in big gestures. "She hated him. He cheated on her and gave her VD. That's how she found out."

"Gina said he verbally abused her too," the husband added, trying to get a word in.

"Gary was being difficult about the divorce as well." Gloria pressed her lips together. "I felt bad for Gina. Her lawyer was costing her a fortune."

Evans suddenly wondered about Gina's motive in blaming her ex. *Was it simply about revenge? Was Gina mentally unstable?* "You said Gina played music when she was depressed. How often did she get depressed?"

"When she first moved in, we heard the classical stuff a lot. Then she started getting out more and we could tell she felt better. Until that day, she hadn't been depressed in weeks."

"Did you ever meet Gary Bekker or see him here at the complex?"

"Oh yes. He used to sit out in the parking lot just to upset her. And he succeeded." Gloria leaned forward. "That wasn't the first time Gina overdosed."

CHAPTER 10

Tuesday, September 7, 8:35 a.m.

Jackson parked in front of 2353 Emerald, turned off the engine, and drank his coffee. His car windows were down and the smell of dew-covered grass filled the morning air, reminding him of the lawn-mowing business he and his brother had operated in this neighborhood when they were kids. Two years older, Derrick had been bigger and stronger and always won when they wrestled for control of shared possessions. Yet Derrick had let him tag along on many adventures with his older friends. Careening down Green Hill Road on their bikes, jumping off the bridge near Fern Ridge—they were Jackson's favorite childhood memories.

Derrick's sedan was still in the driveway, so his brother had to be home. It was time to barge in and confront him. This visit wasn't about their estrangement. It was about finding their parents' killer. Jackson climbed out of the car, and the sun warmed his back, promising the day would be another hot one.

He rang the doorbell once, then pounded loudly. "Derrick! I have to talk to you. It's important."

No response. Jackson shouted again, then looked for the ceramic frogs tucked into the ferns along the front window. He lifted the middle frog and found a key under it. Jackson tried the key in the door and it worked, so he entered the house. "Derrick, it's Wade. We have to talk."

A sour smell assaulted his nostrils. Spilled beer, Jackson guessed. He stepped out of the foyer into the living room. The shape of the walls was all he recognized of his childhood home. Beer cans littered the area around the couch, and an empty Jack Daniels bottle stuck out between the cushions. Dirty plates covered the coffee table, with congealed food adding to the stink. Heavy blankets hung over the picture window, blocking out the light. To his left, dirty laundry and newspapers were piled on the kitchen table.

In his head, Jackson heard his father's voice holler, *What in tarnation is going on here?*

He strode down the hall, thinking his brother might still be in bed. "Derrick, are you here? We need to talk." A cold wave of apprehension spread across his chest. What if Derrick slept with a gun and woke up drunk and mad? Jackson instinctively reached for his weapon, then just as quickly pulled back.

He pushed open the master bedroom door at the end of the hall and prepared to hit the ground. His brother was sleeping facedown on the bed, wearing only white boxers. Jackson shook the bed and shouted his brother's name until Derrick rolled over.

"What the fuck?"

"Sorry to barge in, but I've been trying to contact you since Sunday." Jackson stepped back to give the man space. "I'll go put on some coffee." Derrick muttered something as he left the room.

In the kitchen, a small garbage container overflowed onto the floor and fruit flies buzzed around two blackened bananas on the counter. Jackson found a can of coffee in the refrigerator and had to clear dishes out of the sink to access the faucet. He hadn't known Derrick was drinking this heavily. *That's because you haven't called in ten years*, a guilty voice in his head countered.

He heard the shower running, and it made him feel a little less bleak, but he wasn't sure why. While the coffee brewed, he loaded the dishwasher and planned what he would say.

When Derrick entered the kitchen ten minutes later, they had a long moment of silence while Jackson poured coffee. He was pleased to see his brother's clothes were clean, but he hadn't shaved in days and his hair had grown to his shoulders.

"What do you want, Wade? After ten years?"

"I'm sorry I didn't contact you in all this time, but you didn't call me either." *Oh shit. Why had he said that?*

"You told me not to, remember?"

"That was a long time ago, and we'd been arguing. I didn't mean it."

"Why are you here now?"

"I've reopened our parents' case." Jackson looked around for somewhere to sit.

"What the hell are you talking about?"

"Hector Vargas contacted me, and I went to see him. He says he took the money but didn't kill them, so I'm starting over with the investigation."

"Oh come on, the bastard confessed!" Derrick's cobalt-blue eyes blazed and his wide jaw tensed. They both had their mother's features, only Derrick was blond and better looking.

"Vargas was abused and coerced into signing a confession. He's dying of cancer and has nothing to gain by changing his story."

Derrick rubbed his face with both hands. "I'm not ready for this." He lurched to the table, grabbed the pile of dirty clothes, and tossed them through the laundry-room door. They took seats on opposite sides of the table. Derrick gulped some coffee, then said, "You think you'll find the real killer after all these years?"

"I'm going to try."

Derrick shook his head. "Wade to the rescue. Do you always have to be such a goddamn Boy Scout?"

Jackson was taken aback. Derrick resented *him*? He started to respond, then caught himself. He was here as an investigator with a job to do. "I need to know about the time before the murders. Did you see Clark or Evelyn the day they died?"

"Clark or Evelyn? That's cold, brother."

"I'm trying to make this less emotional for both of us."

"You can't." Derrick spit coffee as the words flew out of his mouth. "Our parents were shot dead in this house. People we called Mom and Dad, not some strangers named Clark and Evelyn. It is emotional, no matter how many years have passed."

"This isn't easy for me either. I had to look at the damn crime-scene photos and stop at the lab to see the blood stains on Mom's sweater. Now I need your help."

"What do you want to know?"

"Did you see them the day they died?"

"I saw them that morning before I left for work. When I came home, the cops were here and they were dead."

"You moved in here with them the day before they were murdered. Why?"

"My girlfriend and I had just broken up. I needed a place to stay." Derrick got up, found a piece of bread, and wolfed it down. "To settle my stomach," he said, sounding defensive.

"Who did Mom and Dad know that drove a dark-blue sedan?"

"Seriously? You have a lead?"

"The Graysons saw a dark-blue car parked near the house that day. Mr. Grayson saw it drive away after he heard the shots."

Derrick rubbed his face again. "That was so long ago."

"Think about it. Who did they hang out with?"

"They spent time with Dad's friend from work, Charlie Bledsoe. He drove a black midsize car. Mom's book-club friend Kathy drove a blue minivan." Derrick shook his head. "I only remember that because she was kind of hot and I helped her load some flowers into the back of the van once."

"Had something changed recently for Mom and Dad? Did they seem worried about anything?"

"Mom always looked worried to me." Derrick shrugged. "I had that effect on her."

"What about financial concerns? Did they talk to you about anything specific?"

"They never talked about money. You know that."

"The medical examiner found a hundred-dollar bill under Mom's body."

Derrick's thick brows lifted. "We know Vargas took their cashbox. He must have dropped some on the way out."

"He says the box was locked and he smashed it open when he got home."

"He's a thief and probably a murderer too, so I don't put much stock in anything he says." Derrick gulped his coffee. "You got any aspirin? I ran out days ago."

Jackson dug in his bag for a small bottle of naproxen, which he'd been taking since his surgery. "It's not aspirin, but it should help." He wanted to comment on the source of Derrick's headache, but he wouldn't risk alienating him. Not until he had what he'd come for.

"I need to look through Mom and Dad's paperwork if you still have it."

"It's in the small bedroom that used to be yours."

"You brought it in from the garage?"

Derrick gave him a half smile. "When Mona moved out, I brought all their stuff into the house just to be spiteful. Mona didn't even want it in the garage. She kept bugging me to get rid of it."

"I'm glad you didn't." Jackson stood. "I'm sorry about your marriage. What happened?" Derrick and Mona had eloped to Vegas, so Jackson hadn't even attended the wedding.

"It doesn't matter now." Derrick pushed up more slowly. "I heard you got divorced too."

"Renee's drinking became such a problem I had to kick her out. Worst day of my life." His wife and daughter had cried and called him names as he packed Renee's belongings. He wondered if Derrick's wife had left him for the same reason.

Without commenting, his brother started down the hall. Jackson followed him to the small bedroom that had once been his. The room had been painted pink and turned into a sewing space long before his parents' death, so Jackson was past being sentimental about it. Now it held a large set of weights and a pile of dusty boxes, all sealed with tape and labeled in his own handwriting. He dreaded this process, which would be both tedious and disturbing. He turned to Derrick. "Would you like to help?"

"Maybe in a minute. I have some things to do first."

Jackson wondered why Derrick seemed to have Tuesday off. "Where are you working these days?"

"I've been unemployed for a year." Derrick held out his hands in a gesture that said, *Look around here, idiot.* "Eugene has no middle-management jobs, or anything else, but I only recently quit looking." Derrick abruptly walked out, leaving Jackson to face the memories alone.

Eventually, he would examine everything in the boxes, but he wanted to start with personal letters and the contents from his mother's desk. She had been a hoarder who could never throw out anything she thought might be important. Derrick obviously had inherited that gene. Jackson found a box labeled *Letters* and used his utility knife to cut open the tape. Sitting cross-legged on the floor, he pulled out bundled stacks of letters. Some dated back to his mother's years in college. Others were from his various aunts. Many were Christmas cards only. Jackson remembered sitting in this house with Derrick, boxing up everything and hoping to cauterize the wound of their death. He had suggested they throw away the old letters, and his brother had refused.

Starting with the most recent stack, he untied the blue ribbon holding the letters together and pulled the top one out of its envelope. It was from his Aunt Irene. Jackson skimmed it, thinking that reading incoming mail might be less revealing than reading his mother's outgoing mail. Unless the killer had written to her. His parents had purchased a computer about three months before they died, but neither had set up an e-mail account. They claimed they bought the PC for shopping online and checking the news and weather in Missouri, his father's home state.

After a half hour of skimming through family updates, Jackson stood to stretch his legs. Not only did it feel wrong to read personal information intended for his mother, it also seemed like a waste of time. He opened the bedroom window and sat back down with a box marked *Financial*. He decided to switch back and forth to keep from getting burned-out.

He'd seen some of the bank statements a week or so after the funeral. He and Derrick had consulted his parents' lawyer and accessed their finances. They'd had less cash in the bank than Jackson expected. At the time, he'd felt guilty, because they'd paid for two years of community college for him and later loaned him money to put Renee into a treatment program. They'd acted like they had plenty. Was that a facade or had they spent large sums on something else? Had someone been blackmailing them? Even more unthinkable, did one of them have a gambling problem?

Either way, Jackson didn't see why any of those circumstances would lead to murder. None of it made sense.

After an hour of reading through bank statements, IRA paperwork, and canceled checks, Jackson had discovered nothing of significance. None of the cash withdrawals seemed large enough to be important. He learned that his father wrote checks to the Mission and that his mother had given money regularly to Planned Parenthood. He would have to tell Kera that. She was a nurse at the local Planned Parenthood clinic and knew how important those donations were.

Jackson's stomach grumbled, making him think it was time to get some lunch. Yet he felt like he had missed something. What would he be doing if this were a current case? Then it hit him. He would have subpoenaed the victims' phone records in addition to their financial statements. Knowing his parents, they had kept all of their monthly bills for at least seven years. Jackson dug around until he found a box labeled *Bills*. He almost laughed out loud. He had tried to convince Derrick to throw all this away, and any normal person would have.

He cut open the box, found a bundled stack of phone bills dating back to January 1993, then realized that landline phone statements back then didn't include a detailed listing of every call going in and out, just the long-distance calls. *Crap.* He wondered if Qwest would still have the records and if the company would release them without a court order. It was worth a call. Jackson grabbed the box of personal letters and carried it out to the hall, planning to go through the rest that evening.

Derrick sat at a computer in the bedroom across the hall. A bottle of dark ale was open on the desk next to him. Jackson called out to his back, "I'm taking some letters with me so I can look at them at home."

Derrick spun around. "Why can't you look at them here?"

"Because it's a long and tedious task and I don't want to spend my work hours doing it. I'll bring the letters back, unless they become evidence in the case."

"I know I have to let go of that stuff eventually, but it's all I have of them."

Except their house, Jackson thought. "What do you have going on today?"

"What's that supposed to mean?"

"I thought we might go out to lunch."

"Now we're going to be pals? Like the last ten years never happened?"

"We have to start somewhere."

"Maybe some other time." Derrick took a long pull of beer.

"I called you a couple times over the years, but you didn't answer and I didn't leave a message."

"I'll have to take your word for that."

"What happened, Derrick? How did you get like this?"

His brother let out a bitter laugh. "You mean drinking at home on a Tuesday morning?"

"That's what I'm asking."

"Let's see." Derrick mockingly held a finger to his mouth as if pondering the question. "My parents were murdered. My brother stopped talking to me. My wife left me, and my employer laid me off after seventeen years of loyal service. I've applied for a hundred and sixty-two jobs in the last year, and in response, I received three phone calls, two no-thank-you e-mails, and one interview."

"A hundred and sixty-two?" Jackson was stunned—and skeptical.

"I'll show you the damn Excel file." Derrick was working up some hostility.

"I believe you. I just didn't know the job situation here was that bad."

"I don't want your pity. Why don't you get out of here?" His brother pivoted back to his computer. "I've got porn to watch."

At a loss for an intelligent or snappy comeback, Jackson walked away.

Out in the yard, he heard voices in the house next door that belonged to the Brickmyers. Jackson cut across the lawns and knocked on the door. He'd stopped by late yesterday afternoon, but no one had been home.

A woman yanked open the door, her face transmitting exasperation. "Yes?"

"I'm Detective Jackson, Eugene Police. I need to ask you some questions about a crime that happened next door ten years ago."

Confusion replaced her exasperation, but only for a moment. "Can it wait? I'm trying to get three kids ready for school. They have a late start today, but they still need to be on time."

In the background, a child yelled, "I'm telling."

Jackson had a flash of guilt about interrupting her busy schedule, but he suspected there would never be a better time. "Sorry, but this can't wait. I'm investigating a homicide."

Her face softened. "I remember it. Come in." She stepped back and let him pass through. "We'll talk while I make lunches."

As Jackson followed her to the kitchen, a boy of around ten scampered up to his mother, asking where his backpack was. She told him to check the laundry room. Jackson sat at the table, which was still covered with half-empty cereal bowls, and took out his notepad. "What's your name and how long have you lived here?"

"Angie Brickmyer. We bought the house in February of 2000. That was before we had kids." She gave him a rueful smile.

"Your neighbors were murdered on September 23, 2000. Where were you that day?"

"I was home sleeping. I'm a nursing assistant, and I worked a lot of graveyard back then." She frowned suddenly. "They caught the guy and he went to prison. Why are you asking this now?"

"New evidence has been discovered and the case is open again."

"Did the guy have an accomplice?"

The idea hadn't occurred to him. "What makes you ask?"

She shrugged. "The killer confessed, so what else could it be?"

"Did you hear anything unusual that afternoon?"

"No. I woke up when I heard the sirens coming down the street." Angie spread peanut butter on a row of bread slices as she talked. "That was before the kids. I was a heavy sleeper."

"Did you see a car parked outside your house that day?

"Not that I remember."

"Did you know Clark and Evelyn Jackson?"

"Not really. We'd only been in the neighborhood a couple of months. I'd met them both and they seemed real nice, but we didn't socialize."

"Had you noticed any change in their behavior? Any new visitors at the house?"

"No. Sorry." She looked up at him with a hint of sadness. "We were shocked to learn our neighbors had been shot dead in their living room. But then they caught the guy right away and it wasn't some random home invasion, so we decided to stay."

"Did the police question you?"

"Briefly, but I didn't know anything then either."

"Did you call the police and report seeing someone leave the victims' house?"

"No. Like I said, I was sleeping that afternoon."

A different young boy ran into the kitchen, crying. Jackson thanked Mrs. Brickmyer and left. The source of the anonymous tip mystified him. None of the neighbors had made the call. Jackson started to think the man in the blue sedan had reported seeing Hector Vargas leave the house. But why? Unless he was the killer and hoped to frame the handyman for the crime.

CHAPTER 11

Tuesday, September 7, 2:35 p.m.

Evans jogged down the stairs, pulling on her jacket, then blinked in the bright sun. She was discouraged to learn Gina Stahl had attempted suicide in the months before the alleged attack. Now she had to seriously consider that Gina may have tried to kill herself, ended up in a coma instead, and was now seeking revenge on her ex-husband by blaming him.

Gina's neighbors had reluctantly relayed the story of the first attempt. Gina had called them in a sleepy voice to say she had taken too much medicine. They'd come running over and rushed Gina, still conscious, to the emergency room. They told the admitting nurse it was an accident but afterward, they had their doubts. When Gloria found Gina the night she went into the coma, she assumed it was a suicide attempt and reported it that way to the 911 operator. Now Gloria believed Gina's accusations about her ex, but Evans was trying to stay open-minded. Anyone who took an overdose of tranquilizers had some kind of problem. What had Dragoo said about Gina? *Crazy as a box of weasels.* It didn't make Bekker any less revolting, but he might not be a killer.

As Evans moved up the sidewalk toward the Geezer, the apartment manager came running out of her unit. "Detective." Evans saw that she had a small paper sack in her hand.

The manager shoved it at her. "I remembered after you left that I had some of Gina's mail. The new tenant collected it for a while and turned it in to the office, then I forgot about it until now. Will you please give it to Gina?"

"I will. Thanks."

In the car, Evans riffled through the envelopes. A utility bill, two letters from Chase Bank, a bill from Oregon Medical Group, and a plain white envelope with no return address. It struck her as odd, and she itched to open it. Gina had given her permission to go through the mail at her parents' house, so she figured it extended to this mail too. She tore open the plain envelope. The letter was from a local credit union, requesting payment on a $4,000 loan, with the threat of turning the debt over to a collection agency. Evans started the car, cranked on the air-conditioning, then promptly opened all the mail. She discovered Gina had been overdrawn at the bank and behind on her bills. She owed Oregon Medical Group $2,246 for doctor visits and lab fees.

Evans started to rethink her assumptions. Had Gina's financial troubles somehow led to an attempt on her life? Was Gary Bekker a convenient, but still evil, scapegoat? It was time for another chat with the victim.

On the drive to Rosehill Care Center, Evans left Jackson a message, asking him to call back. She often worked homicides in which Jackson was the lead, and she missed having him and the other detectives to brainstorm with. As much as she'd learned from him already, she felt in need of guidance. She still had two law-enforcement men to question: the retired officer who had given Bekker his alibi and the detective who had seen Bekker at a prostitute's house. She had to keep chipping at the blue wall of silence.

She pulled off the freeway onto Q Street in Springfield and witnessed a homeless man urinating in the parking lot of an insurance office. She understood the sentiment, but thank god his lawlessness was not her problem. She'd had her fill of drunks and assholes as a patrol officer.

Once inside the care center, she learned Gina was in a session in the heated physical-therapy pool. Evans went to Gina's room to wait. She read through her notes and ate a few more bites of her Luna bar. When her phone rang, she wanted it to be Jackson but she didn't recognize the number.

A male voice said, "This is Pete Casaway, returning your call. How are you, Evans?"

"I'm good. Thanks for getting back to me." She hesitated. "I need to talk about an old case. Will you meet me somewhere?"

"What's it about?"

"Sergeant Gary Bekker."

"What has the prick done now?"

His hostility gave her spirits a lift, so she plunged right in. "You provided Bekker with an alibi for the night his wife went into a coma. I'd like to hear about that evening." Evans dug in her bag for her recorder as she talked.

"You're asking me if I lied?" Casaway scoffed. "Even if I did, why would I admit it now?"

"Gina woke from her coma and says Bekker tried to kill her. I'm investigating, and I need to know the truth." Evans held the recorder up to her cell phone, doubtful that it would be effective.

"You'll never pin it on him, and I have no intention of setting myself up for an obstruction-of-justice charge." Someone started talking in the background and Casaway said, "I've got to go."

"Wait." Evans frantically searched for the right thing to say. "You won't be charged, I promise. You're not in the brotherhood anymore, so you don't have to worry about retaliation. I'm putting my career on the line here."

"Why?

"Bekker is a criminal and needs to be stopped, but I won't even be allowed to question him unless his alibi falls through."

After a long silence, she heard a door close, as if Casaway had stepped outside. "This is officially off the record, okay? I'm only telling you because I came to despise Bekker and the way he treated people."

Evans wanted to know about the people Bekker had mistreated, but first she had to hear Casaway recant the alibi. "It's off the record."

"I saw Bekker that night at the Sixth Street Grill. That was true, but I saw him around seven o'clock and not again after that. He came to me a few days after his wife was hospitalized and asked me to make a statement and fudge the time a little. Gina's parents had gone to IA and accused Bekker of trying to kill her. At the time, the claim seemed outrageous and I wanted to help put it to rest."

"But it doesn't seem outrageous to you now?"

"I have less respect for him now. That doesn't mean he's a killer, but you deserve a chance to interrogate him."

"Anything specific you'd like to share with me?"

He ignored the question. "You'll never build a case against him after two years, but you may get him fired and that would be good."

"Tell me about the people you said he mistreated."

"I don't have time. I've got a security shift to work. Good luck." Casaway clicked off.

Evans shut off her recorder and hoped she had something to play for Lammers. She quickly made notes of the conversation. While she was writing, Jackson called back. "What's up?"

"I've got a case that's getting ugly and I could use your guidance. Can we meet today?"

"I'm on hold with Qwest, trying to track down old phone records. What about five or so?"

"Should we have dinner? I'll be working late."

"I'll check with Katie. If she has other plans, we'll go somewhere to eat and talk."

"Sounds good. Keep me posted."

The thought of having dinner with Jackson in a restaurant gave her a surge of pleasure. It might just be a business meeting, but still, it would be their first meal alone together.

Evans was feeling upbeat when Gina rolled into the room in a wheelchair with her physical therapist pushing. Gina smiled when she saw her. "Hey, detective. I got into the pool and moved my arms and legs. I can't tell you how wonderful that felt."

"That's great. It sounds like your recovery is going well." Evans felt like an asshole for what she was about to ask.

"She's making stunning progress," the physical therapist said. "She'll be using a walker in a few days." The therapist flipped the side of the wheelchair down, helped Gina into bed, and left.

"I talked to your old neighbors, the Hutchins," Evans said gently. "They told me about Gary Bekker stalking you. They also said you tried to kill yourself before."

Gina's cobalt-blue eyes flashed with anger. "That was an accident. I was upset and I forgot I'd already taken a Valium. That's why I called the Hutchinses. I wanted to go to the hospital for help."

"Are you accusing your ex-husband just for revenge?"

Gina's eyes didn't waver. "Someone attacked me. He was the same size as Gary and he was a smoker like Gary. And Gary had threatened to kill me."

"Why didn't you tell me that before?"

"I thought I did."

"Did anyone else hear his threats?"

"He's too careful for that."

"What exactly did he say?"

"He said, 'If you fuck with me, I'll kill you, and I'll get away with it.'"

"When did he make the threat?"

"A week before the attack. I think he spotted me following him, so I quit for a while." Gina sounded tired.

"I have to ask about your finances."

"What do you mean?" Gina's face registered concern.

"The manager at the Riverside Terrace has been holding some of your mail." Evans felt awkward. "You said I could go through your personal stuff, so I opened it.

Gina's eyes narrowed.

"You were overdrawn at the bank and behind on your bills. Did you owe money to individuals too?"

"No. I'd had health problems and wasn't able to work much for a few months. And I lost my health insurance when I left Gary. I was just going through a tough spot."

"I'm looking for another possible suspect. Could your financial troubles have led someone to harm you?"

Gina closed her eyes and didn't answer.

"Did you hear my question?"

"I need a nap." Gina struggled to respond.

Evans stood by the bed, watching her face. Had Gina purposely avoided the question, or was she simply tired after pool therapy? Either way, she was done talking for now. Evans grabbed her shoulder bag and left.

As much as she wanted to give herself more time, Evans knew she had to update Lammers immediately. If the sergeant heard through the grapevine that she was investigating another officer, her boss would feel blindsided and Evans could kiss her detective career good-bye.

Lammers was in a meeting when Evans returned to the department, so she took a minute to type her notes into a Word document. Jackson always created such a file, and it made sense to follow the lead of the investigator with the best track record of closing cases.

As five o'clock loomed near, Evans worried Lammers would head out after her meeting and their talk would have to wait until tomorrow. She was eager to question Bekker, but it would never happen without the involvement of both their supervisors. There was still the huge possibility that Lammers would take the case away from her and put someone else in the lead. If that happened, she hoped it would be Jackson. She trusted him to go after Bekker with the same determination he pursued any other suspect. Yet it would probably be Ben Stricklyn in IA, who'd only been with the department for a year.

Lammers' laugh came booming down the hall, and Evans figured this was her chance. She hustled over to intercept the boss at her office door. "Sergeant, I need a minute."

The big woman looked at her watch. "You know I'm always available to my team, but really, Evans, can't this wait until tomorrow?"

"It's important."

"Then come in and give me the short version."

Evans pulled case notes from her bag as she sat down. The office door banged shut, and she jumped at the sound. *Damn.* She didn't want to look skittish. She sat up straight, wishing for the millionth time she were taller. "This is about the coma-woman case you assigned me."

"The short version."

"Gina Stahl says her ex-husband tried to kill her. His name is Gary Bekker and he's a patrol sergeant with our department."

"Oh, for fuck's sake." Lammers looked ready to throw something. "What do you mean, 'she says he tried'? Is she filing a complaint against him?"

"The man who attacked her was wearing a ski mask. Gina says he was the same size as Bekker and she has reason to think her ex wanted to kill her."

"Ex-spouses often feel that way, so that's not much to go on. Have you investigated other possible suspects?"

"Of course. But I haven't come up with any yet."

Lammers abruptly jerked forward. "You haven't contacted Bekker, have you?"

"No, but I want to question him."

"Just slow down." Lammers tapped her pencil, her face scrunched in concentration.

"There's more I have to tell you."

"Oh, christ." Lammers looked at her watch. "Excuse me." She made a call on her cell phone and told someone she would be late. Evans would have felt bad about keeping her boss, but she planned to work for another three hours, so the sympathy didn't materialize.

When Lammers hung up, Evans launched into the speech she'd practiced. "Gary Bekker used his authority as a police officer to coerce women into sex. Gina, his ex-wife, started documenting his activities. She even talked to one of his victims. Gina believes that's why he tried to kill her."

Lammers started to swear again, then stopped short. "This is a very serious accusation."

Evans glanced at her notes, looking for a name. "I talked to Trisha Cronin. She said Bekker threatened to put her in jail unless she gave him oral sex. Trisha complied. Eventually, he came back and raped her." Evans pulled out her recorder but held on to it. "I can play the conversation for you."

Lammers bolted from her chair, making Evans feel small. "You shouldn't have gone to see her before talking to me. The sexual abuse is a separate investigation."

"I know, but I needed to determine if Bekker had real motivation in my attempted-homicide case, and I believe he did."

"What a fucked-up mess."

Evans forced herself to stay quiet.

Finally, Lammers said, "The abuse of his authority will need to be investigated by internal affairs. I'll set up a meeting with Ben Stricklyn for the morning. I want you to update him and turn everything over."

"What about the attempted homicide?"

"We can keep that case here in the unit, but I want Jackson to take the lead. You can work with him, but you don't have the experience to handle this alone." Lammers help up her hand. "Don't argue. I want to be briefed every day, and I want to participate in the interrogation. I'll talk to the chief and get him to compel Bekker to surrender to questioning."

Evans tried to hide her relief. Working the case with Jackson was a best-case scenario.

Lammers plopped back in her chair and stared hard at Evans. "Do not discuss this case with anyone in the department except Jackson. Do not contact Bekker yet. We have to do this carefully."

"Do you know Bekker? Is he a friend of yours?" Evans couldn't believe she'd just blurted that out.

"I know Bekker. And he's no friend."

CHAPTER 12

Earlier that day, Tuesday, September 7, 9:15 a.m.

Sophie Speranza's headache was making her cross-eyed. Some days the stress of trying to do two people's jobs made her wish she had lower standards. The newspaper kept laying off people to cut costs, but the workload didn't shrink with the staff. Now she had to write obituaries and short pieces for the city section as well as cover politics and crime, which her new girlfriend kept joking were one and the same. To top it off, she had to open all the e-mail—meaning press releases—that came to the news desk. She hated the task even more than writing obituaries, but she loved being a reporter and would hang on to her job until the paper's owner dragged her kicking and screaming from the building.

Grudgingly, she started opening e-mails. A local author had a new book contract (so what?), a yard-products company was moving to a new location (snoozeville), and a charity was holding a walkathon to raise money (couldn't drag her there if they served free champagne and Euphoria chocolate).

The fourth e-mail announced that Roger Norquist, a local businessman and ex-senator, had started raising campaign money to run for the Senate again next year. He planned to hold a fundraiser at the Eugene Hilton in late October and charge a hundred dollars a plate. The name and announcement caught her attention. Norquist had lost his reelection race in 2006 by a narrow margin and apparently didn't want that to happen again, so he was starting early. That had been her first year on the paper, and she vaguely remembered an allegation of sexual misconduct from Norquist's first Senate race, which he'd won. She would have to dig that up if she wrote about him. Sophie googled Norquist's name while she called the number listed for his campaign manager.

A woman answered, "Patty Smith speaking."

"This is Sophie Speranza with the *Willamette News.* I'd like to get a quote from Mr. Norquist to run with this little fundraiser story. Is he available?"

"Not at the moment, but I'm sure the senator would love to talk to you. I'll check with him about his schedule and give you a call back."

"We'll probably use this press release as filler in the next few days, so he should get back to me quickly."

"I'll let him know."

Sophie glanced at her monitor. Norquist's web page had loaded with an oversize smiling picture of him. He had an aging-surfer look, with delicate features and intense blue eyes. She moved the press release to her *Maybe* file, then opened the next one.

The e-mail came from Rosehill Care Center, and she expected some trumped-up occasion meant to attract attention. Dutifully, she scanned the text, and her heart fluttered with excitement. A woman who had been in a coma for two years had come out of it, thanks to the attentive and professional care administered by the dedicated staff…blah, blah, blah. Sophie read the pertinent part again. The press release didn't name the patient, but she didn't care. A woman had come out of a coma after two years. This was a story.

She threw her recorder into her big red purse that complemented her short red hair, e-mailed her supervisor about where she was going, and headed out to her Scion. Every time she left the building, she wondered if she would have a job when she got back. The newspaper was slowly dying, and she'd been looking for employment elsewhere, but nobody was hiring print journalists. Sophie had moved to Eugene to attend college and, although she liked the town, she had no real loyalty to it. Her last boyfriend had wounded her deeply, and she'd considered moving out of state, as well as giving up on men for a while. Now she was dating a bright, beautiful woman, and leaving Jasmine would not be easy.

As she drove down Q Street, Sophie noted the care center was rather close to the freeway. She wondered if the patients even noticed or cared. Still, the property had nice landscaping and some trees for the old folks to gaze at through the windows of their little medical prisons. She pushed the buzzer and trotted inside, bracing herself for the experience. She loved old people and found them more honest and humorous than most others. Yet she believed the country needed to implement radical changes to keep Medicare and Social Security solvent.

Inside, she popped some peppermint gum in her mouth, then greeted the receptionist. "I'm Sophie Speranza with the *Willamette News*. I received a press release about a patient who came out of a coma. I'd love to interview her, if that's possible. Or one of her caregivers."

"Let me check with Gina's nurse."

Now she knew the patient's name. Sophie was dying to learn the circumstances of her coma. Car accident seemed most likely. She wondered if she could find the original story on microfiche at the newspaper.

The receptionist paged someone named Jeri and they both waited. A nurse dressed in blue scrubs came hurrying up to the desk, looking annoyed. "How did you find out about our patient?"

"The care center sent me a press release."

The nurse rolled her eyes. "Our marketer is new and young, and I don't know what the hell she was thinking."

"Still, I'm here, and I'd like to talk with Gina."

"You're not family, and I don't think it's a good idea." The nurse looked around, as if to find someone who would back her.

"If I got the press release, then the TV reporters probably did too. At least I'm not shoving a camera in your face. I just want a statement from the patient or from you."

"The patient is doing well and should make a full recovery."

"What was the cause of Gina's coma?"

"I can't discuss a patient's private information with you."

"Will you please ask Gina if she'd like to see me?"

"I'm sure she wouldn't, but I'll tell her you were here." The nurse spun around and walked away.

Sophie turned back to the receptionist. "How do you spell her name?"

"G, I, N, A, S, T, A, H, L."

Sophie suppressed a smile. She'd meant the nurse's name for the quote. Now she knew the patient's last name too. "What about the spelling of the nurse's name? I plan to quote her."

The receptionist spelled it out as well, then looked up. "Here come Gina's parents."

Sophie's headache vanished. She turned and smiled at the older couple who'd just entered through the glass door. They were both gray, but the woman was tall and lean, while her husband had rounded shoulders and a potbelly. "Are you Mr. and Mrs. Stahl? I'm Sophie Speranza."

"I know that name," the woman said. "You write for the paper. You did a great job on that story about the Young Women's Outreach Center."

"Thank you. That's nice to hear." Sophie held out her hand.

The older woman shook it. "I'm Sharon and this is my husband George. What brings you to the care center?"

"I'm here to see your daughter, Gina. I'd love to do a story about her recovery."

They both seemed taken aback. The old man spoke up. "I'm not sure Gina's ready for that."

"I understand. Would the two of you be willing to answer a few questions?" Sophie could see they needed encouragement. "The fact that she came out of a coma after two years is so amazing. It'll be nice to do an upbeat story for a change. People need some good news."

"Boy, that's the truth." Sharon Stahl turned to her husband. "Besides, some media coverage might put pressure on the police to fully investigate this."

The words *police* and *investigate* gave Sophie a jolt of adrenaline. *What had she lucked into?* She turned back to the receptionist. "Is there a visitors' room where we can sit down?"

"It's down that hall." She pointed left. "It's right next to the dining room."

The beige room was windowless, but they were near the kitchen and the yeasty smell of baking bread made it bearable. Unable to hold back, Sophie clicked on her recorder and jumped right in. "What happened to Gina? Why do the police need to investigate?"

Sharon took the lead. "Two years ago, our daughter ingested an overdose of Valium and Demerol. She had a prescription for Valium, but not Demerol. Her neighbors found her and called an ambulance. They told the cops and paramedics it was an attempted suicide. We never believed that."

Sophie hoped she wasn't drooling with eagerness. "What do you think happened?"

"We think her ex-husband tried to kill her. Gina had filed for divorce, but it wasn't final yet."

"What makes you think that? Had he threatened her?"

"He stalked her too," George cut in. "He's a prick. One of those guys who can't stand losing."

"Did you tell the police this at the time?"

"We did," Sharon said. "But they told us Gary Bekker had an alibi and that the doctors said it was a suicide."

"Has Gina talked about the incident since she woke up? Does she remember what happened?"

"She says a man in a ski mask attacked her in her apartment and she blacked out." Sharon lowered her voice. "Gary must have forced the pills down her throat or given her some kind of injection."

Sophie suddenly got a these-people-might-be-crazy vibe, but it didn't change anything. This was still a good story. "Is Gary a medical professional?"

"He's a cop, but he used to be a paramedic, so he has medical skills."

A cop? Sophie practically came in her nice linen pants. *How juicy was this story?* "Is Gary Bekker still working as a police officer?"

"He's even been promoted," George said, showing distress for the first time.

"Have the police assigned someone to investigate?"

"A young detective named Lara Evans has been here to ask questions," Sharon said, "but we worry nothing will come of it."

Sophie paused her recorder. "Do you think Gina would be willing to talk to me?"

"Let's go ask her."

When they arrived in Gina's room, the patient was sleeping. Her parents each took a seat, prepared to wait. Sophie was less inclined. She turned to Sharon. "Can I take her picture? Not a close-up. Just a shot of the room and the bed."

"I don't think Gina would want that."

"Fine." Sophie stepped near the hospital bed and made a few mental notes for her story: long gray-streaked hair, pale but beautiful skin, strong jaw line. *Had she met this woman before?* "What does Gina do? I mean, where did she work before the coma?"

"She's a clothing designer. She ran her own business, Goddess Garments."

"How old is she?"

"Forty-six."

Sophie jotted it down, then decided to turn her recorder back on. "What was it like for you during those years?" It was an idiot question, but she had to ask it to get some good quotes.

The couple glanced at each other, then Sharon spoke for both of them. "We visited Gina almost every day and talked to her for hours. We thought the sound of our voices would help keep her connected to us and to the world around her." Sharon cleared her throat, holding back tears. "We played her favorite music too, hoping that would help."

"What kind of music?"

"She loves funk and rock and anything she can dance to."

Gina's father spoke up. "We paid for daily physical therapy as well. That's why she's recovering so quickly. They said we could take her home in the next day or so."

"Wow. That's fast."

"She doesn't have any brain damage." Sharon beamed. "We're so excited. We still have to bring her back every day for the therapy pool and the special treadmill, but Gina really wants to come home."

"Do you think she'll be awake soon?"

The nurse Sophie had spoken to earlier strode into the room and glared. "Gina needs rest. Will you please leave?"

Sophie ignored her and dug in her wallet for a business card. She handed it to Sharon. "Here's how to contact me when Gina comes home. I'll be in touch. Thanks so much for your time." She gave the nurse a friendly smile and left. If she hurried, she might get the preliminary story into tomorrow's paper.

CHAPTER 13

Tuesday, September 7, 4:45 p.m.

Jackson took two naproxen and stood, to relieve the pain in his intestines. He'd been on hold with the phone company for fifteen minutes and was glad he'd used his desk phone. The manager at Qwest headquarters finally came back on. "I think I've found the phone records you need, but my computer is being really slow. I'll fax them to you as soon as they load."

Jackson breathed a sigh of relief. "Thanks. I appreciate your effort." He'd been prepared to get a subpoena for the documents, but the manager had been so skeptical about finding ten-year-old data she hadn't even asked for one.

Jackson pulled on his jacket and headed out. It was time to connect with his family.

In the car, he checked the time on his cell phone and called his daughter. Katie surprised him by answering. "Hi, Dad. I'm glad you called."

Jackson laughed. "That worries me. Where are you and what are you going to ask for?"

"I'm at the mall with Zoe and her mother, and we want to see a movie. Can I have dinner here with them, please? I'll be home by eight thirty or so."

Having a meal together every day was an important routine that kept him in touch with his daughter. In the past, he'd missed more than a few dinners when he worked tough homicides. Now Katie was more likely to be the one who wanted out of their time together. "I'd rather you came home. You can see the movie this weekend."

"Why do you get to excuse yourself from our dinner plans whenever you have a hard case, but I never get a pass? That doesn't seem right."

The truth was, Jackson felt a little relieved that she had other plans, because he wanted to meet with Evans, which also made him feel guilty. "For starters, I'm the parent. Second, my job is rather important. But to be fair, I'll let you have a pass this time."

"Thanks, Dad."

"You're welcome. I'll see you around eight thirty."

"Okay. Later."

Jackson missed the sweet little girl his daughter had been, but he liked this new spunky version too. He just didn't trust her as much as he used to. No matter how responsible Katie was about homework and chores and checking in, she was still a teenager, and Jackson remembered what that was like.

He called Evans and arranged to meet her at the Sixth Street Grill. He was pleased she wanted his help with her investigation, and he looked forward to talking about his parents' case. He would have liked to discuss the investigation with Kera, but some details he just couldn't share with a civilian. Tonight, his girl-friend was volunteering at a veterans' rehab center so she wasn't available, anyway.

The restaurant was only a few blocks from the department and offered little parking, so Jackson left his cruiser under city hall and walked over. The warm breeze felt pleasant on his face, and he was grateful for the chance to be outside. As he crossed Eighth Avenue, a nearly naked man with dreadlocks to his waist bicycled past, pulling a homemade rainbow-painted trailer with a small dog inside it. Jackson smiled. Summer in Eugene was especially colorful.

Inside the eatery, nearly every booth was filled, reminding him that Tuesday was burger-and-brew night. Not the best timing for an important conversation, but they'd make it work. The hostess sat him near the front window, and he saw Evans cross the street. Her heart-shaped face was animated and the wind tousled her freshly cut hair. He'd come to really like working with Evans. She was insightful and energetic and a visual change of pace from looking at Schak and McCray. Jackson was glad he'd met Kera soon after Evans joined the unit. Taking the Evans option off the table made their situation easier. Department romances usually ended in disaster, with one person being terminated or transferred.

Evans slid in across from him and grinned. "You haven't ordered us a beer yet?"

"I just got here. Rough day?"

"Sort of. I've got a stressful case." Evans had a light sheen on her face, and Jackson found it oddly attractive. She signaled a waitress, who came straight over. "I'll have a Ninkasi Radiant."

The waitress looked at him, and Jackson hesitated. He almost never drank, a by-product of being married to an alcoholic for fourteen years.

"Come on, have a beer with me," Evans cajoled. "It'll replenish your electrolytes after a hot, sweaty day." She laughed at her rationale, and Jackson laughed too.

"I'll have the same." He probably wouldn't finish the beer, but it sounded good.

Evans, on the other hand, took a long pull the minute their server set down the beers. They both ordered burgers with salad instead of fries, to take advantage of the special.

"I'll have to run another five miles tonight," Evans said. "But I don't care. They make the best burgers here."

"I haven't had one in months, so I'm due."

"Thanks for meeting me. Lammers wants you to work with me on this case.

"The coma woman? Do you have any leads?"

"I do. The victim says her ex-husband tried to kill her." Evans gave him a peculiar smile. "Guess who her ex is?"

Jackson waited.

Evans leaned forward and lowered her voice. "Sergeant Gary Bekker, Eugene Police Department."

"I'll be damned." Hearing the name of one of the cops who'd browbeaten Hector Vargas surprised him. Jackson wondered if he should tell Evans. If it were his case, he'd want to know.

"What is it? Don't tell me you and Bekker are friends."

"We're not. I've got some information for you, but first tell me about your case. Have you told Lammers about Bekker?"

"An hour ago. That's why she wants you to get involved. She thinks I don't have the experience to interrogate Bekker."

As much as Jackson wanted to focus exclusively on his parents, Evans' investigation intrigued him. "Is this case going to come down to a he-said, she-said situation for the jury?"

"It's worse than that. The attacker was wearing a ski mask, so Gina can't say for sure it was her ex."

"The DA won't want to press charges."

"I know, but there's more." A wave of disgust passed over Evans' face, then she caught herself. "Here's our food. I'll update you in a moment."

While they ate, Evans told him about Gary Bekker's sexual-predator visits and how his ex-wife had documented them, thus leading to her near-death experience. Jackson put down what was left of his burger, no longer hungry. "You're saying the sexual coercion has been going on for years."

"For one of the women, it started in 2006. We have to nail this guy." Evans' voice had an edge he'd never heard before.

Jackson sipped his beer, trying to decide how much he should tell her about Bekker's involvement in his own case. Lammers had asked him not to discuss it, but how could they work together if she didn't know? "I'm working a case from the past too. My parents' homicides."

"What the hell? Wasn't that a decade ago?"

"Yep." Jackson explained about Vargas' letter, the coerced confession, and Bekker's role in it. "You can't tell anyone else in the department about the allegations of abuse. Lammers wants to keep this under wraps."

"What a total bastard. We have to get him off the force." Evans reached over and squeezed Jackson's hand. "It must be painful for you to work your parents' case. Since you're going to spend time on my investigation, let me help with yours. Do you have any leads? Is there anything I can do?"

Jackson told her about the guy in the sedan sitting outside the house and leaving shortly after the sound of gunshots. "I hope to have phone records soon, so maybe I'll find something."

"Do you have the old case file? Did they investigate anyone besides Vargas?"

"I have the folder but it's slim. They focused on Vargas immediately, forced a confession, and never looked at anyone else."

Evans raised her nearly empty beer in the gesture of a toast. "Here's to our cold-case success."

Jackson tapped glasses with her, thinking they would both need to catch a lucky break to bring justice to any of the victims.

Later at home, he carried in the boxes he'd gathered from Derrick's. As he removed his Sig Sauer, jacket, and shoes, he wondered what his brother was doing at that moment. He pictured him sitting in front of the TV, alone, drinking. Jackson considered asking Derrick over for dinner some night, then anger flared. Why was his brother wallowing in his troubles instead of fighting for a good life?

Jackson set a box labeled *Personal Papers* on the table and sat down to his task. As an investigator, he often spent hours scanning through bank statements and phone records and he'd learned to be patient with the process. This time it was personal. He was digging through his parents' private life. He wished he'd finished his beer.

His first task was to prioritize. He set aside his father's sports scores and crossword puzzles and his mother's family recipes. Seeing his father's familiar neat print and inhaling the faint scent of cigar made Jackson realize why Derrick had not been able to throw all this in the recycling. It would have been tantamount to pushing away a warm hug.

Jackson started with a little yellow notebook that had a dollar sign on the cover. In his mother's handwriting was a list of charitable contributions and the date of the donation. They'd given money to the Mission, Food for Lane County, Planned Parenthood, and Womenspace. The list went on for pages and dated back three years. He started to set down the notebook, then flipped through the empty pages to see if he'd missed anything. Near the back was another list of dollar amounts and at the top of the page, his brother's name. Were these loans or gifts to Derrick? Jackson mentally added up the entries: $1,500, $3,000, $1,500. All the notations were dated and had been recorded in the two months before the murders.

Why had Derrick needed $6,000? His brother had been working and making decent money. The timing of the loans and the homicides was too close for Jackson to write off as coincidence. He reached for his cell to call Derrick, then changed his mind. This needed to be handled face-to-face. It was too easy to lie over the phone. The money given to his brother unsettled him. How much of a burden had Derrick been? Had his parents made sacrifices in their own lives to help him?

Jackson checked the time: 7:35. Katie wouldn't be home from the movie for an hour. Since he wasn't technically on duty, he decided to take his personal car. Still, he grabbed his weapon and shoulder bag before heading out to the garage. In the harsh fluorescent light, he took a moment to admire his midnight-blue '69 GTO. He'd spent years restoring the vehicle on weekends, buying the materials one paycheck at a time.

Next to the muscle car sat the trike he'd recently completed with the help of his daughter. He'd been so pleased when Katie had decided to join him on the project and even learned to weld. The three-wheeled motorcycle had a Volkswagen engine/rear end and a Goldwing front end, which they'd welded together with a homebuilt frame. He'd painted the body a dark burgundy at his daughter's request, and he loved riding the damn thing. Especially when Kera or Katie rode with him. He knew he hadn't done a professional job, but he got compliments from everyone who saw it.

Jackson was tempted to take the trike, wanting Derrick to see it, but again, his instinct told him to be prepared for anything. He climbed in the GTO, and the engine roared on the first turn of the key as always. The rumble warmed his heart.

Only a dim light shone in the back of Derrick's house, but his Town Car was in the driveway, so Jackson knew his brother was home. He pounded on the door, assuming Derrick was drinking and watching TV and would not hear anything less.

After a short wait, Jackson pounded again, then used the key he'd found earlier to let himself in. Since Derrick had never bought him out, Jackson still had half ownership in the house. It was odd, and frustrating, to be in that position with both his brother and his ex-wife. He would be glad to get at least one of the situations resolved.

"Derrick." Jackson stepped into the house as he called out, but his brother didn't answer. Jackson moved through the foyer into the living room.

Derrick, who'd been half-asleep on the couch, jerked upright. "What the fuck?"

"Sorry, but I pounded on the door and you didn't answer."

"So come back later. You can't barge in here like this." Derrick tried to sound angry, but he lacked the will. "What do you want?"

Jackson pushed an empty pizza box off the recliner and sat down. "You borrowed money from Mom and Dad in the weeks before they were killed. I want to know about it."

"What makes you think that's any of your business?"

"I'm investigating their homicides. I have to look at every possibility."

"Forget it. The money had nothing to do with their deaths."

"Don't make me subpoena your financial records. What was it for?"

"Don't go all authoritative on me, you little shit." Derrick rubbed his face. "Why do you always get like that? You're so self-righteous."

"I'm just doing my job. Why did you need six thousand dollars?"

"It was for a business I bought into."

"What business?"

"Eco Solar Panels. A guy at work decided to start his own company, and he asked me to come in as an investor. I didn't have the money, so I borrowed it from our parents."

"I'm surprised they loaned it to you. Mom and Dad didn't usually take financial risks."

Derrick was quiet, then looked away.

"What are you not telling me? Did you lie to them about what it was for?"

"Mom gave it to me, and Dad never knew."

Jackson didn't believe him. "Tell me what really happened. Mom didn't keep things from Dad."

Derrick made a snorting sound. "You'd be surprised."

"What does that mean?"

"Nothing." Derrick pushed himself off the couch, moving like an old man. "Want a beer?"

"No thanks. What happened to the business?"

"It went to shit, like everything else in my life."

"You lost your investment?" *Mom's investment*, Jackson mentally corrected.

"Yep." Derrick shuffled into the kitchen and came back with a bottle of beer. "None of this matters now. Can you let it go?"

"How can a solar-panel business not survive in Eugene? Especially ten years ago? That was ahead of the curve."

"Sam was killed in a car accident a few months after I gave him the money. The business fell through."

"Sam who?"

"Forget it, Wade. It has nothing to do with their deaths."

"How do you know?" Irritated, Jackson raised his voice. "What if Sam invested the money in a drug deal that went bad? What if Sam's associates came here looking for you?"

Derrick rolled his eyes. "His name was Reinhart, but he's dead and you're wasting your time."

"How do you spell it?" Jackson would have to search the databases, because Derrick was clearly not going to help him.

"It doesn't matter." Derrick shifted in agitation. "This isn't about Sam. He's not the bad guy."

Something in his tone caught Jackson's attention. "Who is the bad guy? You got involved in something shady, didn't you?"

"You're like a pit bull, Wade. You get your teeth into something and you don't let go. You were like that as a kid too."

"And you're evasive as usual, trying to turn this on me instead of answering the question." Jackson wanted to say, *You were like that as a kid too*, but he resisted. "Who did you owe the money to?"

Derrick took a long gulp of beer. Jackson watched him try to decide what to tell him. Finally, his brother said, "Ray Durkin."

"Who is he and how did you meet him?"

"Seth Valder introduced me to him at Lucky Numbers one night."

The name slammed into Jackson like a fist. "I had a run-in with Valder recently, and he's a heartless son of a bitch. How did you get mixed up with him?"

"I met Valder at the club, and he seemed like a decent guy. I was talking to him one night about the business I wanted to invest in, and he introduced me to Durkin. Durkin offered to loan me the money, so I borrowed it."

"At what cost?"

"Ten percent interest on the cash and one percent of the business."

"What happened when you didn't pay?"

Derrick's shoulders sagged. "Durkin threatened me, so I borrowed money from Mom to pay him off."

"Did he know you got the money from your parents?"

"No." Derrick's mouth turned down, and Jackson didn't believe him.

"You owed more than six thousand, didn't you? Durkin came here looking to collect the rest." Jackson bolted out of the chair, heat building in his chest. "Our parents were murdered over your asinine debt, weren't they? And you've known all along!" At the end, he was shouting.

Derrick stood and shouted back. "Bullshit! I paid Durkin, and it was over." His brother stepped toward him, shoulders tensed. "You're out of line, and I want you to leave."

"I'm trying to find out who killed our parents. Don't you give a shit?"

"Of course I do. Like everyone else, I thought Vargas did it. Now I don't know what to think."

"Are you going to help me? I need the truth, Derrick, the whole ugly truth."

"I told you everything about the loan, which had nothing to do with their deaths."

"Let's sit down and talk. Maybe there's something else."

Derrick shook his head. "It's late and I'm tired. They've been dead for ten years. What's your rush now?"

"I only have a few weeks to work this investigation, then I'll have to take new cases. This one will get shuffled to the back burner. It's a limited window of opportunity."

"It's probably a waste of time too." Derrick threw up his hands in mock defense. "Don't come at me for saying that. It's just been too long."

"The dead are patient. They don't care how long it takes, but they want justice."

CHAPTER 14

Tuesday, September 7, 7:05 p.m.

Evans watched Jackson drive away, then started across the parking lot. She felt energized, happy, and horny. She and Jackson had walked back from the restaurant together, making jokes about his disappearing-corpse case. It felt almost like a date. She suspected Jackson wasn't totally happy with Kera and wondered if she should make a play for him. She pushed the thought aside and focused on her priority. Tomorrow she would have to turn over the sexual-coercion investigation to IA. Gina's notebook with its list of victimized women called to her from her shoulder bag.

Evans wanted to interview at least one more victim and hear her story firsthand, but she wasn't sure if she should. They weren't officially part of her main investigation, yet Lammers hadn't forbidden her from talking to them. As an occasional volunteer for Womenspace, where she taught self-defense skills to victims of domestic abuse, Evans was learning to listen without judgment and to offer guidance without expectation. It still frustrated her when women didn't fight back, but she understood and would continue to empower others whenever she had the opportunity.

She jogged upstairs into the department and photocopied each page of the journal. Ben Stricklyn from internal affairs would take possession of it tomorrow, and she didn't know him or trust him to fully investigate Bekker. If the notebook *accidentally* went missing, Evans would have a backup. She made copies of her handwritten notes as well and noticed Stuart Renfro's name. She hadn't talked to Gina's boyfriend yet. Typically, she would interview coworkers as well, but as a self-employed seamstress, Gina hadn't had any.

Evans went to her desk, looked up Stuart Renfro, and gave him a call. He answered on the second ring, sounding breathless. "Yes?"

"This is Detective Evans, Eugene Police. I need to talk to you about Gina Stahl."

"Gina? I haven't seen her in years. What's this about?" A treadmill hummed in the background.

"She came out of her coma and I'm investigating."

"Investigating what?"

"Her assault. Can I come over? I'd like to ask you a few questions."

"I didn't know she was assaulted." The treadmill stopped. "I barely knew her. We went on two dates, then she disappeared. I heard later she tried to kill herself. There's nothing else I can tell you."

Evans was inclined to believe him but wasn't giving up yet. "Do you know anything about her finances? Was she a gambler?"

Renfro let out a sigh. "I knew she was broke. She'd developed rheumatoid arthritis in her hands and couldn't work for a while, but I can't comment on the gambling one way or another."

"Do you know anyone who might want her dead?"

"You mean besides her ex-husband? No. Everybody liked Gina."

"Who is everybody?"

"Her friends, her clothing customers, the people at the clinic."

"What clinic?"

"The medical-marijuana clinic she volunteered at. That's where we met."

"What's the name and where is it located?"

"The Compassion Center at 2055 West Twelfth."

Evans scrawled the information in a quick flourish. "What was your business at the clinic?"

"I'm a nurse. I work there. How is Gina, by the way?"

"She's going to fully recover."

"Tell her I wish her well. Now I'd like to get back to my workout."

"Please call me if you think of anything that might help my investigation."

"It's not likely." He hung up.

Was the clinic still open this late and was there any point in checking it out? Evans felt like anything she did that wasn't focused on Gary Bekker was just going through the motions. But if she didn't investigate every possible lead, Bekker's defense attorney would claim the police never looked for anyone else.

Evans looked up the Compassion Center in the online yellow pages and gave it a ring. A recorded voice informed her that clinic hours were between ten and five on Tuesdays and Thursdays and from noon to five on Wednesdays. The limited hours indicated the clinic was staffed mostly by volunteers.

Evans jumped up, feeling restless after a day of mostly sitting. She still had a five-mile run to do that evening, and she wasn't ready to quit working yet. If Gina were a newly dead homicide victim instead of a two-year-old assault case, a team of detectives would be working round the clock. She owed Gina a similar diligence.

Heading downstairs to her car, Evans decided to go back to the beginning and look at the case as if Gina were dead and Jackson were investigating. What would he do that she hadn't done yet? Write subpoenas for phone and bank records? In this case, she didn't need a judge's signature, because she had Gina's consent.

Some of the paperwork was still boxed up at the Stahls' house. She just hadn't looked through much of it yet, because she'd found the notebook about Bekker's victims. Would Gina's parents mind if she showed up later tonight? She wanted to grab some boxes and bring them back to the department. Before starting her car, Evans pulled out the notebook and glanced through it. Joni Farmer's apartment was only a mile away. *To hell with protocol*, Evans thought. She would stop and talk to Joni on her way to the Stahls' house. If internal affairs decided to make the whole thing go away by asking for Bekker's resignation, these women needed a backup plan.

Joni Farmer lived in a small apartment complex near Tenth and Chambers. Evans nearly missed the building, because it had almost no exterior lighting, and large trees and shrubs dwarfed one end. Evans parked in the alley between the two complexes, then went upstairs to unit four. A thin young woman with ridiculously long hair answered the door. A little girl was wrapped around the woman's legs, making happy high-pitched noises. Evans started to regret stopping by. Through gritted teeth, she asked, "Are you Joni Farmer?"

"Are you a cop?"

"I'm Detective Evans, Eugene Police, but I'm not here to harass you. I want to ask a few questions about Gary Bekker."

Joni's eyes filled with tears. She motioned Evans to come in, then carried the noisy child to another room. Evans was relieved when she returned without the little girl.

"What do you want to know?" Joni sank down on a battered couch with no legs.

Evans pulled a chair over from the small table nearby and clicked on her recorder. "How did you first meet Bekker?"

"He arrested me for possession. I was with my boyfriend, who was carrying three grams of heroin. Bekker took the dope off Jake and let him go. I didn't know what the hell to think." Joni rocked herself as she talked. "He put me in his car, drove me to a parking lot behind a warehouse, and said I had two choices: give him a blow job or be charged with distribution." The young woman fought back tears. "What else could I do? The state would have taken my little girl while I did six months. Bekker took me to jail anyway, but my paperwork said I had less than a gram, so I got probation."

"Bekker kept the rest of the heroin?"

She nodded. "He's evil."

"Did you see him again?"

"Two weeks later, he showed up with the H and offered it to me in exchange for sex." She begged Evans to understand. "Do you know what that was like for me? I was trying to get clean, and I hadn't been high in days. I was in a world of hurt. So I screwed him for drugs." A pent-up sob burst from her throat.

"How many times has he been back?"

"Dozens."

"Does he bring heroin every time?"

"Sometimes it's Demerol or methadone."

Rage forced Evans from her chair. She visualized putting a bullet in Bekker's head, then throwing his body to a pack of hungry dogs. Taking a deep breath, she said, "Are you willing to tell this to another detective? And testify in court?"

"Only if you promise I won't go to jail. I can't lose my little girl again."

"Are you still using?"

"Sometimes."

"You need to get help. Have you tried the methadone clinic?"

"I don't have insurance and I can't afford it, but I'm on a waiting list for a free inpatient clinic in Eastern Oregon."

"That's good to hear, but it's not enough. Your daughter will grow up to be a better person if you're a better mother."

"I know." Joni hung her head in shame.

Evans handed her a business card. "I'll be in touch."

Some people don't deserve to live, Evans thought, pounding down the stairs. No trial either. Just a bullet between the eyes. It was something her dad used to say. One of the many redneck things that came out of his mouth, but in this case, she agreed with him.

Evans jogged down the dark alley between the two apartment complexes. The Geezer was parked at the end, next to a tall hedge of laurel. Her body burned with anger and adrenaline. She decided to skip going to the Stahls and head straight home for a run.

As she reached her car, she sensed movement from the thicket. Evans spun, but not fast enough. A club came down on her head, wielded by a tall blur. She blacked out for a split second and landed on her knees. The attacker grabbed her hair and slammed her head into the side of her car. Pain and rage exploded in an animal fury. Bellowing like a wounded bear, Evans shot to her feet and punched her assailant in the groin as she came up. Her other fist slammed into his sternum, and he doubled over, gasping for air.

Evans jumped back and reached for her weapon. The man in the ski mask lunged just as her Sig Sauer came free of its holster.

He slammed her with the full length of his body and knocked her to the ground. Crushed under his weight, she could only move her arms. Evans grabbed his hair with one hand and slammed her gun into the side of his head with the other.

"Bitch!"

He pressed his forearm against her throat and straddled her so he could bear down. Evans yelled, but nothing came out as her windpipe was crushed under his arm.

A window banged open in an apartment above them and a voice hollered, "I'm calling the cops."

Her attacker leaned close to her face, his breath reeking of cigarettes and alcohol, even through the knit mask. "Back off, or next time I'll kill you." He pushed off her and, in the cover of darkness, moved toward the street.

Evans struggled to her feet, head pounding. The mother-fucker! She considered shooting him in the back but couldn't do it. She didn't have enough light and it was too cowardly. She sprinted after him, pain and instinct driving her actions. The bastard was not getting away. In a few seconds, she was within striking distance. Evans leaped, twisted in the air, and landed both feet in his lower back. The assailant went down on the asphalt with a thud. She landed nearby on her knees, weapon still in her hand. She pushed up, scrambled back out of his reach, and aimed her Sig Sauer at his prone body.

"Don't move, or I'll shoot you," she shouted, her voice weak from the choking.

Breathing heavily, he started to crawl away.

What the fuck? Evans considered plugging him in the leg, but she couldn't bring herself to shoot someone crawling on the ground either. She rushed in and smacked him on the back of the head with her gun. His body went limp. She planted both knees into his butt and reached in her pocket for the handcuffs she always carried. He struggled as she pulled his arms together, but she managed to cuff him.

Evans holstered her weapon and held her head in her hands. The raw pain made her breath shallow and a lump formed under her fingers. The motherfucker. It took every ounce of self-control she had not to kick his groin while he was down.

Through the pain, she tried to figure out what to do next. The dickhead belonged in jail, but could she get him into her car? Even cuffed he could be dangerous. Evans grabbed her phone from her other pocket and hit redial. While she waited for Jackson to pick up, she looked around for her bag, which she'd dropped near her car.

Finally, Jackson answered. "Evans. What's going on?"

"Someone just attacked me. I subdued and cuffed him, but I need help getting him to the jail."

"Did you call for backup?"

"Not yet. I need someone here I trust."

"Where are you?"

Evans gave him the address, then heard the wail of a siren. The onlooker from the window must have followed through on his threat to call the cops. "I hear patrol units now, but I'd still like you to be here."

Her assailant struggled to his knees. "Gotta go." She hung up and kicked him in the shoulder. He fell to the ground, landing on his side. Adrenaline still pumping, she yanked up his mask.

Bekker!

CHAPTER 15

Wednesday, September 8, 7:55 a.m.

Evans crossed the breezeway, feeling apprehensive. She had a nasty headache, an abrasion on her cheek near her hairline, and her bruised knees hurt with every step. After booking Bekker into jail, she'd spent hours in the ER at Jackson's insistence, waiting for a CAT scan of her head, which revealed nothing. He'd come with her to the hospital, making it bearable, but she hadn't slept well or had enough coffee yet this morning. She worried that Bekker's attack would somehow be used against her.

Jackson had called Lammers from the jail to update her, and their boss had set up an early morning meeting. The conference was being held in the building next door, which housed internal affairs, and Evans felt out of her element. She straightened her posture, tightened her face to mask her pain, and entered the small gray meeting room.

A tall, gorgeous man with a shaved head stood and smiled warmly. Evans' heart took a little leap. *Who was this?*

"Hello. I'm Ben Stricklyn, internal affairs." He reached out to shake her hand.

"Detective Lara Evans, violent crimes." She smiled, hoping he wouldn't notice the lump on the side of her head.

"That looks like it hurts. Are you all right?"

Reflexively, she touched her facial abrasion. "I'm fine. You should see the other guy." It was lame, but they both laughed and sat down. Evans was pleased to have a cushioned chair instead of the hard chairs they used next door.

Lammers burst into the room, sucking up the moment with her built-in tension. "Where's Jackson? He's supposed to be here too."

"I'm sure he's coming." Evans wished she'd stopped for coffee, but she'd been running late after a rough night and didn't have time.

"Let's get started. We have a lot to cover." Lammers grabbed a chair at the end of the table. "Despite last night's incident, we still have to keep the investigations involving Bekker as secure as possible. It's imperative that neither of you discuss these cases with anyone else in the department." Lammers looked at Stricklyn. "You especially can't talk to your IA partner and you'll know why in a moment."

Jackson hurried into the room and slid into a chair as the sergeant spoke. Lammers paused, gave him a look, then continued. "Much to my disappointment, Sergeant Gary Bekker is suspected of sexual coercion, attempted murder, and now assaulting an officer."

"He's been accused of assaulting a detainee as well," Jackson added.

"Yes, but considering the magnitude of the other charges, that incident is not our focus."

"Rick Santori was involved in that interrogation," Jackson said, turning to Stricklyn. "That's why he can't participate in the investigation of Bekker."

"Santori assaulted a suspect?" Stricklyn looked skeptical.

"Ten years ago," Jackson said. "Santori and Bekker were assigned to investigate the murder of Clark and Evelyn Jackson. They picked up Hector Vargas, a handyman who worked for the Jacksons, and according to Vargas, they kept him detained for three days without food. They verbally and physically abused him until he confessed to murder."

"This is disturbing," Stricklyn said. "It must be especially difficult for you."

"They also failed to properly investigate the crime," Jackson answered. "Now the case is cold and some of the evidence is missing. I'd like to see them held accountable."

They discussed the Vargas situation for a few minutes, and Stricklyn said he would make a trip to the prison to interview the inmate. Evans waited for them to come back around to her case.

"Interrogating Bekker while he's in custody is a priority," Lammers said. "We'll strategize about that in a minute. But first, Evans will bring everyone up to date on her attempted homicide investigation."

Evans launched into her prepared statement, giving a brief summary of her conversations with Gina's parents and neighbors, then described her visits to Bekker's sexual victims. "As I left Joni Farmer's apartment, Gary Bekker attacked me."

"Bekker did that to you?" Stricklyn's mouth dropped open, and he reached over and grabbed Evans' arm.

His touch gave her a jolt of pleasure. She met his eyes briefly and kept talking. "Bekker struck me in the head with his baton, bashed my face into the side of my car, and pressed his forearm against my throat." Evans fought to keep her emotions in check. "But I prevailed and arrested him. He's in the county jail."

Stricklyn stared at her with admiration, followed by a small grin. "You subdued him and brought him in? Too bad you didn't have a taser with you."

"I hope to be assigned one soon," Evans said, looking at her boss.

Lammers cleared her throat. "We have two separate but linked investigations. The attempted homicide from two years ago and the ongoing sexual coercion. I'm not optimistic we'll convict Bekker of the attempted homicide, but now that he's facing a slam-dunk assault conviction, he might cooperate or plead to the other charges."

"Let's go interrogate him right now." Stricklyn stared at Evans, and warmth spread through her body.

Lammers said, "I've arranged with Sheriff Waters for Bekker to be brought here for questioning, so we can videotape and watch each other's interrogations."

Eager to participate, Evans said, "You'll let me question him about Gina's case?"

"No." Lammers slapped her leather folder closed. "It's too personal now." The sergeant locked eyes on Evans, daring her to contradict the statement. Lammers continued, "You can work the case and watch the interrogation, but you will not come into contact with Bekker. Understood?"

Evans nodded, wishing she'd hit Bekker harder, since she'd never have another shot at him.

Jackson spoke up. "I'd like to question Bekker about my parents' case. He was one of the investigators. Maybe we should start there, get him talking about something that won't make him defensive."

"Let's go round him up." Lammers stood. "While you're gone, I have to meet with our spokesperson and decide what the hell we're going to say publicly about all this."

Jackson and Stricklyn walked out together, discussing their trip to the jail. Evans felt like she was watching an X-rated movie. Why did good-looking cops make her so weak in the knees? She hoped it was just a perk and not the reason she'd joined the department.

She realized Sergeant Lammers was watching her watch them, so she distracted her boss with a question. "Why does Jackson get to work his parents' case, which is as personal as it gets, and I can't participate in Bekker's interrogation because it's too personal?"

Lammers stepped over to the door and closed it. "If you repeat this to anyone, I'll have you transferred to sex crimes, clear?"

"Yes."

"I'm letting Jackson investigate his parents' homicides because it's only a matter of going through the motions. He needs to believe he tried. But those murders were ten years ago, and his chances of closing them are slim to none. If it wasn't the handyman, then it was some crackhead who knew they kept cash in the house. The killer is either dead, in jail, or long gone."

* * *

Stricklyn rode with Jackson to the jail, and they talked about an interrogation strategy on the way. The IA detective wanted to use a linear approach, working from one crime to the next. Jackson wanted to mix it up and keep circling back to the important points of each case. Stricklyn agreed to let Jackson take the lead for the first round and see how it went.

After parking near the front doors of the redbrick building, they went up the stairs together. The night before, when he and Evans had dropped off Bekker, they'd entered through the side bay in their vehicles, so Bekker would be stripped and processed like any other detainee. Jackson had driven Bekker in the back of his car, and the man had been silent until they'd arrived at the jail. As Jackson pulled him out, Bekker had casually offered to resign if they would forget his "little altercation." Evans had shown restraint and only said, "Not a chance in hell."

Today in the public waiting area, a young woman who looked as if she'd never known joy sat stiffly on the wooden bench. He and Stricklyn walked to the reception desk, now walled off with plexiglass, showed their badges, and asked to transfer Bekker.

"Has he been arraigned yet?" Jackson asked.

"Let me check." The female deputy looked like she might burst out of her beige uniform. "At eight this morning. The judge set bail at two hundred thousand."

"Oh crap." Jackson turned to Stricklyn. "He'll probably come up with ten percent of that before the day is over. This may be our only chance to get anything out of him."

The deputy said, "I'll have someone bring Bekker out." She made a call, and they waited for ten minutes. Finally, the door opened behind her and Bekker came through with cuffed hands and shackled feet, followed by an older male deputy. Bekker had dark circles under his eyes, and the prison-green scrubs made the rest of his face look pale. A red gash showed through his near-buzz-cut hair.

"You're wasting your time," Bekker said, as they escorted him to the car. "But what the hell, it gets me out of the box for a while."

At the department, Jackson escorted the handcuffed sergeant to the claustrophobic gray room while Stricklyn went to round up Evans and Lammers, who would watch from the conference room. The plan was to give Jackson some time alone with Bekker to talk about the old homicide case. After Jackson got what he needed, Stricklyn would join him to question Bekker about his ex-wife. Then Jackson would exit and Lammers would come in, and she and Stricklyn would ask questions about the sexual coercion and the earlier abuse of a suspect. They had no idea if Bekker would talk at all.

Jackson clicked on the video recorder and announced the day and time for the camera, then identified himself and his suspect.

"This is a waste of time," Bekker complained. "I'm not telling you anything until I consult a lawyer."

"I need your help with an old case." Jackson's plan was to get Bekker talking about something other than his crimes. "We've reopened the homicide of Clark and Evelyn Jackson. You and Santori handled it in 2000."

Bekker seemed genuinely puzzled. "Why? We had a confession. It was a slam dunk."

"Vargas recanted and new information has come up, so I'm starting from scratch."

"What new information?"

"A man in a dark sedan, sitting outside the Jacksons' house the day of the murders. Did any witnesses mention it?"

"No." Again, Bekker seemed surprised.

Jackson wanted to point out the many ways in which the investigation had been shoddy, but that would be counterproductive. "I'd like you to describe the crime scene, since I have no way to see it for myself."

"We took photos. They're in the file."

"These are my parents' murders. Help me out here."

"I think you're wasting your time, but what the hell." Bekker seemed to realize that talking about an old investigation was better than anything else on the menu of crimes to discuss. "I'll never forget the case. It was my first double homicide and we found the bodies in the living room. The woman was on the floor with a bullet hole in her forehead, and the old man was slumped against the couch with two holes in his chest. They were dressed like they'd just come back from church."

Jackson's parents always looked their best in public, and until he was thirteen they wouldn't allow him to leave the house in a T-shirt. "What was your initial impression?" he asked. "Before the tip got called in. Do you remember?"

"It looked like a home invasion, except we soon realized nothing was stolen, including two rifles in a bedroom closet. Then I started to think it was a professional hit."

Jackson was intrigued. "What made you think that?" Eugene almost never had that kind of homicide. The local crime element was definitely not *organized*.

"Bullets in the forehead and the chest. Kill zones. Like someone who practiced at a shooting range."

"Do you mean law enforcement?"

"I didn't think that at the time, no." Bekker shifted uncomfortably.

Jackson found it unlikely as well, so he moved on. "What about the money under the woman's body?"

"Oh yeah." Bekker cocked his head. "That was odd. The ME found a hundred-dollar bill when his crew moved her."

"What happened to the money?"

"I bagged it as evidence and turned it in to the crime lab."

"Did they dust it for prints?"

"Yes, but they didn't find a match. Not to Vargas, or the victims, or anyone in CODIS."

"That seems odd."

Bekker didn't respond.

"The bill is no longer in the evidence crate."

Bekker smirked. "I guess I'm not surprised. I'm sure some technician found it hard to resist."

"Tell me about the anonymous tip."

"Dispatch got a call from a pay phone. The caller said he heard shots, then shortly after, he saw a handyman come out of the house, jump in his truck, and take off. A patrol officer responded to the address, found the bodies, and called us."

"How did you come up with Vargas' name?"

"There was a check made out to Hector Vargas sitting on the kitchen table, and we had a description of him and his truck. Patrol units picked him up twenty minutes later."

"Was there anything about the tip or timing that seemed odd to you?"

"Nope. Just a citizen doing his duty."

"Did you check Vargas' hands for gunshot residue?"

"We did, and they were clean. But he had time to wash them. He had the victims' money. He admitted to being in the house."

"Did you look for the gun?"

Bekker glared. "Of course."

Jackson decided to mix it up. "Why did you try to kill your ex-wife?"

Bekker jerked back. "Why is this old shit coming up?"

"Gina thinks it's important. Tell me about your relationship with your ex."

"What is there to say? We were in the middle of a divorce. She left me for another guy."

That was not what he'd heard. "Really? Who?"

"Some pansy-ass nurse." Bekker shook his head in disgust.

"So you were angry with her?"

Bekker scoffed. "Hell, yes. But she tried to kill herself. I had nothing to do with that."

"Why would she try to kill herself?"

"She was depressed and crazy."

"Is that why you stalked her and threatened to kill her?"

Bekker shifted in his chair. "I didn't stalk her. I just wanted to see who she left me for."

"You admit you threatened her?"

"I admit nothing."

"Where were you that night?"

"Drinking at the Sixth Street Grill with Pete Casaway. This has already been established."

Jackson tried to remember what Evans had reported. "Casaway now says he didn't see you after seven that night."

"I don't believe that."

"Evans recorded the conversation. You have no alibi."

"Why is that bitch Evans suddenly all over me?" Bekker's eyes and nostrils flared, and Jackson got a glimpse of his hatred for women.

"Does Evans remind you of Gina?"

"Fuck you."

Jackson sat quietly, staring down Bekker. The small gray room seemed to shrink, and he breathed from his diaphragm to counteract the tension. The more time he spent in this closet, the more difficult it became. After a minute, Stricklyn strode in.

Bekker laughed. "IA? Really?"

Stricklyn stood over Bekker, his voice deadly quiet. "You're charged with assaulting a police officer. You'll get five years just for that. Throw in attempted homicide and sexual assault, and you're looking at twenty years, minimum. It's time to cooperate."

Jackson watched Bekker process the charges and calculate how much they knew. Finally, the inmate said, "I didn't assault a police officer. Detective Evans struck me, and I defended myself."

Jackson let his disgust show. "Why would she do that?"

"She's an aggressive bitch."

"What were you doing outside that apartment?" Stricklyn asked.

"Minding my own business."

"Tell us about the altercation. How did it start?" This was Stricklyn's interview now.

"Why should I tell you anything? What's in it for me?"

"We'd like to keep your cases from going to trial and becoming a media frenzy. The DA is willing to drop the assault-of-an-officer charge if you plead to assaulting your wife. We'll knock it down from attempted murder. It's a sweet deal and you should take it."

"I didn't assault anyone, so no thanks."

Stricklyn glanced at his notes. "Let's talk about Trisha Cronin. When did you first meet her?"

A flash of panic registered in Bekker's eyes. "I'm not answering any more questions until I see a lawyer."

"Right now, the whole department thinks you're a rapist. That's going to stick unless you tell us your side of the story."

"They believe a hooker?" Bekker tried to look scornful, but Jackson heard distress in his voice.

"And a heroin addict. These women are glad to tell their stories now that someone is listening." Stricklyn tapped his notepad on the table. "Attacking Evans outside one of your victims' apartment made you look guilty as hell. Judges and juries hate dirty cops, so your lawyer will advise you to stay out of court." Stricklyn stood. "I'll get you a glass of water and let you think about how you want to play this."

Jackson was glad to get out of the room, yet he hated to give up the interrogation before they'd made progress. Still, Bekker was not his focus...unless he was the man in the blue sedan... who had assassinated his victims with kill shots, then came back later to investigate the crime. It was possible, but so far, he had no reason to think that.

"Did you get anything useful?" Stricklyn asked, as they stood in the hall.

"I'm now considering the possibility that my parents were a professional hit, as unlikely as that seems." Jackson started toward the break room. "I'll get Bekker some water while you confer with Lammers."

Stricklyn laughed. "We're not getting him anything. Let's see how he likes it."

* * *

"That motherfucker! I can't believe he's saying I hit him first." Evans now realized why Lammers wouldn't let her in with Bekker. She might thump him.

"Would you stop bouncing? You're making my blood pressure spike." Lammers turned to her as they stood side by side in the conference room, watching the monitor. "You got pictures of your injuries, correct?"

"Jackson took them when I was in the ER, so I have a paper trail too."

"Good." Lammers touched her shoulder. "Don't worry. Bekker has lost all credibility. He'll do time for assaulting you."

Evans watched Jackson and Stricklyn leave the interrogation room and struggled to get her emotions under control. She had to stay professional. She'd gone over to Full City for coffee while the guys had picked up Bekker, and now the caffeine was working against her. "Even without the shit he's saying about me, Bekker seems a little off, like he might have a mental problem."

"You think?" Lammers cast skeptical eyes down at her.

Evans ignored the sarcasm. "His hostility toward me is irrational. What if he makes bail? If he does, I want a twenty-four-hour watch on both him and Gina."

"Don't worry, if he makes bail, we'll pick him up on new charges."

"Good to know."

On the monitor, Bekker suddenly turned to the camera and made a kissing gesture.

Evans hated and feared him more than anyone she'd ever known, including her father, who'd beaten and ridiculed her for sport. "Is Bekker setting himself up to be incompetent to stand trial?"

"We'll see."

Jackson and Stricklyn came into the conference room, and they all sat at the new table the department had recently brought in. The hard metal chairs had not been replaced.

"What do you think?" Jackson asked. "Did you pick up anything we might have missed?"

Lammers responded, "When you asked Bekker about stalking and threatening Gina, he got very uncomfortable. He squirmed in his chair, then tried to cover it by leaning back and acting casual. I think we can assume Gina is telling the truth about that."

"I'll hit that subject again in the next round," Stricklyn said.

"He also seemed upset when you mentioned that his peers in the department thought he was a rapist," Evans commented. "I think you can use that as leverage too." She looked at Stricklyn. "You told him the DA was willing to drop the charge of assaulting me. Have you talked to Slonecker?"

"I made that up. We're not dropping it."

"Damn straight. He threatened to kill me if I didn't back off. He's a psychopath."

"Exactly why you're not in there," Lammers said.

After another ten minutes of strategizing, Lammers and Stricklyn headed to the interrogation room.

Jackson and Evans stood near the monitor watching Bekker. His eyes were closed and his body slack, as if he had dozed off.

"Look at that fucker," Evans said. "Only the guilty can sleep in an interrogation room."

"True enough. The innocent are too worried."

Evans used the opportunity to pick Jackson's brain. "Now that Bekker's in custody, what should I do next on this case?"

"Have you talked to all the possible witnesses who might have seen Bekker in the vicinity the night Gina was assaulted?"

"I haven't tracked down the neighbor who moved yet."

"See if you can find him or her. What about video? Does her apartment complex have cameras? Maybe Bekker or his vehicle got caught on tape somewhere."

"Great ideas. What's next for you, Jackson?"

"Going through my parents' phone records and questioning a loan shark."

They watched as Lammers and Stricklyn got Bekker talking about the women he'd victimized. Only, in his warped perspective, they were just friends. Fuck buddies. Evans felt queasy listening to him.

"I'm going back to work," she said, heading for the door.

CHAPTER 16

Wednesday, September 8, 8:25 a.m.

Sophie flashed her ID badge at the security camera, entered the *Willamette News* building, and hurried into the lunchroom to pick up a copy of the morning's paper. The cafeteria had been closed a year earlier after the bulk of the layoffs, but they'd left the lunchroom open. She grabbed a newspaper from one of the tables, said hello to the entertainment reporter, and trotted up the open staircase. On the way, she noted all the empty workstations on the first floor. So many people had been laid off, the newspaper had moved the remaining support staff upstairs and was trying to rent out the first level for cash. The once busy, noisy office was dying, and it was damn sad. But the truth was, she wouldn't trade her iPhone, iPad, or Kindle to get it all back. She loved new technology, and she'd find a way to keep her career going too.

She clicked on her computer, then laid the paper open on her desk. Her story about Gina Stahl was on the front page of the city section, and Sophie scanned it to see how it flowed. She quickly realized the layout editor had cut selective chunks of her copy to make it fit a limited space. *Shit.* She hated when they butchered her careful transitions. She read the paragraph referencing Gina's accusations.

Stahl says her attacker wore a ski mask, but the victim believes the assault was carried out by her ex-husband. Stahl says she was collecting evidence about her ex-husband's criminal activities and that he tried to kill her to silence her. The police are investigating various leads.

It was a little choppy, because someone had edited out the fact that the victim's ex was a police officer.

Sophie grabbed her phone and called Detective Evans again. She wished she had Evans' cell number instead of her desk phone, because so far, Evans had not called her back. Sophie wanted to know the names of the women Gary Bekker had victimized so she could interview them, but she suspected the detective wouldn't tell her. She would have to visit Gina again and reassure her that she would not use the women's names in print. The paper had a policy of not naming the victims of sex crimes, and Sophie fully supported it.

"What are you working on this morning?" Karl Hoogstad, her editor, clumped up behind her. He was round in the middle and bald on top, except for a strip of gray hair across the back of his head. Sophie tried not to hold it against him.

"I'm heading over to the care center to talk to the coma woman again. I want to dig into the sex crimes she says her ex-husband, the cop, committed. I think this could be the biggest story we follow this year."

"I trust your instincts."

Sophie's heart about burst with pride. It had taken her years to earn some respect at the paper. Her intuition on the story of two missing women last spring had netted her an eyewitness account of the perp's apprehension. Hoogstad had apparently not forgotten. "Thanks. I appreciate that."

"I'll still want to see each story before it goes to layout."

"Yes, sir."

As he walked away, her phone rang. Hoping it was Evans, she grabbed it. "This is Sophie."

"Roger Norquist, returning your call. You're going to run a story about my fundraiser?"

"Just a short piece." Sophie had lost all interest in the politician, but decided to get a quote while she had him on the phone. "Why are you starting your campaign so early? Are you worried about your ability to win next year's election?"

"I'm not officially campaigning, just fundraising, and I'm not worried. I plan to start early, work hard, and win this time."

"You lost the Senate race in 2006. What's different for you now?"

"I'm more in tune with voters, and the mood of the public is turning more conservative. Voters are tired of big government and big spending. My platform—"

Sophie cut him off. "I'm sorry, but I only have the space for a sentence or two. Next fall, when your campaign is in full swing, we'll talk again."

"Thank you."

She hung up, glad to get off the phone and back to her juicy story about the psycho cop.

* * *

At his desk, Jackson keyed the loan shark's name into the criminal database and discovered Ray Durkin had served three and a half years in the Oregon State Correctional Institution on charges of assault and extortion. He'd been incarcerated in October of 2003 and released in April of 2007—which meant Durkin had gone to prison years after his loan dealings with Derrick. Jackson was relieved that his brother's judgment wasn't completely worthless. Still, Derrick had borrowed a chunk of cash from someone he'd met in a strip club, who later went to prison. Sometimes it was hard to believe he and Derrick had the same DNA.

Durkin had fulfilled his parole terms and had no criminal history since. After failing to find Durkin in the citizen database, Jackson googled his name and was surprised to discover the ex-con was working as a mountain-bike-race promoter. Jackson searched the Cascade Mountain Races website but couldn't find a phone number, only an e-mail contact. "Crap."

"What's going on?" Schak heard him swear and rolled his chair over.

"My only lead has no address and no phone number that I can locate."

"Who is it?" Schak knew Jackson was working his parents' case.

"Ray Durkin. He was a loan shark back then. Now he's a promoter for mountain-bike races."

"Ray Durkin was a loan shark?" Schak looked stunned, an expression Jackson had never seen on his face before.

"Do you know him?"

"I've met him. He's not just a promoter. He hosts mountain-bike races on his property and donates a percentage of the profit to the Big Brothers program."

Jackson suppressed a groan. "How do you know this?"

"Remember when my son was into mountain biking? I watched a couple races up there." Schak looked over Jackson's shoulder at the website on the monitor. "I'll be damned. Durkin's an ex-con."

"And a suspect in my parents' homicides."

"What's his connection?"

"He loaned money to my brother, then threatened him when he didn't pay. Derrick moved in with Mom and Dad the day before they were killed."

"Jesus." Schak shuddered. "Are you going up there to see Durkin? He has a cabin on his property off Murdock Road."

"How do I find it?"

"Take Fox Hollow to Murdock, then take the second or third gravel road on the left. I think there's a sign."

"Thanks." The fax machine near the hallway jumped to life and started spitting out paper. "Maybe that's my phone records."

Searching and sorting phone numbers was the most tedious aspect of his job. His parents had not made or received that many calls in the weeks prior, so it wasn't a worst-case scenario. Nearly a third of the calls were to or from Derrick. Jackson knew his brother and mother had been close, but he hadn't realized they talked on the phone that much. He tried to remember how often his mother had called him. Maybe once a month, to invite him and his family over for Sunday dinner.

He suppressed the thought and kept keying in numbers. The outgoing calls were to his mother's sisters, to a doctor's office, and to the utility company. Some of the numbers for the outgoing calls were no longer listed or no longer in service. The incoming calls were more diverse. On the evening before the murders, they'd received a call from a company called Valley Fresh. Jackson googled the name and discovered it was a bakery and cereal business that had been in Eugene for sixty-five years. The call had come in at 6:07 p.m., and he assumed it was some kind of sales pitch. Earlier that day, they had also received calls from an insurance company and the Democratic headquarters.

On September 21, two days before the murders, only two calls were listed. One at 5:17 p.m. from EWEB, the utility company where his father had worked. Most likely his dad was calling home to see if his wife needed anything at the store. A second call came in at 8:15 that evening. Jackson entered the digits. A business name popped up and gave his heart a little jump. Lucky Numbers. The strip bar owned by Seth Valder, an associate of Ray Durkin. Had Durkin called from the bar looking for Derrick? Or had he started harassing Derrick's parents for the money?

Jackson spent another twenty minutes keying in phone numbers, then lost patience with the process. He was eager to talk to Ray Durkin, so he mapped Murdock Road on the computer to see where it met Fox Hollow Road, then headed out. It was a long trip, and he hoped like hell Durkin would be around.

Jackson drove out East Amazon, a long, narrow street heading toward the south hills. The weather had cooled a little, so he opened his window and enjoyed the end-of-summer air. He turned on Fox Hollow and tried to remember the last time he'd been in this part of Eugene. As he passed the Cascade Raptor Center, where they rescued and nurtured birds of prey, he realized what it was. He'd taken Katie and a friend to see the owls and falcons on Katie's twelfth birthday.

Murdock turned out to be a hard-packed gravel road, and Jackson drove it slowly, watching for the Cascade Mountain Races sign. He spotted it tucked into a V in the road, and laurel had started to grow over it. Jackson turned onto a loosely packed gravel road and slowed down even more. He wondered how often Durkin made a trip into town.

A half mile later, the road dead-ended into a large gravel parking area. Off to the right sat a large white truck with KSL

Construction lettered on the side. Beyond it, the framework for a two-story house rose toward the sky, and Jackson heard the rhythmic pounding of hammer on nails. A log cabin was nestled into a grove of fir trees at the other end of the gravel lot.

A dark-blue sedan was parked in front of the cabin. A shiver ran up Jackson's spine. It had been ten years, and Durkin had spent three of them in jail. Was it possible this was the car that had been parked outside his parents' house that day?

Jackson climbed out of his vehicle, touching his weapon out of habit. Barking dogs descended on him in a mad rush. He reached for his taser and realized he'd left it in the car. Two tan pit bulls and a big black mixed breed formed a half circle around him, barking aggressively. The noise was nerve-racking.

"Back off!" Jackson yelled and drew his Sig Sauer to take some measure of control. The scar through his eyebrow was compliments of an angry unleashed dog.

A man came running up from the direction of the construction. "Quiet, boys!"

The dogs went silent but didn't move.

Muscles bulged under the man's T-shirt, and his brow dripped with sweat. He was forty-something with a dark-blond ponytail, sun-bronzed skin, and tinted glasses. "Sorry about the dogs," he said. "Who are you?"

"Detective Jackson, Eugene Police. Are you Ray Durkin?"

"Yes. What do you want?"

"I have some questions about a loan you made ten years ago."

Durkin looked amused. "Are you serious?"

"As a heart attack. Can we go inside somewhere?" Jackson wanted to get out of the sun and away from the dogs.

"Sure. Let's get this over with." Durkin started toward the cabin, and the dogs followed. Jackson glanced back at the construction site to see if they were being watched. A second man tossed wood scraps in a big green trash bin and seemed to pay no attention to Jackson's presence.

At the door of the cabin, Jackson said, "I'd like the dogs to stay outside."

"They're harmless." Durkin grinned.

Jackson started to dislike him. "Leave them outside."

"Stay."

The dogs plopped on the low-slung deck.

Inside, the cabin was cool and the main room held three couches. A big fireplace took up one wall, and the interior reminded Jackson of a ski lodge. Durkin went to the small adjacent kitchen and grabbed a beer out of the refrigerator. He sat at the table and gestured for Jackson to join him.

"What loan and why now?" Durkin asked, as Jackson sat down.

"In 2000, you loaned money to Derrick Jackson. I want to know the details."

Durkin looked blank. "That was a long time ago. Give me a clue."

"He borrowed the money for a solar-panel business."

Durkin's eyes clouded, as if he remembered something painful. "He's your brother, right?"

"Yep."

"I loaned him ten thousand and he only paid back six of it. But I don't care anymore. I've got a whole new life here."

Either Derrick had lied about the amount of the loan or Durkin was lying now. "You just let it go? Four thousand dollars?"

"Circumstances changed."

"Like what?"

"You know what I mean." Durkin took a long pull of his beer. "We both know your parents were murdered around that time.

Suddenly the cops and the media were all over that house, and Derrick was grieving and dysfunctional. I wrote off the four thousand and moved on."

"Bullshit. Derrick says you threatened him."

"That was before. It's also the nature of the alternative loan business."

"Where did you get the ten grand?"

"I was doing a nice business. I had cash in the bank."

"You called the Jacksons' house two days before the murders. Who did you talk to?"

"I don't remember." Durkin glanced away.

"Don't lie to me. What did you say to Evelyn Jackson?"

"I never spoke to her."

Jackson decided Durkin was a pathological liar. "Why did you call her house?"

"I was looking for Derrick. He still owed me money and he was hiding."

"What did you threaten my parents with?"

Durkin sat forward and tried to look earnest. "I admit, I broke a few fingers and I cheated a few people. I also did time for it. But I never threatened anyone's family."

"Where were you on the afternoon of September 23, 2000?"

Durkin's mouth opened in surprise. "You think I killed them?"

"Where were you at the time of the murders?"

"I don't remember. It was ten years ago."

"What kind of car were you driving then?"

"The same one I have now. I had just bought it. Why?"

"Someone saw it parked outside my parents' house the day they were killed."

Durkin shook his head. "Not my car."

"Then you won't mind submitting a DNA sample for comparison. It's an opportunity to clear yourself."

"Sorry, but I'll pass. I don't trust the system." Durkin took another drink of beer.

Jackson thought about the ex-con's fingerprints on the beer bottle and made a note to have the crime lab compare Durkin's prints to those at the scene. "Were you ever in the house at 2353 Emerald Street?"

"No."

"When I come back with a subpoena, I'll have to take you down to the department for a cheek swab. Why don't you save us both the trouble?"

"I didn't kill anyone, and I don't have to prove it." Durkin bolted to his feet, sounding frustrated. "I run a legitimate business now and I donate ten percent of my profits to the Big Brothers Big Sisters program for kids. I also sponsor teenagers to come up here and race. The idea is to help young people stay out of trouble so they don't make the same mistakes I did. I don't appreciate being hassled."

"I'm just doing my job."

"I thought they caught the killer and he went to jail." Durkin vibrated with impatience.

Jackson didn't budge from his chair. "It turns out they didn't. What did you think of my parents?"

"I never met them." Durkin gestured toward the door. "I've got to get back to work."

"That's a big house you're building."

"It's a lodge. A lot of people come here to race."

"Did the money come from your loan-shark days?"

"It's none of your business."

"Are you still in contact with Seth Valder?"

"Not since I got out. I gave up the old life."

Jackson sensed he'd been lied to again, but Durkin seemed to be done talking. "Do you have a cell phone?"

"Yes, why?"

"I want the number."

"I don't want to be harassed."

Jackson waited him out.

Durkin sighed and gave him the number.

Jackson stood to leave. "Keep your dogs under control when I walk out so I don't have to shoot them."

CHAPTER 17

Wednesday, September 8, 2:16 p.m.

Evans checked her notes for Gina's neighbor who had moved. The name wasn't there. *Shit.* How could she have been so sloppy? She used her desk phone to call the Riverside Terrace and was relieved when the manager picked up.

"This is Detective Evans again. I need the name of the neighbor who lived on the other side of Gina Stahl at the time of her assault. You told me she moved."

"Give me a sec and I'll look." After a while, the manager said, "Alison Bertram. I have her forwarding address, but it's in Salem. Do you want her phone number too?"

"Thanks, I'll take both."

Evans made a note of the name and number. "I noticed a camera mounted on the front gate. Do you still have video footage from 2008?"

"You'll have to call the company that maintains the camera. It's Secure Systems West."

Evans thanked her and made the next call. She asked to speak to the manager, and a moment later, a man came on the phone. "This is Chuck Summers. How can I help you?"

Evans introduced herself. "I'm investigating an assault that took place a few years ago at the Riverside Terrace. Do you have security film from August 3, 2008?"

"Of course. Which cameras do you need?"

Yes! "The front gate and anything that would show the exterior of apartment sixteen."

"Would you like me to download the files to a disk?"

"That would be great. Can I pick it up now?"

"Sure. We're always happy to work with the police department."

A surge of adrenaline pulsed in her veins. Evans stood and began to pace. What if the cameras had caught Bekker driving into the parking lot or walking up to Gina's apartment? By itself, it wasn't enough for a conviction, but it could give them leverage for a plea bargain. Then she remembered the attacker had worn a mask. When had he put it on? What kind of vehicle had Bekker driven two years ago? Would he have taken his city-issued car?

The quickest route to that information was the department of motor vehicles. She called Stacy Garrett, Jackson's contact at the DMV, and introduced herself.

"How can I help you?" The woman sounded annoyed.

"I'd like to know every vehicle Gary Bekker has owned since 2008."

"It's crazy-busy here today. Can I call you back on my break?"

"Bekker is a dangerous man who's about to make bail. I need this info to keep him locked up."

The overworked state employee sighed. "Give me a minute."

Syrupy pop music filled Evans' ear. She set her cell phone on the desk while she was on hold and mentally kicked herself for not doing all of it yesterday. She'd been sidetracked with contacting Bekker's sexual victims. Evans snatched up the phone when she heard Stacy talking.

"Gary Bekker has owned a 1997 red Chevy truck since 2002. In 2007, he appeared as a co-owner on a white Ford Fiesta that is no longer registered to him. That's it."

"Can I get the license numbers?"

Stacy rattled them off, then hung up before Evans could thank her.

Impatient to pick up the video disk, Evans quickly called the number for the neighbor who had moved and was subjected to an annoying voice message from a young man named Troy. Obviously, it was not Alison's number anymore. She keyed Alison into the database and came up with the old address at Riverside Terrace. *Crap.* She had no intention of spending an hour driving to Salem without contacting the woman first.

Evans googled the address for the security company, pulled on her jacket, and headed out.

Forty minutes later, she checked the disk into the crime lab and went to look for Joe. She found him in his office, comparing fingerprints.

"Hey, Joe." Evans had once called him Berloni, the way law enforcement called everyone by their last names, and Joe had strongly objected. She waited while he finished his scrutiny. "What case are you working on?"

"The woman who was buried in her backyard. They found the murder weapon, and I'm checking the prints." Joe looked up. "What happened to your face?"

"An altercation with a suspect. I'm fine. Any luck with the prints?"

"Not yet. I keep getting interrupted." He smiled to soften his words. "What can I do for you?"

Evans handed him the disk, now in a plastic bag with labels. "This is camera footage of an apartment complex where a woman was attacked and given an overdose of drugs. She went into a coma for two years, then recently came out of it."

"I saw the story in the paper this morning."

"What the hell?" Evans immediately thought of Sophie Speranza, who'd been leaving her messages, asking about the case. "Who would give a reporter information? Thank god my suspect is in jail."

"Is the woman in danger?"

"If he gets released on bail, she could be." Evans didn't want to believe Bekker was that stupid or irrational, but he'd already proved her wrong. "What I need you to look for on the footage is a red Chevy truck driven by a man. He's around five-ten and one ninety. He may be wearing a ski mask. I'm looking for him in the vicinity of apartment sixteen around nine in the evening." She hesitated. "He could be driving a department-issued vehicle."

Joe raised his eyebrows. "An officer?"

"Maybe."

"I'll get one of the assistants to start wading through the footage, but we're pretty swamped. It may be a day or two."

"The suspect is in jail on unrelated charges but he was arraigned this morning. If he makes bail, I need a good reason to pick him up again."

"We'll do it as fast as we can."

At the department, Evans went straight to the break room, hoping to find a newspaper, but she found someone's uneaten lunch instead—one of the joys of working with mostly men. She wanted the news story in front of her when she called Sophie Speranza to give her a verbal ass kicking. Evans jogged over to Full City, where they had a newspaper stand nearby.

She bought a paper and hustled back to City Hall, her weapon bouncing against her ribs as she ran. She laid the paper out on her desk, found the story on the front page of the city section, and quickly scanned it. At least the reporter had not given Gina's name. Yet Speranza had named the care facility, so anyone who knew Gina was there would know she was now conscious. The story quoted Gina and her parents, so they had obviously consented to the coverage. The quotes mentioned the ex-husband and Gina's effort to document his criminal activity, but didn't give his name or occupation. The reporter had been careful to let her interview subjects make the unsubstantiated accusations. *Crafty.*

Evans called the *Willamette News* and asked to speak to Sophie Speranza. The reporter didn't answer her phone, so Evans left a message. Trying not to sound hostile, she simply asked for a call back on her cell number. Next, she searched Salem's online white pages and found a new phone number for Gina's unaccounted-for neighbor. She called and left Alison a message as well.

Frustrated by her lack of progress, Evans read through her notes and mentally retraced the steps of her investigation. What had she not done yet? She visualized the visit to Gina's parents and the boxes full of her personal belongings. Was there any value in digging through the rest of it? She was no longer looking for a suspect; she was in the phase of building a case. Would she find anything in the pile of stuff that would incriminate Bekker?

She couldn't just sit and wait for people to call back, so Evans decided to see the victim again.

Gina was out of bed and sitting in a chair by the window. A petite, slender woman with short red hair and a digital recorder sat next to Gina, leaning forward and looking earnest. They both looked up.

"Detective Evans. Oh my god, what happened to you?" Gina's smiled faded.

"An altercation with a suspect. I'm fine."

Gina gestured at the redhead. "This is Sophie Speranza from the *Willamette News.*"

The reporter jumped up and stuck out her hand. Evans ignored it. "I need to talk to you outside."

"Sure. I've got some questions for you anyway."

The ballsy little bitch. Evans gestured for the reporter to move through the door. She followed and closed it behind her. In the hall, an old man with a walker moved slowly past, so Evans waited. When he was clear, she yelled at Speranza, but without raising her voice. "You put Gina's life at risk by printing that story this morning."

Speranza blinked and rocked back, but she quickly recovered. "The care facility sent out a press release and both Gina and her parents consented to an interview. They think the publicity will pressure the department to do something about Gary Bekker."

"We are doing something, but you could jeopardize our investigation."

"I don't buy that. If you want Gina to be safe, arrest Bekker."

"We did, but we still have to build a case. I need you to stay away from Gina and her parents until we have something solid on Bekker."

"What about all the women he sexually coerced? That seems like a solid reason to keep him in jail."

Evans struggled for the right thing to say. "That investigation is even more critical. Please leave it alone until we've made some progress."

"Maybe I can help you." Speranza still had her pen, tablet, and recorder in hand. "If I run the story—without naming the women—maybe more victims will come forward. The more accusers Bekker has, the more likely he'll be convicted."

Evans had to admit she liked the logic. "I can't let you name me as a source."

"Fine. This is off the record. What can you tell me?" Speranza clicked on her recorder.

"No recorder."

She clicked it off.

"Gary Bekker is being investigated by internal affairs for inappropriate contact with detainees. We have the testimony of two women so far."

"Will you tell me their names so I can interview them? I promise not to release their identities. I also know a lawyer who will be happy to take their case. "

"I can't. But I will give your name to the victims so they can contact you if they choose."

"How long has Bekker's behavior been going on?" Speranza's young face was a mask of determination.

"At least two years. Beyond that, we don't know."

"You said you arrested Bekker. What is he charged with?"

"I can't say."

"No problem. I can look it up." The reporter pulled a cell phone from her jacket pocket and quickly accessed the Lane County Jail website. She looked up, startled. "He has a pending charge of assaulting an officer. Is that who hit you in the face?"

"I can't comment. I'm going in to talk to Gina now. Alone."

"Let me grab my laptop."

Speranza went back in the room and sat next to Gina for a moment. "I'm not leaving yet. I'm just stepping out for a few minutes. We'll finish up after the detective leaves."

"Okay."

Evans took her chair as she left. "How are you doing? Still making progress?"

"The doctors are stunned by how quickly I'm regaining strength. In fact, I'm going home this afternoon." Gina gave a sad smile. "I mean to my parents' house. But I'll have my own place again soon."

Evans was surprised by the suddenness of it, but happy for Gina. "That's great news. In fact, I'll escort you. I want to look through more of your paperwork. We have to build a case against Bekker."

"What do you expect to find?"

"I honestly don't know, but I've run out of other sources."

"Have you talked to Gary's brother?"

Evans was crushed by her oversight. In avoiding contact with Bekker, she hadn't talked to any of his citizen associates. "No. You didn't mention his family."

"His parents are in San Diego, but his brother lives here. His name is Doug Bekker. He's a slacker, but a nice guy."

"Where can I find him?"

"He used to live in a trailer park not far from here. It's called Meadow View and it's near Thirty-Second Street just off Q. Doug had the green single-wide at the very end." Gina shrugged. "I don't know if he's still there, but most likely."

"Would he talk to me about his brother?"

"Oh sure. He loves Gary, but he also hates him. They have a weird relationship."

Evans understood that. She felt somewhat the same about her own brother. Charged with a new lead, she stood. "What time are you leaving here today?"

"Around five. My parents are out buying me a walker and doing some last-minute preparation at the house."

"I'll be back at five." Evans touched Gina's arm. "Be careful about what you tell reporters."

Gina smiled. "Sophie is going to help me launch a comeback. The publicity will be great for my clothing business."

Apprehension crawled up Evans' spine. "Bekker is in jail for now, but if he makes bail, I'm worried he'll come after you."

Gina nearly dropped her water bottle. "That seems crazy."

"I know, but he's not acting rationally. I requested a guard for you, but I didn't get it."

"How much is Gary's bail?"

"Two hundred and fifty thousand, but he only needs twenty-five of it."

"He'll never come up with that unless he cashes out his retirement, and that would take weeks."

"Just keep your eyes open and your doors locked. I will make sure patrol units circle by your house as often as possible."

"Thanks."

"See you in an hour."

Evans found Doug Bekker sitting on the deck of his shabby trailer, drinking from a two-liter bottle of soda. Boxes loaded with mechanical parts surrounded him, and a rusted kitchen stove took up the rest of the space. Doug wore shorts and sandals and nothing else. With the same ash-blond hair and broad chest as his brother, Evans identified him immediately. But while Gary Bekker looked like a man on permanent stress duty, Doug looked tanned and relaxed. Not a care in the world on a Wednesday afternoon.

Evans noticed two teenage boys across the cul-de-sac and a group of Hispanic men clustered around a food truck nearby. She locked her car and strode over to the man in the lawn chair.

"I'm Detective Evans, Eugene Police. Are you Doug Bekker?"

"I am." He stood and shook her hand. "You sure are pretty for a cop. Even with that bruise."

Evans tried not to jump to conclusions about him, tempting as it was. "I'd like to ask you about your brother, Gary Bekker." She grabbed her recorder from her bag, held it up for Doug's consent, and clicked it on.

"Did he do that to you?" Doug asked, sounding more curious than concerned.

"Does Gary have a history of assaulting women?" She used Bekker's first name as a courtesy to his brother.

Doug gave her an odd look. "Not exactly. But I hear he's in jail on assault charges and here you are looking assaulted."

"Did you ever see him hit his ex-wife, Gina Stahl?"

"Nope, but I heard him threaten to kill her."

Excellent. More corroboration. "When was that?" Sweat pooled in her armpits, and Evans wanted to get out of the sun, but she didn't want to break the flow of information.

"The first time was at a backyard barbecue at their house. Gary had too much to drink and Gina tried to cut him off. They got into a fight and he threatened to kill her. She left him shortly after."

"Were there other threats?"

"One night Gary and I were drinking at the Keg. He started talking about the guy Gina was dating and how he'd like to dump them both in the river."

"Can we go inside and narrow down the dates? I'd also like to get his verbatim statements, if you can remember."

As soon as they stepped into the trailer, Evans understood why Doug had been sitting outside. Stuff was piled everywhere. Stacks of newspapers and magazines filled the space under the coffee table and lined up against the walls. Laundry covered the couch, and open plastic bags full of empty food packages were stuffed in every crevice. The room smelled like a giant recycling bin. Evans fought the urge to run outside. *Jesus!* Gary Bekker was a predator and Doug Bekker was a hoarder. Had their parents been brother and sister?

"I know. It's a little overwhelming, but I'm getting help." Doug gestured for her to come into the kitchen.

Evans told herself it would only take five minutes. She'd been inside homes that were more disgusting. At least Doug had no animals or dirty diapers. He pushed a massive pile of mail to one side of the kitchen table, and Evans reluctantly took a seat.

"Would you like something to drink?"

"No."

"You can relax. There's no garbage in here, so it may be cluttered, but it's sanitary."

Who was he kidding? "What was the date of that family barbecue when Gary threatened Gina?"

"It was late summer, probably September, the year before Gina went into the coma. So 2008."

"What about the time at the tavern? What was the date of that threat?"

"That was July 7, 2008. I remember because it was my birthday. That's why Gary was having a beer with me."

Evans jotted down the dates. "Do you and Gary get along?"

"Sometimes."

"Do you have a grudge against him? Is that why you're talking to me?" She had to ask. This was too easy.

"He has serious issues, and I can see no reason to lie for him."

"Was he a delinquent when he was teenager?"

Doug laughed. "He was a Boy Scout. Being a cop and having control over people is what ruined him. The power made him mean."

"What do you think happened to Gina?"

Doug shook his head. "I really don't know. She was always kinda moody, so I wasn't too surprised to hear she tried to commit suicide. Yet here you are implying Gary tried to kill her. And that doesn't surprise me too much either."

"Did Gary talk to you about the women he had sex with? Other than his wife?"

"Sometimes he bragged about getting all the pussy he wanted, but the truth is, I don't see him that often."

"Why not?"

"We don't have much in common."

"What do you do for a living?" Evans thought she knew the answer, but she wanted to see if it made him uncomfortable.

"I'm disabled. I hurt my back logging when I was twenty-seven and I have chronic pain." He showed no sign of embarrassment.

"Does Gary have a current wife or girlfriend?"

"He dated a young girl for a while after Gina, but I don't think he's had anybody serious since. He was crushed when Gina left him."

The idea of Bekker as a wounded soul was hard to swallow. "Does Gary have access to Demerol?"

"He might. He has recurring pain from an old football injury, and I know he takes something for it."

"Does he inject it?" It was the easiest way to get drugs into an unconscious person.

"I don't know."

"Has Gary ever been diagnosed with a mental illness?"

Doug gave her a hurt look. "I know Gary is troubled, but he's not crazy. He has a good side, you know."

"Yeah? Tell me."

"Gary was married once before Gina. They had a boy with Down syndrome and Gary ended up raising him after his wife died. He does yearly fundraisers for the Special Olympics and he's really good with the kids."

Evans would have hated Bekker a little less if her head didn't still hurt from where the bastard had smacked her with a baton. Still, the information was interesting. "Would you testify in court about his threats to Gina?"

"Not if I could avoid it."

CHAPTER 18

Wednesday, September 8, 1:12 p.m.

On the drive into town from Durkin's cabin, Jackson checked his watch. It was after one and he'd missed his opportunity for lunch with either Kera or Katie. He stopped at Taco Bell, bought a burrito at the drive-up window, then parked at the back of the lot. He called Kera between bites.

Her hushed tone told him she was at the clinic. "Hey, Jackson. Nice of you to call."

What had he missed? "I'm sorry. You know what it's like when I'm on a new case."

"I do." She paused, then softened her tone. "How's your day going?"

"I'm having lunch in a parking lot. I thought if I talked to you while I was here, it wouldn't seem as pathetic."

Kera chuckled. "That depends on what you're eating."

"A burrito."

"You're at Taco Bell, aren't you?" She laughed again. "You know their beef is sixty percent filler, right?"

"Yeah, but it's cheap, fast, and salty, so it's working for me today."

"How's your investigation coming?" Kera asked. He heard a voice in the background, then a door close.

"I have a lead, but I need a subpoena to get his DNA and I'm not optimistic."

"But you have a lead. That's terrific." She was no longer whispering. "What's his connection to your parents?"

"He's a loan shark, and my idiot brother borrowed money from him."

"Have you talked to Derrick?"

"Yes, and he lied to me. I'm going over there again now to confront him."

Kera paused. "Try to be reasonable, maybe even empathetic. He's your brother."

"He's an unreliable source of information in this investigation."

Kera changed the subject. "How is Evans doing?"

Jackson had called Kera from the hospital the night before to let her know he wasn't coming over. Maybe that was why she was irritated with him. "Evans is a little beat-up, but she seems fine. Lammers wouldn't let her into the interrogation room with Bekker this morning." He laughed. "I think the boss was afraid for Bekker."

"Rightfully so. I've got to get back to my patients. Will I see you tonight?"

"I don't know. I'll call you. I love you."

Jackson hung up, feeling guilty for leaving Kera hanging about his schedule. He pushed his lunch sack to the floor and started the car. *What had Kera meant by 'rightfully so'?* Did she feel threatened by Evans?

Not likely. Kera was the most secure and rational person he'd ever known. Jackson pulled out of the parking lot and headed for Derrick's house. On Hilyard Street, the traffic seemed to crawl and he made aggressive lane changes to stay ahead of it. Despite Kera's caution to be reasonable, Jackson was still furious. Derrick hadn't told him the truth about the amount of the loan. What else had he lied about?

He didn't bother calling, because Derrick never answered. His brother's car was in the driveway, as usual. Jackson jogged up the walkway, pounded on the door twice, then waited sixty seconds. Just as he reached for the knob, the door swung open.

"I knew it was you. I could tell by the angry knock." Derrick had shaved and looked ready to go out.

"We need to talk."

"It has to be fast. I have an interview this afternoon."

The news pleased him, but he couldn't be distracted by it. Jackson stepped into the foyer, forcing Derrick to move back. "If you stick to the truth, this conversation shouldn't take long."

"Here we go again." His brother rolled his eyes.

Jackson cut through the kitchen to reach the dining-room table, noticing that Derrick had cleaned up a little. "I talked to Ray Durkin yesterday. He says he loaned you ten grand and you only paid back six. Why did you lie to me?"

"Because I was embarrassed by the whole thing and six thousand sounds less foolish than ten thousand." Derrick reluctantly sat across from him. "I'm sorry, Wade, but you were blaming me for their deaths, and that was hard to take."

You brought a killer into their lives! Jackson found the will to keep the thought to himself. "When Durkin threatened you, what did he say?"

"He said he would break my fingers. At the time, I was still working out in the warehouse, so it would have meant lost wages."

"Durkin called here from Lucky Numbers two days before the murders. I'm sure Mom answered the phone, because Dad never did. I think he pressured her for the money."

Derrick was silent.

"You knew! What did that scumbag say to Mom?" Jackson shouted, his cheeks burning.

"You're making too much of this." Derrick's hands were on the table, and they were shaking.

"What did he threaten her with?"

"Durkin told Mom he would hurt *me* if he didn't get his money in twenty-four hours. Naturally, that upset her, and she called me."

"And?"

"She said she couldn't get her hands on any more money without bringing Dad into it. I told her not to do that. I couldn't let Dad know I'd screwed up again." Derrick glanced over at the fridge, like a man longing for a beer. "I told Mom not to worry, that I would get the money somewhere else."

"But you didn't."

"I didn't have time! Mom and Dad were murdered the next day, and I was devastated. Mom was my best friend."

"How did you plan to pay off the additional money?"

"I sold my car and started driving Dad's Buick."

Jackson remembered that soon after the funeral, Derrick had claimed his car was stolen. "You lied to me about your car."

"I know. I'm sorry." Derrick pushed his hands through his new haircut. "I never wanted you to know about the loan."

Jackson wasn't in a forgiving mood. "Ray Durkin drives the same blue sedan that he owned back in 2000. Mr. Grayson saw a blue sedan parked outside the house the day of the murders. I think Durkin came here looking for cash and ended up killing Mom and Dad."

"Oh, christ." Derrick covered his face.

The remorse was a breakthrough, but it didn't change anything. "What kind of gun did Durkin own?"

"I never saw him with a gun or heard him talk about owning one."

"But he came here with a weapon and shot our parents. I'd sure like to know what he did with it afterward. Any ideas?"

"I don't think he brought a gun." Derrick stared at his hands, still shaking.

"Why not? What do you know?"

"I think they were killed with Dad's Jennings."

"What are you talking about?"

"Dad kept a handgun for self-protection, but it wasn't registered, which is why he never told you about it. It disappeared after that day, and I always assumed it was the murder weapon."

Jackson was stunned. "Did you tell this to the investigators?"

"No. They arrested Hector Vargas, he confessed, and I didn't think it mattered who owned the gun."

Jackson slammed his hand on the table before he could stop himself. "Of course it matters! It's about motive. If the killer didn't come here with his own weapon, then the murders may not have been premeditated." He stood and fought for control. "Goddammit, how can I solve this crime without the right information? What else have you not told me?"

"There isn't anything else."

They stared at each other in silence. Finally, Derrick said, "I don't know if this is important, but right before the murders, Mom was really upset about something in the news. I heard her mumbling that she couldn't let it happen again. I asked her what was going on, and she wouldn't tell me."

His brother glanced at the clock. "I have to go." Derrick stood and waited for Jackson to do the same. "Listen, Wade," his brother continued, "I made some mistakes back then and I tried to hide them from you and Dad. I also had some bad breaks too. But I got it together after that. I worked hard and I got promoted. I settled down and got married. I really tried to be someone you would respect."

Jackson nodded but he wasn't listening. *What had his mother tried to stop that might have cost her life?*

On the drive back to the department, he made a difficult call. Sophie Speranza picked up right away. "Jackson. Good to hear from you. This must be important."

"I need a favor."

"You name it. I'm all over it."

She wasn't just being nice. He would owe her something in return. "I need you to look back through old newspaper stories to September 2000. Specifically, the week before September 23. I'm looking for anything a middle-aged woman might react to emotionally."

"That's a little vague. Can you tell me why? I could be more effective in my search."

"This is confidential. You can't write about it."

"Fine."

"My parents were murdered on September 23, 2000. I just learned that my mother was upset about something in the news right before they were shot. She said something about not letting it happen again."

Sophie made a sympathetic noise. "I'm sorry for your loss and I'm glad to help." Voices in the background spoke to Sophie, and she was gone for a moment. "Sorry. I'm with Gina Stahl in the care center right now. She's getting ready to go home."

"Is Detective Evans there?"

"No, but she'll be back soon to escort Gina home. I'll start your search in the microfiche first thing in the morning."

Jackson stopped at a traffic light and pressed speed dial #7. He knew using a cell phone while driving could be dangerous, but if he didn't multitask, he'd never get his job done. Jasmine Parker didn't pick up, so he left her a message: "It's Jackson. Please compare the fingerprints from the double homicide back in 2000 to an ex-con named Ray Durkin. I hope to have DNA for you soon."

On the way up to his desk, Jackson tried to visualize the murders from a new perspective. Someone, probably Durkin, had come to the house and threatened his mother, or maybe both his parents. In fear, his father had pulled out his handgun, but the assailant had taken it away and shot them both. His father had died first, maybe during a struggle for the weapon, accounting for the bruises. Yet even if his father's death had not been deliberate, the bastard had then executed his mother with a bullet to her brain.

Grief and anger threatened to overwhelm him. Jackson suppressed his emotions and played the scene again. The killer brought his own weapon, but didn't use it because his father had surprised him by pulling a gun. Why had the perp taken the murder weapon from the house? Were his prints on it? Had he not worn gloves? Was it simply easier to carry the gun out and throw it away rather than spend a few seconds wiping it down?

Jackson opened a form on his computer and began to write a subpoena for Ray Durkin's DNA. As he keyed in his rationale, he realized how little circumstantial evidence he had. Derrick's testimony about Durkin's threats would help. He'd have to try Judge Cranston and play on his sympathy.

As he crossed the underground parking area, heading for his city-issued Impala, Jackson suddenly stopped. He drove an unmarked dark-blue sedan and so did every other detective in the department. Bekker had said he first thought the homicides were professional hits, committed by someone who practiced at a shooting range. Good god. Had an officer of the law murdered his parents? It made no sense and Jackson didn't want to believe it, but he couldn't ignore the possibility.

Once inside his car, he froze again. *Did Bekker commit the murders himself?* If he did, it would explain why the investigation was so sloppy and why he'd pressured Vargas so ruthlessly to confess. Jackson used his cell phone to call the reporter again.

"Hey, Sophie. When you search the September 2000 newspapers, pull stories that involve police officers."

"This sounds juicy. You will give me an exclusive at some point, correct?"

"When I can."

"Does it involve Gary Bekker?"

Surprised again by her ability to make connections, Jackson hesitated. "Why do you ask about Bekker?"

"I spent the afternoon listening to Gina, his ex-wife. So I know what he's capable of."

"This is a completely different case."

"I'm headed back to the office now. I'll try to get to the microfilm this afternoon if I can."

"Please print everything and fax it to me."

"Of course. Thanks for trusting me with this."

Jackson could visualize her pixie face grinning, maybe even smirking. "I didn't say I trusted you, but thanks for your help."

Judge Cranston was not available, so Jackson reluctantly entered the office of Marlee Volcansek. He'd seen her once at home with her hair down and snug-fitting clothes, and that's how he visualized her now. The fact that she was attractive didn't make her any easier to persuade. She was liberal and protective of an individual's rights.

"Detective Jackson," she said, looking up. "I'd ask how you've been, but I read the news. We've had a lot of homicides this year."

"We passed our annual record, and it's only September."

"What can I do for you?"

"I'm investigating a double homicide from the year 2000. The wrong man was convicted, but I have a good lead on the right suspect and I need you to sign this subpoena for his DNA."

She scowled and took off her glasses. "What case was that? And who presided over the trial?"

"The Jackson murders. Hector Vargas confessed and entered a plea. Judge Ramusson was in court that day."

"The Jacksons are your relatives?"

"My parents."

"I'm disappointed to hear that justice was not served in our courts." She held out her hand. "Let me read your subpoena."

Jackson handed it over and held his breath.

Volcansek read quickly, then asked, "Ray Durkin is currently a law-abiding citizen?"

"As far as I know."

"This is weak, Jackson. You're basing your supposition on a threatening phone call and a matching vehicle description." She drummed her fingers on the desk. "I'm going to sign it anyway, because if it were up to me, every convicted felon would have his or her DNA processed and logged into the system. It would save all of us a lot of work and prevent countless crimes."

A wave of relief washed over him. "Thank you. Everyone in law enforcement feels the same."

"Good luck with your investigation." She handed him the signed paperwork.

Jackson resisted the urge to run from the room. If Durkin's DNA matched the unidentified hair found on his mother or the saliva from the cigarette butt, it was enough to convict him.

CHAPTER 19

Evans stood next to the Geezer and breathed in warm September air. She'd never been so happy to exit someone's house. Except for the home where the triple homicide had taken place. She'd never get those mutilated bodies out of her mind. Doug Bekker's hoarding was mild in comparison.

One last deep breath and she climbed in her car and drove back toward the Rosehill Care Center. She couldn't get Bekker and his pain medication out of her mind. Did he use Demerol? Had he tried to kill Gina with his own meds? Or had he taken the opioid from one of the drug addicts he victimized? Bekker's doctor wouldn't tell her without a subpoena, but the department might have some information. Evans was tempted to pursue the lead, but she'd told Gina she would escort her home from the care center and it seemed important to be there. She'd learned from Jackson that making connections with the victims and their families could be critical in solving a case. Yet it was more than that. She felt protective of Gina.

As Evans pulled into the Rosehill parking lot, she saw Mr. and Mrs. Stahl enter the building, pushing an empty wheelchair. Evans checked her cell phone: 4:27. She hoped to wrap this up in an hour or so, then grab some dinner. Her stomach ached from drinking coffee and not eating all day.

Inside the facility, food smells from the kitchen mingled with the stink of unflushed toilets. Her stomach heaved. *Goddamn. Why couldn't they do something about that?* She flashed her badge at the receptionist and strode down to Gina's room, where she was happy to find the reporter had left. Gina sat in her new wheelchair, dressed in street clothes, still gaunt, but flushed and happy. Her mother took photos and blinked back tears, and her father kept saying, "We've been praying for this day."

The emotion in the room was too much for Evans, and she felt embarrassed to witness it. Her own parents had not been inclined to hug or cry. She was relieved when Gina's doctor stopped by to give her patient some final instructions and the family had to be serious for a moment. Two nurses came in to say good-bye and the emotions flowed again.

Finally, George pushed Gina out of the room she'd lived in for two years and Sharon held her gray-haired daughter's hand. Evans followed. Part of her wished she'd skipped this drama fest and another part was jealous that no one had ever cared for her that lovingly.

* * *

A warm wind caressed Gina's face and the sun felt glorious on her exposed arms. Tears of joy welled in her eyes. She was leaving the medical center and resuming her life! She had months of rehab still ahead to build up her strength, but she was functional. She could get around with a walker for a few minutes at a time, and her hands were already strong enough to draw sketches for five minutes at a time. In a few months, she would be back to normal, and she couldn't wait to start making goddess clothing again.

They reached the minivan, a new vehicle she didn't recognize. Her mother opened the backseat door, and her father lined up her wheelchair as best he could. Detective Evans stood by, squinting in the bright sun and looking uncomfortable. Gina thought it was sweet for her to be there. With Gary in jail, she felt safe, so Evans' presence wasn't really necessary.

"Ready, honey?" her dad asked.

"I'm so ready."

Her parents lifted her from both sides, and Gina pushed as much as she could with her weak legs. Standing felt glorious too. The pain of her bedsores was already receding. Her mother let go and moved out of the way. Gina shuffled sideways to get closer to the van. Her legs shook but held. Stepping into the car and lowering herself down to the seat took every bit of strength and coordination she had gained. Even with her father hanging on, she flopped over at the last minute and ended up lying on the seat with her legs sticking out the door.

Her mother drew in a startled gasp, but Gina burst out laughing. "I'm okay. Just pull me up please and seat-belt me in."

Detective Evans opened the opposite door and climbed into the car to help. "Are you sure it's not too soon? You seem a little floppy."

"I feel like a rag doll, but I couldn't stay in that room for another minute." Gina wanted to tell Evans what it had been like, the half wakefulness, the dreams, the inability to communicate. Yet she kept it to herself. She hated seeing pity in people's eyes. It was time to put the coma behind her and reclaim her life. "It may not seem like it, but I'm getting stronger every day."

"I'm happy for you." Evans gave her a tight smile. "I'll follow in my car."

On the ride home, Gina rolled down the window and let the warm air blow on her face. God, it was good to be alive and fully awake.

The sight of her parents' house with the ducks waddling in the front yard filled Gina with happy memories—barbecue dinners on the deck, followed by long Scrabble games. Could she still play? Would her brain ever be that sharp again?

The van came to a stop in the driveway, and Gina unbuckled, pleased by every small thing she could do for herself. She heard Evans pull in behind and shut off her engine. Her father retrieved the wheelchair from the back of the van while her mother opened the door and helped get her legs out and her feet on the ground. Her mother held out her hands, and Gina grabbed them tightly, grateful that her parents were still healthy for people in their seventies. Together, they got her upright on the driveway.

"Let me take a few steps," Gina said, feeling confident.

Her mother looked worried, but she stepped to the side. Gina heard a car pull up on the street behind her. She turned to see who it was. A masked man in a dark vehicle idled near the curb. Terror grabbed Gina's heart and squeezed hard. The man shoved a gun out the window and fired right at her.

* * *

As she climbed from her cruiser, Evans heard a car drive up. She spun toward the street. Her own vehicle blocked most of her view, but she saw the back end of a dark SUV idling at the curb. Panic rising, she ran toward the sidewalk, fumbling under her jacket for her weapon. The driver came into view. A ski mask covered his head and his arm snaked out the window. As she brought up her gun, he fired his. Two quick shots, muffled by a silencer. Evans fired four shots at the driver as he gunned his engine and raced away. The blasts ripped through the quiet trailer park and shattered a side window in the vehicle. Evans started to sprint after him to fire another round, but a small truck was suddenly coming down the street toward her. *Shit!* She couldn't endanger the other driver.

Evans spun back, unsure of what to do next. Every nerve in her body wanted to jump in her vehicle and chase down the shooter. The fucker! Yet Gina's life had to be her priority.

Weapon still in hand, she charged up the driveway. Gina was on her back on the ground and blood flowed freely. Sharon knelt next to her daughter, cradling Gina's head and making an odd humming sound. George frantically searched his pockets, presumably looking for his cell phone. Evans grabbed hers from her jacket and dialed 911, noting the time was 5:17.

"Detective Evans here. I have shots fired and a woman down. I need an ambulance at 466 Pondview Park near the corner of Royal and Echo Hollow. The shooter is driving a dark SUV, possibly a Ford Explorer. He was last seen wearing a ski mask and a dark long-sleeved shirt. He's about six feet tall, armed and dangerous." She handed the open phone to George, because Sharon seemed to be in shock. "Answer any questions they have."

Evans examined Gina's damage. Two bullets had pierced her chest, one directly in the heart, and blood soaked through her pale-yellow shirt. A small gurgling sound came from Gina's mouth, and her eyes rolled back in her head. Evans understood that Gina was moments from death, and there was nothing she could do. Her experience as a paramedic felt worthless, yet she holstered her weapon, peeled off her jacket, and used it to stem the flow of blood.

For a long moment, time stood still. The sun beat down, the wind blew, and Gina's blood flowed. The neighborhood was eerily quiet, except for the sound of Sharon Stahl's humming. Gina's father sat nearby, eyes closed and lips moving in prayer.

A siren pierced the stillness and Evans breathed a sigh of relief. More sirens followed. A patrol car raced up the narrow street. Evans spoke sharply to Sharon. "Put your hands here and keep pressure on her wounds."

The woman numbly did as instructed. Evans bolted to her feet and ran for the patrol car. She held up her hands, forcing the driver to stop twenty feet away. The officer shut down his engine as Evans ran up to the vehicle. He stepped out and she yelled, "The shooter was parked in front of the driveway. Don't let anyone near the scene until I've searched for casings."

"Got it." He didn't question her authority, and she assumed it was the Sig Sauer strapped to her side.

Evans ran back to where the SUV had been parked and dropped to her hands and knees. She scanned the area as she crawled, ignoring the sting of the rough asphalt. She found a copper casing near the curb. *Yes!* Evans ran to her car to retrieve her shoulder bag. She dug out latex gloves and pulled them on over her bloody hands, then found two evidence bags and her camera. She hurried back to the casing, took pictures where it lay, then bagged it.

The patrol officer stood nearby, and she heard him warn someone to stay back. Moments later, an ambulance wailed down the street. Evans moved toward the house and took photos of Gina lying on the driveway. She used her zoom lens so she didn't have to disturb the distressed parents, who still believed their daughter would pull though. Two male paramedics charged up the driveway with a gurney, and Evans stepped out of the way.

While they attended to Gina, Evans paused on the sidewalk and tried to catch her breath. Her heart pounded like a cylinder about to blow, and her mind raced with scrambled thoughts. *Fuck!* Gina had been shot right in front of her, and she'd failed to protect her charge. Had Bekker done this? Did he make bail or did he have an accomplice?

Another patrol car raced up the street and parked near the ambulance. Evans took a deep breath. She needed to take charge of the scene. She jogged out to meet the officer, a thirty-something woman named Connie Perez she'd known from her patrol days. "Officer Perez. Start checking with the neighbors. See if anybody got a license-plate number or a decent description."

Perez pointed in the direction of Bertelsen Road. "There's a dark-green Ford Explorer at the end of Mira Court near the bike path. Another officer is with the vehicle, and it looks empty."

"Shit." The perp had ditched his vehicle. Evans called dispatch. "The shooter has abandoned the Ford Explorer. He may be on foot, probably on the bike path that runs along Roosevelt." She visualized the big space in the back of the SUV. *Did he bring a bike with him?* "He may be on a bicycle and no longer wearing a ski mask." *Oh fuck. He was getting away.*

Evans hurried back to the driveway. The Stahls were on their feet now, hugging each other tightly. Sharon sobbed as a paramedic draped a cloth over Gina's face. The man looked up at Evans and shook his head. "She's gone."

CHAPTER 20

The abandoned SUV sat just off the street in a gravel turnout. Ten feet away, an asphalt feeder path led to the West Eugene bike route. A patrol unit was parked directly behind the vehicle, and an officer stood near the Explorer. Evans stopped in front of a nearby house and hurried over, noticing the SUV had no license plates. The right front fender was dented, rust spots showed through the paint on the hood, and a side window was shattered. She took photos of the vehicle as she approached.

"I'm Detective Evans," she said, walking up to the officer. "This is my case."

"Richard Anderson. I was a first responder at the Walker murders."

Evans nodded, but she didn't remember him. "Have you searched the vehicle?" She caught him staring at her chest and suddenly felt self-conscious without her jacket. Her snug-fitting sleeveless top left her breasts and weapon on full display.

"It's locked," he said. "I conducted a visual search with a flashlight but the interior looks empty."

"Locked is not good." The crime-scene technicians would be happy to know the vehicle had not been contaminated, but Evans needed to get inside and search for any kind of identification, including the VIN. What if the killer had dropped something that could lead her to him? She couldn't wait for the crime-scene techs to find it tomorrow. The perp could be long gone by then. She had to do a quick but thorough search and get back to the main crime scene.

She peered in the windows, taking pictures of the spotlessly clean interior. The bastard had planned the murder and his escape carefully. He obviously knew where Gina's parents lived. Had he followed them from the care center or had he been watching their house? Evans dug in her carryall bag and pulled out a slim jim, a thin metal tool used to break into vehicles. A guy she'd dated once had locked his keys in his car repeatedly, and she'd learned to break in as fast as any junkie could.

"Do you know how to use that?" the officer asked.

Evans gave him a scorched look and set to work. In less than three minutes she popped the lock. She pulled on latex gloves and yanked open the driver's door. Squatting in the V, she copied down the vehicle's identification number. She handed the notepaper to the patrol officer. "Call this in, then start interviewing the neighbors. We need to know if anyone saw his face." She enjoyed giving him an order, the sexist little shit.

Her time was limited. She'd called Lammers from the shooting scene, and the sergeant said she would send Jackson out to take charge. He was probably at the Stahls' house already and needed an update. This was the first time she'd worked an active crime scene without Jackson present from the beginning.

Evans leaned into the vehicle and ran her gloved hands in the space between the seat cushions. She searched the floor and under the seat and found only a thick owner's manual. Even the console between the seats was empty. She went around to the other side and opened the glove box. It too was empty. The SUV seemed to have been recently detailed and the backseat had been folded down for carrying a load.

Frustrated, she stood back from the vehicle and visualized the shooter's activity. He'd pulled over, then hauled the bicycle out of the back. Next, he'd yanked off the ski mask and probably his dark shirt as well. The clothes weren't in the SUV, so he'd taken them with him. He'd probably brought a backpack or a bicycle pack with him. The killer had stuffed the mask, the shirt, and the weapon into a backpack, jumped on the bike, and pedaled off.

Evans stared at the feeder bike path that ran between the houses. She visualized a slightly different scenario. The killer had left the ski mask on while he rode away, not wanting the neighbors—who may have watched him drive up—to see his face. As he cycled into the visual safety zone of the bike corridor, he'd pulled off his mask and stuffed it into his pack. By the time he reached the main bike route, he was just a guy in a T-shirt riding his bike.

Evans jogged to the feeder path and started down it. She walked briskly, glancing right and left, scanning the grass along the edges as well as the asphalt. She ignored the beer cans and food wrappers, looking for something the shooter may have dropped or discarded. More than anything, she hoped to find wet blood. Even more than she needed the DNA, she wanted to know she had wounded the bastard.

A young guy on a bike passed and said, "Nice gun."

Reflexively, she touched her weapon, now exposed because her jacket was back at the Stahls, soaked with Gina's blood. She would have to start carrying an extra jacket in her car.

Near the end of the feeder corridor, where it formed a T with the main bike route, Evans spotted something dark in the grass.

Her pulse quickened. She ran toward the object and knelt next to it. *Hot damn.* A black ski mask. The bastard had dropped it. Adrenaline pumping, she grabbed the mask with a gloved hand. Now if only the killer's hair was clinging to the inside. Getting DNA from hair was tough but not impossible. An attached follicle would make it easy. *Oh shit.* She'd forgotten to take photographs. Evans set the mask exactly where it had lain and stepped back to take pictures of its relationship to the bike path.

She bagged the mask, then looked east and west on the path. Had he gone toward Beltline or Highway 99? Or had he crossed Roosevelt and disappeared into the industrial area? Evans jogged a hundred feet in both directions, looking for a dark shirt or perhaps even a weapon, but saw neither. Those items likely ended up in a trashcan somewhere.

Evans hustled back to the Explorer and called Lammers. "Sergeant. It's Evans. I think I found the mask the shooter wore."

"Excellent work."

"I need more officers here to search along the bike route and to search trash cans for a mile in each direction. The feeder path is off Mira Court, just off Elmira, where the killer abandoned his vehicle."

"Do you know who the owner is yet?"

"The plates are stripped off, but we called in the VIN and should have it soon."

"It's probably stolen, but even knowing the location of where he picked up the vehicle could help."

"I'll call dispatch and see if they have an ID yet."

"Keep me posted." The sergeant hung up.

While Evans waited to speak to a patrol officer who had just driven up, dispatch called her. "The VIN belongs to a 1996 Ford Explorer registered to Joel Greer at 324 Clark Street."

Evans wrote it down, feeling disappointed. She hadn't expected the vehicle to be registered to Bekker, but somehow she knew Greer would be a dead end. "Put out an attempt-to-locate on Greer and send an officer to his house. When he's detained, call me."

Another patrol unit raced into the short street. Evans gave search directions and her business card to the officers, with instructions to call her if they found anything. When a third arrived, she instructed him to guard the Explorer until the crime technicians came to tow it away. They would haul it to the big bay at the crime lab and dust every surface for prints.

Feeling she'd done everything she could at the secondary scene, Evans climbed in the Geezer, preparing to drive back to the Stahls' house. But first she had to know: was Gary Bekker still in custody?

Evans called the jail and identified herself. "Is Gary Bekker still an inmate? It's spelled with two Ks."

"Let me check." After a moment, the deputy said. "No, he's not."

"When was he released?"

"At four fifty this afternoon."

CHAPTER 21

Wednesday, September 8, 4:38 p.m.

With a signed subpoena, Jackson was eager to drive back up to Durkin's property and bring him in for a DNA cheek swab. Yet instinct told him to stop at home first and check in with his daughter.

When he reached his house, a silver Toyota and a red minivan were parked in his driveway. Jackson recognized the little car that belonged to his real-estate agent. He hoped the minivan represented a buyer. The thought also filled him with dread. He parked on the street and climbed out.

Katie rushed down the walkway, wearing a short denim skirt and a tight pink blouse he'd never seen before. She seemed taller and thinner than he remembered. What had happened to his pudgy little girl in the last year?

"Hey, Dad. I think we have a buyer." Katie was surprisingly excited.

"Are they talking about an offer?"

"Not yet, but this lady really loves the location. I think she has a job at the university."

"We should stay out here and let them have some privacy while they look." Jackson leaned against his vehicle, enjoying the sun on his face.

Katie leaned against the car too, her shoulder touching his. Together, they stared at the house they loved.

"How was school?"

"Now that I know my way around, I'm starting to like high school. The teachers seem both smarter and friendlier than those in middle school."

"What's your favorite class?"

"Algebra."

Jackson raised his eyebrows in mock surprise. "Since when?"

"Since Mr. Ferguson started teaching it."

"He must be cute."

"Oh yeah."

"In that case, I expect to you to get an A."

"He's not *that* cute." After a minute, Katie said, "It'll be strange not living here, but I think I'm ready for a change." She looked at him with wounded eyes. "I still associate this house with Mom."

"Me too." Jackson put his arm around her shoulder and gave a quick squeeze. "It's good we're getting out of here."

Katie suddenly gave him a puzzled look. "Why are you home so early?"

"I just stopped in to see you. I have to go back to work for another couple of hours."

"I knew it." She gave him a friendly shove. "You'd better get going. I'll go do my homework." She started up the sidewalk, then turned back. "And if you believe that…"

The sound of her laugh filled his heart with joy. Jackson watched her until she disappeared into the house.

Twenty minutes later, he was driving up Fox Hollow for the second time that day. Just before he reached the Murdock turnoff, his cell phone rang. He checked the ID: Sergeant Lammers. His gut told him it would not be good.

"We've had a shooting. Gina Stahl is dead in her driveway. Evans was with her at the time, and she's handling the case until you get there."

"The shooter got away?"

"For the moment. I need you at the scene to make sure everything is covered."

"I'm up on Fox Hollow, so it'll take a while, but I'm on my way."

Jackson kept driving. A flood of emotions raced through him. He was stunned that Gina had been killed and felt guilty the department hadn't protected her better. His adrenaline kicked in, and he was eager to get to the crime scene and start working it. Yet he resented being pulled off his parents' case just as he was about to break it wide open.

Jackson made the turn on Murdock Road. He was only ten minutes from Durkin's house. He might as well grab him and drop him off on his way. Anyone in the department could collect the cheek swab. If Evans was at the crime scene, then things were well in motion. Her capacity for detail impressed him. Once she had more experience, she'd be the best in the unit.

He made the final turn and pushed his car too fast down the gravel road. At the end, the parking lot was empty. No dark-blue sedan, no white work truck, no sounds of construction. *Damn.*

Remembering the dogs, Jackson stepped carefully from the car, weapon in hand. The beasts did not come running. He strode up to the cabin and knocked, knowing it was a waste of time. The door was locked, so he looked in a window and saw no sign that anyone was home. No jacket over a chair. No coffee cup or beer bottle on the table. Durkin had fled and taken his dogs.

Jackson swore out loud. He'd spooked the ex-con by coming up here and asking questions. He mentally kicked himself for not getting the subpoena first. He should have tried. Yet he didn't believe the judge would have signed it without the support of the matching blue sedan, which he didn't have until he came up here. Now he had a subpoena and no suspect to swab. *Crap.*

Was Durkin lying low or had he fled the state? The ex-con was running a business and building a house, so his sudden disappearance made him look guilty as hell. Jackson hurried back to his cruiser and called in a description and an attempt-to-locate. He asked the desk officer to notify the state police as well. Unless Durkin had already caught a flight out of the state, he would soon be picked up and brought in.

The more he thought about Durkin, the madder he felt. Jackson tried to remember the name he'd seen on the truck earlier. It was a group of initials. KRS or KLS. He would start with the construction company and see what he could find out. But first, he had a new crime scene to process.

Jackson arrived at the Stahls' house just as the medical examiner drove up in his long white station wagon. Rich Gunderson climbed out, dressed in all black, despite the warm season. In the driveway near their car, Mr. and Mrs. Stahl stood on either side of the wheeled gurney, each holding one of their deceased daughter's hands. Jackson swallowed a lump in his throat and joined Gunderson on the sidewalk.

"We've never had one quite like this, with a detective witnessing the shooting," Jackson said.

"No shit." Gunderson shook his ponytailed head. "There's not much for me to do here, but I'll go through the motions and let the paramedics take her downtown." The morgue was in the basement of the hospital and was commonly referred to as Surgery Ten.

"When will you do the autopsy?"

"I'll check with the pathologist. Probably tomorrow afternoon." Gunderson started toward the gurney.

Jackson moved in quickly and took photos of Gina and her position next to the minivan. Evans had probably taken pictures, and Gunderson would too. They often ended up with hundreds of crime-scene shots.

Gina's parents didn't let go of her hands until the ME asked them to step back. Jackson looked around for Evans, thinking she might be talking to neighbors, but he didn't see her. A female patrol officer came out of a house across the cul-de-sac and headed his way.

"Where's Detective Evans?"

"She's examining the vehicle. The shooter abandoned it a few blocks from here."

"Did any of the neighbors see anything worth reporting?"

"Not that I know. Another officer is canvassing over there, so he may have something."

"Do we have a description of the shooter?"

"Not much. He or she was wearing a ski mask. A woman who saw him drive by said she thought it was a man, because he seemed tall."

"Thanks."

Jackson walked over to the Stahls, who were both red-eyed and shaky. To lose a child, at any age, had to be the most devastating pain. Jackson wondered if parents ever stopped feeling responsible.

"I'm very sorry for your loss," he said, knowing the words changed nothing. "We didn't realize Gina was still in danger."

"Detective Evans told us Gary Bekker was in jail."

"I think he still is."

"Then who did this?" Mrs. Stahl burst into sobs.

"I don't know, but we'll find him."

For the first time, Jackson wasn't sure what to do next at a crime scene. Several people had witnessed the murder, so there was little to speculate about. Uniformed officers were questioning the neighbors, and the vehicle had been located. He looked at George Stahl. "Can you describe the shooter?"

The old man's face tightened in pain. "I didn't even know he was there until I heard the shots. All I can say is that he looked about your size."

"What makes you think it was a man?"

"His size. The use of a gun."

"Where was the shooter's vehicle?"

"Right at the end of the driveway."

Jackson searched the area for casings or anything else the shooter may have left behind, but came up empty-handed. He heard the clatter of wheels on cement and looked up to see the paramedics rolling Gina toward the ambulance. He closed his eyes and said a prayer for her as she passed.

The ME came down the driveway. "She took two shots to the chest. One penetrated her heart. I'd say the slugs were likely from a .38, but I won't know for sure until I dig them out."

"Call me as soon as you know." Jackson didn't see any point in attending Gina's autopsy, something he usually did for every victim.

Evans barreled down the street as Gunderson drove away. She jumped from her car and dashed over, her blue eyes sparking with excitement. "Jackson, I'm glad you're here. I can't believe I witnessed a drive-by shooting and failed to apprehend the perp."

"Tell me how it went down."

"I followed the Stahls and parked behind them in the driveway. Gina was already out of the car and standing when I opened my door to get out." Evans gestured at the locations with her hands. "I heard the shooter's vehicle in the street behind me. I spun around, but I didn't have a clear view because of my own car. He fired two shots from right here as I ran toward the street. I returned fire, but he was already driving away. I saw that Gina had been hit, so I called dispatch, then went to assist the victim."

"You did everything right."

"I should have gotten out of the car faster. I was looking for my notebook, so I sat for a few extra seconds."

Jackson related to her sense of responsibility. "It's not your fault. You had no idea this was going to happen. We both thought we had her assailant locked up in jail."

"I've never felt so useless as at that moment." Evans winced. "Bekker was released on bail today at four fifty. The shooting happened at five seventeen."

Jackson thought the timing was too close. "Bekker couldn't have done it."

"Why do you say that?" Evans snapped.

"He would have had to get from the jail to the Explorer, wherever it was, then drive here. I just don't see how he could do that in twenty-seven minutes." They stood at the end of the driveway, facing each other.

"Who else would shoot Gina in broad daylight? I don't have another suspect!" Evans' distress was palpable.

"We have to find one." Jackson reached out to touch her arm.

She pulled back. "I still think Bekker did this. Maybe he stole the SUV as soon as he left jail, then drove straight here."

"Where did he get the gun? How did he know to come here? How did he know when Gina would be released?"

"Maybe he has an accomplice."

Jackson wanted more information. "We need to talk to the registered owner of the Explorer before we jump to any conclusions."

"You're right. If the car was stolen from near the jail, then Bekker is still our man and I'm going to pick him up."

"If it wasn't near the jail, then we need to start over."

"Shit."

"Never get too invested in a single suspect, even if he's a predator like Bekker."

"I still want to pick him up. We've got all kinds of things to charge him with."

"No." Jackson locked eyes with Evans. "Go talk to the vehicle's owner, then call me with an update. Together, we'll decide what to do next."

"I have to drop off the ski mask and the bullet casing at the crime lab first."

"You found a casing? Let me see it."

Evans showed him the evidence bag.

"Smith & Wesson makes copper jackets and Gunderson said the slugs were likely .38s." Jackson held on to the plastic bag. "I'll take the evidence to the lab for you. I have to talk to Parker anyway."

"Thanks. I'll call you in a bit."

Jackson watched Evans walk away. He understood her rage against Bekker, and it worried him. Getting emotional about a case could be dangerous. He hoped she had the good sense not to confront Bekker alone.

Jackson spent another hour at the crime scene, talking to the Stahls and gathering feedback from the officers who had questioned everyone who lived on the street. The Stahls finally went into their house to grieve. Jackson was grateful he hadn't had to start from scratch by asking painful questions such as, *Who had a grudge against your child?* Evans had already covered all that during the last few days.

On the drive to the crime lab, he put in his earpiece and called Kera. "Hey, hon. We had a shooting late this afternoon so I'm not going to make it over tonight."

"Oh no. Was anyone killed?"

"Gina Stahl, the woman who came out of the coma."

"That is so tragic. Her parents must be crushed."

"Evans is taking it pretty hard too." The highway merged into Sixth Avenue, so Jackson cut his speed. "We have a few leads on the shooter, so we hope to make an arrest soon."

Kera was quiet for a moment. "I'll miss seeing you. Do you want Katie to stay here for a few days?"

"Maybe. We'll see how it goes."

"You promised me a weekend at the coast this summer, and we've only got two weeks left before summer is over." She said it with a laugh in her voice, but he sensed she was worried.

"I'll make good on it." Jackson lowered his voice. "You won't have to pack anything. We'll spend the whole weekend naked in the hotel room."

"I'll make a reservation."

"Can you do me a huge favor and pick up Katie for dinner?"

"Sure. We'll go out to Chinese food without you."

"That's mean." Jackson remembered the prospective buyer for his house and started to tell her, then changed his mind. He didn't want to get her hopes up until he had an offer. "I love you, anyway."

"I love you too. Call me when you can."

Jackson arrived at the crime lab just as a tow truck backed the Ford Explorer into the large bay. He watched as Joe and another assistant unloaded the vehicle, thinking the killer must have been confident that he didn't leave any part of himself behind. Only an incredibly bold or desperate person would shoot someone in broad daylight with a police detective standing nearby. The perp probably hadn't counted on a cop being there but had followed through anyway. Or maybe he hadn't seen Evans, because she was just climbing from her unmarked car.

Jackson logged the evidence into the computer system, then climbed the stairs, hoping Parker was still in the building. He caught her in her office as she pulled on her coat.

"I'm not staying late, Jackson. I have a date."

"I'm glad to hear that." He set the evidence on her desk. "I wanted you to know we had two critical pieces from the shooting today. The killer dropped this ski mask, and we're hoping to get DNA. We'll have a sample for comparison soon. Meanwhile, run it against CODIS." Jackson wondered if they would be able to get a subpoena for Bekker's DNA. A judge would be as skeptical as he was about the plausibility of the jailed cop's involvement. "I'd like to make this shell casing a priority too."

"Talk to Joe about it." Parker didn't touch the evidence bags. "Would you put those in a downstairs locker, please?" She grabbed her purse and waited for him to make a move.

Jackson sensed she was tired and annoyed with him. "I'm sorry. I'll follow protocol. Have a good evening." He smiled, picked up the evidence, and walked out.

Downstairs, he went into the little room where he had used the computer and shoved the bags into a locker, which would not open again until it had been released from the other side. The back end of the lockers opened into a room in the crime lab, where a technician would retrieve the evidence and reset the lock. The system, which was new with the building, had been designed to allow officers to drop off evidence night and day and to keep money and drugs from disappearing.

As Jackson left the building, he thought about the hundred-dollar bill that had vanished from his parents' case file. It wasn't the disappearance that bothered him; it was the presence of the money under his mother's body. What was it doing there? Had his mother tried to pay off Durkin with cash? If so, why had he shot her? Maybe his father had gone for his gun and the exchange went sour.

Jackson drove to the department and logged into his computer. While he waited for Evans to call about the Explorer's owner, he decided to spend a few minutes on his own investigation. He opened the online yellow pages and found KSL Construction. As late as it was, he expected to get an answering machine and he did. He told the business a return call was urgent. On a whim, he called Lucky Numbers, the strip bar where Derrick had met Durkin, and asked to speak to the manager.

The voice of an older man came on the phone. "This is the manager. Who are you and what do you want?"

"Detective Jackson, Eugene Police. I'm looking for Ray Durkin. Have you seen him?"

"Not in six years. Why?"

"I need some peace of mind, and I think Durkin is the key."

CHAPTER 22

Evans drove away from the crime scene, then stopped on the corner to use the car's GPS to find the address. Clark Street started near the base of Skinner Butte and ran in segments parallel to West First Avenue. She thought the 324 address had to be near Lawrence or Lincoln Street. Counting squares on the map, she figured the Explorer's owner lived nine blocks from the jail, about half a mile. A healthy person could walk the distance in ten minutes or run it in five. She pulled out into the street and headed downtown, reminding herself to keep an open mind. On the way, she called dispatch and asked for Joel Greer's phone number.

The sun was nearly at the horizon when Evans entered the old neighborhood nestled between the railroad tracks and the river. Without access to the water, the properties had lost value over the years, and many had been beaten down by renters. Evans turned right on First Avenue, and the scent of cooked oats drifted in her open window. She drove past a factory and turned left on Washington, then right on Clark Street.

She parked in front of the small yellow house and took a moment to prepare herself. It was possible Greer was the killer, but Jackson didn't believe it or he wouldn't have sent her here alone. She pushed her jacket back and put her hand on her weapon anyway.

As she strode up the cracked sidewalk, she wondered if Lammers would make her take a leave of absence after today's shooting. Evans hoped not. No lights were on in the house, and she started to think she was wasting her time. After a few knocks and no response, she called Greer on her cell phone. In a stern voice, she left a message. "This is Detective Evans. Your vehicle was used in a homicide and there is a warrant for your arrest. To clear yourself, call me immediately when you get this message, no matter what time." She recited her number and hung up.

Evans considered walking over to the jail to see how long it would take, but she didn't want to leave her car parked in the neighborhood. What she really wanted was to arrest Bekker. Lammers had said they could if he made bail. She hit speed dial #1 and waited for Jackson to pick up.

"What's the update?" He sounded tired.

"Greer, the SUV's owner, lives at 324 Clark, which is near Washington and the base of Skinner's Butte. It's about nine blocks from the jail, or a brisk ten-minute walk. Greer's not home, so I haven't heard his story yet."

"Let's meet at the department. We'll order some food and brainstorm."

"Let's pick up Bekker first. Even if he's not the actual shooter, I still think he's involved. Either way, the bastard shouldn't be walking around free."

"I think it's premature, Evans."

"I'm doing it with or without you. He lives at 1577 Glenn Ellen Drive." She clicked off before Jackson could argue.

A surge of energy pumped through her torso as Evans parked across from Bekker's house. Lights were on and a red Ford truck sat in the driveway. The bastard was in there, ripe for the plucking. It killed her to wait, but she knew Jackson was coming, so she stayed in the car and tried to keep calm.

She'd seen Bekker's address the first time she looked him up in the database, but hadn't realized how close he lived to her. It made her glad she had heavy-duty locks on her house. She'd come to believe every neighborhood had at least one dangerous resident. People who didn't understand that or take precautions were idiots. It made law enforcement's job even harder.

Jackson pulled in behind a few minutes later, and Evans shoved open her car door, adrenaline pumping. The sun had set and she couldn't see her partner's expression until he moved in next to her.

Jackson's jaw was tight and his mouth unsmiling. "I called for patrol backup in case he resists," he said through clenched teeth.

Evans hated that he was angry with her. "This is the right thing to do. Don't forget his sexual-coercion victims. If he's free on bail, he's free to intimidate them into retracting their stories."

"I have a bad feeling about this."

"Do you have your taser?"

"Yes. Let's go."

They moved past the truck in the driveway, guns drawn. Jackson pounded on the door, and it opened moments later. A boy of about fourteen smiled at them. He wore shorts and a Batman T-shirt and had the round face and innocent eyes of someone with Down syndrome. Evans cursed under her breath and let Jackson take the lead.

"We're looking for Gary Bekker. Is he here?"

The young man turned and yelled, "Dad. It's for you."

Bekker came to the door, looking haggard. His face was unshaved and the bags under his eyes were gray. He spoke softly to the boy, telling him to go back to the living room. When his son was out of earshot, Bekker said, "What do you want now?"

"We need you to come in for questioning."

"We've been through this, remember?"

"We have a new crime," Jackson said. "Either come with us voluntarily or we'll have to arrest you."

"What crime?"

"We'll talk when we get to the department."

"I can't just leave my son. Can't this wait until tomorrow when he's in school?"

"Sorry. We'll give you ten minutes to make arrangements. If you can't find someone, we'll call Child Protective Services."

"Fuck that!" Spit flew from Bekker's mouth. "Cody is already traumatized because I didn't come home last night. I will not let him enter the fucking foster system."

"Then start making calls." Jackson stayed firm, and Evans admired him even more. She felt bad for the boy and hoped he had a backup caregiver, because his father might not come home for twenty years.

"Come on, Jackson," Bekker pleaded. "You've got a kid and you know what it's like. Have a heart."

"Think long-term, Bekker. We'll come in while you make calls."

Bekker's shoulders slumped, and Evans could tell he was done resisting. She holstered her weapon, and her pulse slowed.

* * *

Jackson and Evans stood in the living room while Bekker made a call. The boy was engrossed in a crime show on TV. Bekker's call went well. Jackson could tell by the tone of his voice and the look of relief on his face. The sergeant came into the living room, muted the TV, and knelt next to his son.

"Cody, Mrs. Marshall is coming to take you home with her, and you'll be there for a while. Daddy has to go to work. It's a big job, and I may not be home for a few days."

"You're going to sleep at work?"

"Yes. For a day or so. I'll call you if I can."

The boy put his arms around Bekker's neck and said, "I hate it when you're gone."

"Me too, son. I'll go pack some things for you."

Jackson wished he were anywhere else. He hated arresting people with kids.

Bekker got up and turned to Jackson. "I need to make a few more calls."

Jackson nodded and followed Bekker into the boy's room. He didn't really believe it was necessary to shadow him, but if Bekker went out a bedroom window while he stood in the living room, he would kick himself for days.

Bekker loaded a backpack with a change of clothes and called the boy's school to leave a message. Bekker conducted a second conversation that Jackson couldn't follow. He told himself the call was personal and not to worry about it.

After ten minutes, they were back in the living room. Bekker sat on the couch next to his son and Jackson stood next to Evans, who seemed to be struggling to keep her impassive cop face on.

For twenty minutes, they waited, watching Bekker and his son watch TV. It was a long uncomfortable stretch, but Jackson had done even stranger things as a patrol cop. Once he'd changed a baby's diaper while the mother took a shower and washed food out of her hair. Her husband had thrown dinner plates at her, and another officer had taken the offender to jail. Jackson had offered to drive the woman to her mother's home, but she'd wanted to clean up first.

Mrs. Marshall, a heavyset older woman with a sweet voice, finally arrived and Cody left with her. Jackson cuffed Bekker, against his protests, and put him in the back of his car. Evans followed them to the department. Jackson was irritated with her for pushing him to pick up Bekker, but he was also mad at himself for hesitating. The issue for him was that Bekker was not his priority. The patrol sergeant was not a suspect in his parents' murders, and Jackson didn't believe Bekker had shot his ex-wife either. Yet Evans was right that Bekker was a threat to the women he'd victimized, and it was a relief to have him in custody again. Disabled son or not. Damn, that had been uncomfortable.

He asked Evans to order Chinese food while he escorted their suspect to the interrogation room. It was nearly nine o'clock and raw hunger made him irritable as hell. He left Bekker uncuffed with a glass of water, then trudged to the conference room. His legs ached with exhaustion, and his surgery scar felt inflamed, yet he still had hours of work ahead. He bought two Diet Pepsis from the vending machine in the break room on the way.

In the conference room, Evans had a small prescription bottle in her hand. "Want half a Provigil?"

"What exactly is it again?"

"It was originally developed to keep jet pilots awake on long flights. It's also commonly prescribed for people with narcolepsy to keep them awake. I only take it when we're working these late-night cases."

Evans' energy made Jackson feel old, even when she didn't have pharmaceutical help. "Sure."

She broke an oblong tablet in half, and they swallowed the Provigil with their sodas.

"I've been thinking," Jackson said. "If Bekker has an accomplice, then his accomplice is also participating in the sex crimes. Why else would he be willing to kill Gina Stahl?"

"Of course." Evans slapped her folder. "We have to talk to his victims again. Do you think his accomplice is another cop?"

"Most likely. But we have to stay open to the possibility that Bekker has never tried to kill his ex-wife and another suspect is still out there."

Evans made a face. "I don't know who it would be. Gina still has boxes of paperwork at her parents' house that I haven't gone through yet. After we've questioned Bekker, I'll go pick up the boxes and bring them here for us to go through."

Jackson braced himself for a long night of tedium. He remembered the stacks of his mother's letters that he hadn't gone through yet either. He had no idea when he would get back to them.

His partner's cell phone rang and she snatched it from the table. "Detective Evans." After a moment, she set down the phone and put it on speaker. "Thanks for getting back to me, Joel. I need to ask a few questions."

The voice from the cell was scratchy but audible. "I'm on a break at work, so I only have a few minutes."

"This is important. Your boss will understand. Where were you this afternoon at five seventeen?" Evans leaned toward the phone as she spoke. Jackson thought this speakerphone interrogation was yet another strange moment in his law-enforcement career.

"I was right here at work, where I am now."

"Where do you work and what is your shift?"

"I work six to six at Ridgeline Pipe, twelve-hour graveyard shifts."

"Did you loan your Ford Explorer to someone?"

"No. I sold it today."

"What time did that happen and who did you sell it to?"

"I don't know his name. He showed up around noon and gave me five hundred in cash. I gave him the title and that was it."

"Did he call first?"

"No. I didn't have the Explorer advertised. I just parked it on the street with a *For Sale* sign."

Jackson was impressed with Evans' line of questioning.

"Describe the guy."

"He was older, maybe in his fifties, but in good shape."

"Be specific. I want eye color, skin color, hair color, the shape of his face." Evans sounded annoyed.

"I didn't see much. He wore a baseball cap and sunglasses. But he was definitely white, and what little I saw of his hair looked blond or gray."

Jackson heard traffic noises in the background. "Where are you right now? I thought you said you were at work."

"I'm in the parking lot. The break room is too noisy."

Evans picked back up. "What else can you tell us? Did the guy sound crude or educated? Did he have an accent?"

"He seemed smart and smooth, but the whole thing happened in a few minutes. He started the Explorer to make sure it ran, gave me the cash, and went on his way."

Jackson asked, "He drove away in the Explorer?"

"Yes. He came on a bike. After he bought the Ford, he put the bike in the back and drove off."

"We need you to come in to the department tomorrow and work with our sketch artist to create a picture of this guy."

They heard a loud buzzer in the background. "I will," Joel said. "But I need to get back to work now."

Evans warned, "Be here early in the morning so we don't have to come find you."

Jackson loved it when she got into her tough-cop mode.

"I will." Joel hung up.

"White guy in his fifties with blond hair. Sounds like Bekker." Evans jumped up and started to pace. "Yet it can't be, because Bekker was still in jail at noon."

"He either has an accomplice or we need to start over."

"Goddamn it." Evans drummed her fingers. "What if his accomplice bought the Explorer, then picked up Bekker at the jail? They could have driven to the Stahls together in plenty of time."

"Did you see someone else in the vehicle?"

"No, but he could have been lying down in the backseat."

"They would have needed two bikes to get away."

"Maybe one of them was dropped off at another vehicle for the getaway."

"It's possible." Jackson wasn't buying it. "But it would take some planning, and Bekker was in jail."

"This is pretty fucked up."

In the silence, someone knocked on the door and the desk officer stepped in. "This smells incredibly good. What did you guys order?"

"Mongolian beef and egg rolls."

Jackson noticed Evans ordered the same thing Kera always did. It made him smile.

"What?" she asked.

"Nothing. Let's eat, then we'll go see if we can trick Bekker into talking about his accomplice."

Bekker's interrogation proved to be a waste of time. If he responded at all, he simply said "yes," "no," or "I don't know." After twenty minutes, he refused to speak again.

Jackson and Evans stepped out of the tiny room. Jackson checked his watch: 9:35. "I'll take Bekker to jail while you round up Gina's personal papers. We'll meet back here."

Evans touched his arm. "How is your parents' case going? I know you must be frustrated to have to work this one instead."

"My suspect disappeared after I questioned him, so I'm at a standstill until he's located. I'm glad to help with Gina's case."

"We'll make short work of it." Evans gave him a grim smile. "Maybe we'll get lucky with the ski mask. It could have DNA."

"Now all we need is a suspect to compare it with."

CHAPTER 23

Wednesday, September 8, 9:37 p.m.

Evans called the Stahls as she headed down to the parking lot, and Sharon answered, sounding sleepy.

"Sorry for the late call. I need to gather up the rest of Gina's personal papers and bring them in to the department. We plan to look at everything until we find a new lead."

"Are you saying Gary Bekker didn't do this?"

"He was released on bail this afternoon at four fifty. Someone bought the Explorer used in the crime at noon, so we're looking for other suspects, or maybe an accomplice."

"Are you coming over now?" Sharon's voice quivered.

"Yes. We plan to work late."

"Thank you."

Evans crossed the nearly empty parking area and climbed in her car. She looked through her notepad until she found Trisha Cronin's phone number. It was late to be making calls, but Trisha was a hooker, so she probably didn't keep regular hours. It took seven rings, but Trisha finally answered. "Why are you calling so late?"

"I have a murder to solve, so this is important. Did Gary Bekker ever mention a partner or show up with another cop?"

"No."

"Did he ever mention any other adult male to you?"

"He talked about his brother once."

A shimmer of possibility ran up Evans' spine. "What did he say?"

"I don't remember. Gary was drunk and babbling about family."

"Think hard, Trisha. What did he say?"

"Just something about loving his brother even though he was a pain in the ass."

Damn. Evans let out her breath. "Think about the partner idea, please, and call me if you remember anything."

"Sure." Trisha hung up.

Evans visualized Doug Bekker. He fit the description of the man who bought the Explorer. Would he help his brother kill someone? He had talked so freely about Gary's problems. Had it all been a misdirection? She looked up Joni Farmer's number and called her too, but the heroin addict didn't pick up.

Evans made four trips from the Stahls' guest bedroom to her car with boxes, and another four trips from her car to the conference room at the department. The Provigil was doing its job, and she felt great. Jackson was still not back from booking Bekker into jail, and Evans suspected he'd made a stop at home to check on his daughter or maybe a stop at Kera's to tell his girlfriend he didn't have time for midnight nooky. Too bad.

To get comfortable for the long, tedious task ahead, Evans took off her jacket and holster and laid her weapon on a nearby chair. She grabbed one of the boxes from the floor and unloaded the contents on the table. The pile was mostly mail, with stacks of unpaid bills and letters from banks, insurance companies, and medical clinics. Evans hoped to move through it quickly and get into more personal items. She started with correspondence from the two clinics. Both had sent letters telling Gina they were turning over her debt to a collection agency.

Jackson came in a few minutes later. He grinned as he sat down. "The Provigil is quite effective."

"Isn't it? I love my doctor."

Jackson pulled a Reese's Peanut Butter Cup from his pocket, opened it, and handed her one of the candies. "I stopped for coffee, realized I didn't need any, and bought this instead."

"Thanks, I love these."

"I know. That's why I chose it."

He remembered her favorite. Evans didn't try to hide her pleasure. "I'll have to burn off these calories tomorrow."

"You don't look like you have anything to worry about."

"Thanks." That was as close as he'd ever come to complimenting her appearance. Evans didn't know why he was suddenly being friendlier, but what the hell, it was about time. She remembered her jacket was off and the shape of her body more prominently displayed. She hoped it was more than that.

"What are we looking at here?" Jackson asked.

"Mail, mostly bills. I knew Gina was in debt, but her financial situation was even worse than I realized. Look at this." She handed him a letter from the hospital. "She owed North McKenzie more than nine thousand dollars, and they turned her over to a collection agency."

"Unless she borrowed money from a loan shark, I don't see how the debt could get her killed."

"Gina doesn't seem like the type to get involved with lowlifes. What made you say that?"

"My brother, Derrick, borrowed money from a loan shark right before he moved in with my parents. I think it may have gotten them killed."

"Oh shit. Is that your suspect who disappeared? The loan shark?"

"Yep."

"I didn't know you had a brother."

"We haven't been close for years."

"Is he a criminal?" *What made her ask that?*

Jackson looked up, seeming surprised by her question. "He had trouble as a teenager, but as an adult, he just lacks good judgment. And he fails to see how his actions affect others."

"Sounds like my brother. Only Trevor is lazy too."

"Are you in contact with him?"

"Not really." Evans shrugged. "I call him on his birthday. That's it."

Jackson abruptly shifted in his chair and grabbed a stack of mail. "Let's get through this."

It took an hour to scan the mail that had piled up after Gina went into a coma. One collection agency had been relentless in its attempt to contact her, sending fifteen letters in two years. Evans wondered if Gina had fully realized or remembered how much financial trouble she faced reentering the world. She hadn't seemed to.

The next box contained Gina's business documents: client orders, invoices, material costs, letters, and printed e-mails from happy customers. "I wonder if the Stahls still have Gina's old computer," Evans said. "I didn't even think to ask about it."

"Call them tomorrow. If they do, it's worth checking out."

After a few minutes, Jackson said, "Here's a letter from the Compassion Center, thanking Gina for her volunteer work. Did you know she had connections to a marijuana clinic?"

"I did. She dated a guy who worked there. I talked to him and decided it was a dead end."

"Maybe we should revisit that."

"I will." Evans was skeptical, but she didn't have any better ideas.

After another hour, they concluded that Gina's business papers held nothing of interest. Evans stood. "I'm taking a lap around the halls to stretch my legs. Coming with me?"

"Sure."

As they walked the empty halls elbow to elbow, Evans was reminded of indoor gym at her grade school during dark Alaska winters. She glanced at Jackson and picked up her pace. He matched her speed, stride for stride. They rounded a corner and Jackson cut ahead. Evans laughed and ran to pass him. Jackson matched her pace and mockingly elbowed his way in front of her. Soon, they were running and laughing and pushing each other. They reached the conference room door and both tried to step through at the same time. Their bodies mashed together, and electric pleasure jolted through Evans' pelvis. She pivoted toward Jackson, hoping he would kiss her. He reached a hand up to the bruise on her face, then leaned in.

Footsteps sounded in the hall, and they jerked apart. A voice boomed, "What the hell is going on? You're not allowed to have fun in this building." John Bohnert, a vice detective, laughed at the startled looks on their faces. "Just giving you shit. Are you working the shooting?"

"We are," Jackson said. "We just took a break from staring at old paperwork." He nodded at Evans. "Let's get back to it."

Jackson grabbed the third box and dumped it on the table. They dug into the pile without speaking. Evans wanted to say something about their moment, but knew she shouldn't. They worked in mostly silence, occasionally showing each other a document.

After scanning personal letters, Christmas cards, and to-do lists, Evans picked up a handwritten letter that caught her attention. Sentences had been marked through and rewritten as though it were practice. The salutation was also crossed out. The letter said: *I've known who you are for years but I've never wanted to contact you. I'm writing now because I need your help. My health has been poor and I've run up a lot of medical bills. I was also unable to work for a while. If you could loan me $20,000, I would be deeply grateful and keep your secret forever.*

"Holy shit," Evans said. "Look at this. I think we have a very polite blackmail letter."

CHAPTER 24

Thursday, September 9, 5:20 a.m.

Jackson's cell phone jolted him awake. He fumbled in the dark until he found the beeping nuisance on the nightstand and held it to his face. "Hello."

"This is Bobbie at the front desk. A state trooper just brought in Ray Durkin, and he thought you'd like to know. He picked him up in a motel in La Grande."

"Put Durkin in an interrogation room. I'll be there in twenty." Jackson closed the phone and thought it might be closer to thirty minutes. He'd gone to sleep around two that morning. He staggered into the bathroom and took a quick shower, then splashed cold water on his face until his brain started to work.

Jackson arrived at the department twenty-seven minutes later, carrying a cup of coffee he'd bought on the way. He'd been thinking about his flirtatious moment with Evans the night before.

Nothing had happened, and he had no reason to feel guilty. Yet he did. He also blamed the Provigil. Yet he knew that was bullshit. It didn't mean anything, he told himself. He loved Kera deeply, and that hadn't changed.

Daylight was peeking over the horizon as he pulled in. He pounded up the steps from the parking garage and felt an old familiar pain in his gut. *Damn*. He'd forgotten to take his prednisone. He headed for the front desk where Bobbie McCann sat behind the plexiglass.

"Good morning, sunshine." The desk officer gave him a playful smile.

"If you say so." Jackson returned her smile and took the paperwork she held out.

"He's in the deluxe suite."

"Thanks."

He backtracked to the larger of the two interrogation rooms. By larger, he meant a foot or so. Ray Durkin was dressed the same as yesterday: khaki shorts, a blue T-shirt, and sandals. If not for the handcuffs, he would have looked like a tanned man on vacation. Jackson pressed the video to start recording and sat across from Durkin.

"That coffee smells good," the suspect said. "I'd sure like some after spending the night in the back of a cop car."

"We'll see how it goes. Please state your name for the recorder."

"Raymond Durkin."

Jackson identified himself and the date, then said, "Let's start with a DNA swab. Here's the subpoena if you'd like to look it over." Jackson pulled the paper from his file and slid it across the table. While Durkin pretended to read the court order, Jackson dug in his shoulder bag for the swab kit. He stood and stepped around the table. "Open wide."

Durkin hesitated, then gave a little shrug. He opened his mouth, revealing thousands of dollars worth of dental work.

Jackson ran the swab along the inside of his cheek, then bagged and labeled the saliva sample. He left it sitting on the table as a visual reminder to Durkin.

"I told you I was coming back for a DNA sample, and you hit the road, so we both know you're guilty of something."

Durkin started to interrupt, but Jackson kept talking. "If that saliva matches the hair follicle found at the homicides of Clark and Evelyn Jackson, you'll likely get the death penalty. It's in your best interest to tell me what happened and see if we can work a plea deal."

Durkin's tan seemed to fade a little. "I had a family emergency. My sister called and asked me to come out to her place near Baker City. There's where I was headed."

"What was the emergency?"

"Her husband had left her, and she needed help on the farm. Things needed repair, and she didn't have the money to pay someone." Durkin stared straight at him.

Jackson knew it was not the whole truth. "What's your sister's name and phone number?"

"Sue Jacobs. I have her number in my cell phone, which the sheriff confiscated and put into a plastic bag." Durkin nodded at his cuffed hands. "Will you uncuff me, please?"

Jackson decided to go ahead and let Durkin relax. As he uncuffed him, he said, "I expect your sister to lie for you, so you'll have to do better that that."

"Ask her about the dogs," Durkin said. "I had them with me at the motel. The manager had to call her to come get them."

"That doesn't prove anything." Jackson sat back down. "Let's talk about the day of the murders." He forced himself to express empathy with Durkin's situation at the time. "The victims were killed with Clark Jackson's gun, so I know you didn't bring the murder weapon into the house. I'm thinking you didn't mean to kill them. Tell me what happened."

After a long pause, Durkin said, "I wasn't there the day of the murders, I swear."

Jackson heard what he didn't say. "But you admit you were in the house at some point?" He suspected Durkin was afraid they'd match his DNA to the evidence at the scene.

"I went there the day before. I was looking for Derrick, and your mother invited me in to wait. Derrick was in the shower or something." Durkin's voice rose in pitch. "So yes, I was in the house. If my DNA matches, that's why."

Durkin was a lying sack of shit. "Did you interact with Evelyn Jackson?"

"What do you mean?"

"Tell me exactly what happened. Did she take your coat or bring you a glass of water?" The blond hair had been found on his mother's sweater, which would have required proximity. Jackson visualized Durkin grabbing his mother's arm and pulling her close to threaten her. His heart hammered and he worried Durkin would hear it.

"She said I could wait in the living room. I followed her and sat on the couch for a few minutes. Then Derrick and I went outside to talk. Then I left. That's it."

"What time did you arrive?"

"I'm not sure. It was over ten years ago."

"You seem to remember other details. Was it morning or afternoon?"

"Afternoon."

Jackson had a little surge of optimism. Durkin was coming around. "What day of the week were you there?"

"I don't know. But your dad wasn't home, so I think it was a weekday."

Now the suspect had stepped back from the truth. Jackson braced himself to be in the windowless closet for as long as it took. He sipped his coffee.

"Could I have some coffee? Or even a glass of water?" Durkin's voice had an edge of whining.

Jackson started to tell him no, then remembered how Hector Vargas had been treated. He stood. "I'll be back in a minute."

After another hour with Durkin, Jackson had made no progress. The suspect vehemently denied any part in the murders and showed no obvious signs of lying. Yet he was an ex-con who'd spent years in prison. Lying came naturally to him. And like all good liars, he blended the truth with fabrication so seamlessly, it was nearly impossible to pick them apart.

Jackson's stomach growled, he was out of coffee, and the small room had long ago closed in on him. He couldn't justify charging Durkin with a crime, so he had no choice but to let him go. Tempting as it was to leave him in the interrogation room and try again in a few hours, Jackson couldn't do it. Vargas' story had wormed its way into his brain, making him question his own tactics. He was not happy about it.

"I'm going to release you, but I don't want you to leave the county." Jackson stood, relieved to stretch his legs. "I'll have the DNA results in a couple of days and I'll come looking for you. Meanwhile, you'll stay on the watch list. If you get on the road again, a state trooper will be right behind you."

"I have to go get my dogs." Durkin sounded near panic.

Jackson rolled his eyes. "I'll give you twenty-four hours. Check in with me in person tomorrow morning. If I don't see you, I'll put out an arrest warrant."

He escorted Durkin out of the building, then went out in search of breakfast.

* * *

Evans woke before the alarm went off at six, brewed a tall cup of coffee, and called the jail. "This is Detective Evans. When is Gary Bekker scheduled for arraignment?"

"Nine o'clock this morning."

"I'd like to attend and make a statement."

"I'll put you on the list."

Relieved that she had a little time, Evans turned on her computer and scanned the news sites. She was itching to call Gina's parents and ask about the strange letter, but it would not be welcome news and the Stahls were already distressed. She'd wait until eight, then call.

Quickly bored with the news, Evans checked her e-mail. Still nothing from Mason. To hell with him. Evans thought about the delicious moment she'd had with Jackson the night before. Would he have kissed her if not for the interruption? Then what? Would the kiss have led somewhere or simply made their relationship awkward? Her best guess was that it would have ruined their working partnership. Evans vowed to find a new boyfriend and let go of her feelings for Jackson. He kept telling her she needed to date someone in law enforcement. Ben Stricklyn popped into her mind. The IA detective was gorgeous and sexy, and she was certain he'd felt the chemistry too. Should she call him?

Evans jumped up and went to change into workout clothes. Thinking about sex this early in the morning was dangerous. She'd end up doing something stupid before noon. Instead, she would crank up the music and kickbox until she could focus on work.

Evans pulled into the parking lot at the jail and stared up at the redbrick building with the bars across the windows. She dreaded going in. Her incarceration had been brief and long ago, but she still hated to be inside any lockup facility.

She walked away from the Geezer, hating to leave it near the jail. Due to constant overcrowding, any moment the jail would release its daily flood of drug addicts, assholes, and thieves. They would all pass by her car. Some would recognize the Impala as a cop car and might consider it a challenge. She hoped the arraignment wouldn't take long.

The small courtroom inside the jail had room for only a few spectators. Most of the space was taken up with the judge's desk, the court recorder, and a group of inmates who all waited for their five minutes of judicial process. A man in a business suit sat behind the cuffed men in forest-green scrubs. Evans thought he looked too sharp to be a court-appointed lawyer.

She was happy to see Judge Cranston come into the courtroom and plop his skinny butt into the swivel chair. He was a no-nonsense guy and would not be swayed by Bekker's twenty years on the force.

Evans grew impatient waiting for the clerk to announce Bekker's name. She'd called the Stahls before leaving the house and they hadn't answered. Her plan was to drive straight over as soon as she left the arraignment. Finally, the clerk called "Gary Bekker," and he walked up to stand in front of the bench. The judge read the charges Jackson had listed: attempted homicide, assault, sexual coercion, rape, and obstruction of justice. Evans couldn't see Bekker's face, but he shifted his feet and looked at the floor.

"You already have a pending charge of assaulting a police officer." Cranston peered over his glasses. "I can see no reason to grant bail."

The man in the suit sprang to his feet. "Your honor, Sergeant Gary Bekker has served this community for twenty-three years as an officer of the law. He has no criminal record. He was released on bail yesterday, and they've arrested him again on trumped-up charges. Someone in the department has a personal vendetta against him. It would be a travesty to keep this man in jail until he can clear himself at trial."

This was what Evans had feared. She stood and spoke in a loud, clear voice. "Your Honor, Gary Bekker is a violent and unpredictable sociopath. He attacked me without provocation. He assaulted a suspect in his custody. I've heard the personal testimony of the women he coerced and raped. If you release him, he'll have an opportunity to intimidate his victims even further, until they're too terrified to testify against him. I strongly recommend he stay in custody."

"And who are you?"

Disappointed that the judge didn't remember her and embarrassed that she hadn't identified herself, Evans stated her name and rank.

"Sergeant Gary Bekker assaulted you?"

"Yes, Your Honor. He struck me in the head with his baton and smashed my head into my car." Evans touched her bruised face. "He also said he'd kill me if I didn't stop investigating his criminal activities."

Judge Cranston cast a disparaging look at Bekker, closed his folder with a decisive snap, and started to speak.

Bekker's lawyer cut him off. "Your Honor, my client has already posted bail, and you know what it's like in lockup for law-enforcement officers. His life could be in danger. He's innocent of these charges. He was only defending himself against Detective Evans, who has a vendetta against him. That's why she's here." The sleazebag had the nerve to glance back at her. "In addition, Sergeant Bekker has a handicapped child to care for. I strongly recommend that he be released on his current bond, but under house arrest with an ankle monitor."

The judge took a moment to rethink his decision. "That sounds reasonable. House arrest with a monitored release is granted, and a preliminary hearing is set for October twenty-fifth."

Evans bit her tongue and bolted from the room.

CHAPTER 25

Thursday, September 9, 6:00 a.m.

Sophie woke to warm breath on her neck and the sound of a rushing river outside her window. She took a moment to enjoy the sensual beauty of both before crawling out of bed. Jasmine Parker, a lean and luscious crime-scene technician, slept soundly next to her. Sophie was surprised and pleased Jasmine had called late yesterday and suggested they get together. They'd dated for a while earlier that spring, then drifted apart when Jasmine got overwhelmed at work. Over the summer, Sophie had briefly dated a young college professor named Mark, but soon remembered why she'd given up on men. They could be great sexual partners, but emotionally they always held back. Jasmine, on the other hand, was both brilliant and giving. Sophie loved the way her mind constantly analyzed everything. She was also an uninhibited lover. No one who knew Jasmine casually would ever guess that about her. Her coworkers also had no idea she was gay.

Sophie headed for the shower, hoping the noise would wake Jasmine. They both had to be at work by eight, and Jasmine might want to stop at home first.

While driving on Beltline to work, Sophie turned on the radio to listen to the news. The announcer mentioned a shooting in West Eugene and Sophie cranked up the volume. She heard the newsman say, "Gina Stahl had been in a coma for two years. Last Sunday, she came out of her coma and claimed someone had attacked and drugged her. Yesterday, as she arrived home to start her life over, she was gunned down by a masked man."

Sophie's heart missed a beat, and her hands shook on the wheel. *Gina was dead? How?* Gary Bekker had been arrested. What the hell had happened? And why hadn't she heard about it? Sophie longed for a place to pull off the road, but she was on the freeway and had to keep driving.

She took the Coburg Road exit and gratefully came to a stop at the light. Gina was dead. Her mind didn't want to accept it. She had spent almost two hours with Gina yesterday. They'd talked about everything, including Gina's clothing-design business and the story Sophie would write to help her get it up and running again. Gina had said Detective Evans would be there to escort her home. Why hadn't the cop protected her?

Someone honked, and Sophie jerked her attention back to driving. She eased through the intersection and wondered: Did Bekker learn Gina was out of her coma from reading her story? Was it her fault Gina was dead?

Feeling rattled, Sophie drove the last mile to work on autopilot. She needed to call Detective Evans and find out what had happened. This was still her story, and she had to write a follow-up, even if it was difficult for her.

Sophie called Evans from the newspaper's parking lot and left a message. She hurried into the building, feeling strangely guilty, but also frustrated. She decided to get Jackson's research project over with, so she could focus on the new murder story. Jackson had called her a few times and she'd planned to stay late the day before and search the microfiche for him. Then Jasmine had called and asked to meet for drinks, and Sophie had decided the task could wait for the morning. She and Jasmine had been so absorbed with each other that she'd missed the late night news, which had probably reported Gina's murder. *Damn!* She would have to make up for it by getting the full scoop.

A senior editor stopped her on the stairs. "I saw that the coma woman you wrote about was killed yesterday," she said. "Have you found out anything?"

"Not yet, but I will."

"Are you all right?"

"Once I get the details, I'll be fine."

Sophie regretted spending the evening with Jasmine instead of talking to Gary Bekker's victims. Now she had to do this favor for Jackson before digging farther into the backstory. She hurried to her desk and checked her e-mail. Nothing looked critical. She stopped at her editor's office, but he was out. Probably at another meeting about how to cut costs and keep the paper afloat.

Taking her cell phone and notepad, Sophie strode over to the area where they stored the microfiche. The file cabinets were filled with scanned, compressed newspaper stories that dated back nearly twenty years. Newspapers published before that were archived in a basement storage area. Sophie checked her notes for the dates Jackson had given her, then started pulling film for September 2000.

She took a seat at the monitor, fed in the first roll of film, and started scanning. After five minutes, Sophie wished she'd made a cup of tea to keep her company. Eugene was a midsize college town and its front-page news leaned toward crime, sports, and local businesses—except during election periods. In the year 2000, the Bush-Gore contest for the presidency had dominated the front-page news. What had Jackson said? *Look for something a middle-aged woman might react to emotionally.* A George W. Bush presidency would qualify, but Sophie theorized she was looking for something more personal, more specific. She scanned the first couple of pages of each city section as well, just to cover the bases.

She skipped over stories about the 2000 census and the wild-fires in the western states, looking for something more local. She found a news article about a couple in Springfield who'd won a $140 million lottery and a story about the arrest of a man who'd killed his wife and children and dumped their bodies in the ocean. The family had washed up near Newport. Everyone had reacted emotionally to that heinous crime. Next, a series of juicy political stories caught her attention and she sent the three news clippings to the printer. She was skeptical about their connection to Jackson's case, but he could read them and decide for himself.

Sophie spent another ten minutes scanning the last two days before September 23 and only came up with one other possibility for Jackson. A young local comedian had died of brain cancer after spending a year teaching middle-school students about comedy. She printed the story and went to the employee sink to make a cup of jasmine tea. She faxed the news stories to Jackson, e-mailed her boss to give him an update, then called Detective Evans about Gina's shooting.

* * *

Evans pushed out through the jail doors and sucked in a long breath of summer air. A group of scruffy young men loitering nearby stared as she strode past. Evans resisted the urge to give them the finger. She didn't need any more conflict. The judge's decision annoyed her, but she decided she could live with it. Technically, the monitor wouldn't keep Bekker from leaving his house, but if he did, a jail deputy would pick him up soon after.

She climbed in her car and checked her cell phone. The Stahls had not returned her call but she intended to see them anyway. It was pushy and unpleasant to barge in on people who had just experienced the violent death of a loved one, but it was also the nature of her job. She could only hope the bereaved parents would understand that she was trying to bring Gina's killer to justice.

As she drove west, Evans called Jackson. "Hey, I wanted to update you. I attended Bekker's arraignment this morning and asked the judge to deny bail. His scummy lawyer convinced Cranston to release him, but on house arrest with an ankle bracelet."

"At least we'll know exactly where Bekker is."

"That's assuming the jail deputies do their job and monitor him." Evans started to say more, then changed her mind. "I'm headed out to see Gina's parents to ask about the letter we found. Do you want to join me? I'll wait if you do."

"I think it's fine that you handle it. You've talked to them before, and they're probably comfortable with you."

"They *were* comfortable with me. That was before I let their daughter get killed."

"Stop blaming yourself."

Evans didn't think she would ever completely forgive herself for Gina's death. She made a left on Royal Avenue. "What have you got going this morning?"

"A state trooper brought in Ray Durkin, the suspect in my parents' case. I interrogated him but got nowhere. He admits to being in the house the day before the murders, but that's it."

"He must be worried he left some DNA. Smart move."

"I'm a little frustrated with this investigation. If Durkin's DNA doesn't match the crime-scene evidence, I'm at a dead end."

"Why don't you spend some time on it this morning? We'll meet this afternoon to brainstorm Gina's scenario. Maybe the crime lab will have something for us by then."

Jackson let out a small laugh. "Don't count on it. Call me if you learn anything significant."

The Stahls' minivan was in the driveway exactly where it had been the day before. The sage-green mobile home, the tidy yard, the quiet, childless neighborhood—it all looked the same as the first time Evans had visited. She would never have known a violent crime had recently been committed here…except for the huge bloodstain in the driveway.

Evans went around it and hurried to the front door. Sharon opened it before she could knock and silently motioned her to come in. Unlike yesterday, the woman's shoulders slumped, her hair was unbrushed, and she looked every day of her age. Evans thought Sharon might never recover her vivaciousness.

"I'm sorry to bother you, but I have something important to ask. It may help us find Gina's killer."

"Come sit at the table with us. We were having coffee."

In the kitchen, Sharon poured her a cup without asking, and they joined George at the table. He held a newspaper in his hands, but Evans suspected he wasn't processing much information.

"I'm sorry to barge in," Evans said to the old man. "And I'm sorry I didn't do a better job of protecting Gina." She started to say more, then heard Lammers' voice in her head, telling her to shut up. Admitting any kind of responsibility could lead to a lawsuit.

Evans pulled Gina's practice letter from her case file. "We found this in Gina's personal papers last night. First, I need to know if this is your daughter's handwriting. Second, I hope you can help me understand what it's about."

Evans set the wrinkled sheet of paper on the table, and Sharon reached for it, scowling over her glasses. As she read, her lips moved. Finally, Sharon said with trembling voice, "It's Gina's handwriting, but I have no idea what this means." She handed the letter to her husband, looked up at Evans, and fought back tears. "Who was Gina trying to borrow so much money from?"

"I hoped you could tell me."

George folded the letter. "I think I know who she wrote this to." He closed his eyes, as if to block out the pain. "Gina must have discovered who her biological mother was. That's what she meant by 'I've known who you are.'" He took his wife's hand. "I assume Gina didn't tell us because she didn't want to hurt us."

Evans cut in. "What are you saying? Was Gina adopted?"

"Yes." Sharon spoke, but they both nodded.

"And she knew it?" The information was so unexpected.

"We told her when she was ten years old. It seemed like the right age for understanding."

"Did she ever mention she was looking for her biological mother?"

"No. She always said she didn't want to know." Sharon burst into tears. "We didn't know she was in that much financial trouble. We would have helped her. She could have lived with us after her divorce."

Evans braced herself against the crying and plowed ahead. "The letter mentions keeping a secret in exchange for twenty thousand dollars. If Gina mailed a letter like this to her biological mother, the woman might have considered it a threat."

George looked up, startled. "You mean like blackmail?"

"Yes. This letter may be connected to both attacks on Gina."

A long silence followed, interrupted by sniffling sobs from Sharon. Evans couldn't believe Gina hadn't mentioned she was adopted. Had she deliberately kept it from her because of the blackmail attempt? Damn! How could she do her job without adequate information?

"We don't know if Gina followed through and mailed the letter," Sharon said, sucking in a huge breath. "She may have just been thinking about it."

"But if she did, I need to find out who her biological parents are. You have to help me."

"How?"

"Tell me about the adoption. Where did it take place?"

"Right here in Eugene," Sharon said. "The mother was a young girl who couldn't keep the baby. Our lawyer knew her parents."

"What's your lawyer's name?" Evans dug out her notepad.

"He died years ago. The adoption took place in 1965."

The date was crushing. How would she ever find the information? "I still need to know his name."

"Michael Walburg. He had his own law firm." Sharon kept speaking for the couple, but it was taking a toll as she struggled with grief.

Evans wrote down the lawyer's name and gave herself a moment to process. "How do you think Gina found the information? What would she do to track down her birth mother?"

"There are services that help people with these things," Sharon offered.

They had not come across anything in Gina's papers related to adoption or finding biological parents. "Does Gina have more boxes here I haven't looked through? This could be important."

"I don't think so." Sharon seemed uncertain.

George spoke up. "What about the person who shot her? It looked like a man. What are you doing to find him?"

"Everything we can." Evans sat down and forced herself to be patient. "I found a bullet casing in the driveway, and the lab will check to see if it matches other crimes. The shooter also dropped his ski mask on the bike path. The lab will extract any hair or skin cells and analyze the DNA. If the suspect is in the criminal database, they'll find the match."

"What if he's not there?"

"That's why we're looking for someone with a motive to kill Gina."

"What about the car he was driving?" George asked, still demanding answers. "Was there any evidence there?"

"It's been towed to the lab. We believe the suspect bought it just a few hours before showing up here. The man who sold it to him should be at the police department, working with a sketch artist." Evans cringed, hoping it was true. She'd forgotten to check in with Greer this morning. "When we have a sketch of the shooter, we'll put it on the news. Someone will identify him."

"What's your theory? How is the killer connected to this?" George picked up the blackmail letter and shook it. His anger surprised her.

"I don't know yet, but I'll find out." Evans projected more confidence than she felt. She wished Jackson had come with her. "Does the lawyer, Michael Walburg, have relatives or partners I could talk to?"

"I don't know." Sharon shook her head. "It was so long ago."

Evans stood, eager to get moving. "Will you help me by looking to see if Gina has more paperwork here? If she was looking for her birth parents, she should have some documents."

"Maybe her biological mother contacted her," George said quietly. "The search goes both ways."

"Maybe." Evans thought about what Gina had written. "The letter sounds like it was written to someone she'd never had contact with."

"We can look at the stuff we put in her room," George suggested to his wife. The old couple pushed themselves up from the table and moved toward the hall.

"We took some of Gina's things out of the boxes and set them up for her in the guest room," Sharon said. "We wanted to make her feel at home."

The pain in the mother's face made Evans ache to look at her. She stepped into the bedroom she'd grabbed boxes from the night before.

"There are some things stacked in the closet," George said. "Let's look at those."

One box held mixing bowls and old cooking pots, and another was filled with Christmas ornaments. "We stopped decorating for Christmas after Gina was hospitalized," Sharon murmured, as she held up a string of lights.

"I just remembered something," George said. "We threw out a bunch of Gina's papers after the cat peed in a box. We had to."

"Oh yeah, Stinky Boy." Sharon let out a sigh. "He was our last cat."

Evans, who had no use for cats, kept her comments to herself. They opened every box and every plastic tub in the room but found nothing with information. Discouraged, she asked, "Are you sure there's nothing you can tell me about the young mother? Or the lawyer who handled the adoption?"

Sharon tried to be helpful. "Mr. Walburg told us the young woman went to his church and her parents were very religious and didn't want her to keep the child."

"But you never knew the mother's name?"

"Oh no."

Evans accepted that she wasn't going to get anything else out of the visit. "I've got to get back to the department for a meeting. Please call me if you remember anything else."

She moved toward the door and Sharon followed, saying, "Gina's memorial service is on Saturday at ten at the Unitarian church. Will you come?"

"I will." Evans disliked funerals, but she wanted to pay her respects to Gina. Also, they were part of her job. Killers often attended their victims' funerals, so it was important to see who would show up. She said good-bye and left the house.

As she passed the bloodstain in the driveway, she wondered, *What secret could Gina's biological mother or father have been willing to kill for?*

CHAPTER 26

Thursday, September 9, 9:20 a.m.

Jackson tossed his pastry wrapper and started reading through his case notes. With food in his stomach and a second cup of coffee priming his bloodstream, he felt a little less weary. Still, working two cases at the same time was taking a toll, and his brain felt cluttered. He leaned his desk chair back, closed his eyes, and emptied his mind. It wasn't exactly meditation, but in some intangible way, the practice helped him prioritize information. Afterward, he would often make a connection he hadn't seen before. Sometimes, it just gave him a mental rest.

He drifted for about ten minutes, until he heard someone call his name. He quickly opened his eyes.

"What have you got on Gina Stahl's murder?" Lammers towered over him, arms crossed. "The media keeps calling our PR person, and she'd like to give a statement."

"She can tell the press we'll soon have a sketch drawing of the shooter. The man who sold him the van was supposed to come in this morning to work with the sketch artist." Jackson looked at his watch: 9:55. He wondered if Joel Greer had shown up. *Crap.* Why hadn't he remembered to call him?

"Excellent. What else have you got?" Lammers grabbed a chair from an empty nearby desk, pulled it over, and plopped down. A little tension left the room.

"We have a bullet casing from the shooting scene, and Evans found the perp's ski mask on the bike path."

"Tell me something I don't know."

"We dug through the victim's personal papers last night and found an old letter that looked like a possible blackmail threat."

"No shit? Who was blackmailing her?"

Jackson shook his head. "Gina wrote a letter asking to borrow twenty grand, but we don't know who the recipient was. Or if she ever sent such a letter. Evans is talking to Gina's parents now."

"Why aren't you with her?"

"A state trooper brought in a suspect in my parents' case. I had to question him."

Lammers stared at him for a long moment. "You need to focus on Gina's murder. The TV stations will be all over it tonight, and the public will want it solved. Make this case your priority. In fact, call in Schakowski to help. "

Jackson kept his face impassive, but his chest tightened. "You're the boss."

"I'm not asking you to give up your other case, just put it on a back burner for now."

"Okay."

"Let's get the sketch of this guy to the media as quickly as possible."

"I'll call Greer now."

Lammers shoved the chair back to its desk and strode off. Jackson reached for his phone, then realized he didn't have Joel Greer's number. Evans had been the one to contact the Explorer's owner. He realized this must be what it was like sometimes for his team members when they worked his cases. The difference was he was always the one who had to answer to the sergeant.

As he started to call Evans, his phone rang. "This is Officer Rice. I've been working with Joel Greer this morning to create a sketch of yesterday's shooter. Why don't you come see what we've got."

"I'll be right there."

Jackson hustled down the hall to a cubicle near the missing-persons office. Officer Rice, who looked like she could win a bodybuilding contest, sat next to a young man with a long braid and large hoops in his earlobes. He reeked of incense and wore a T-shirt that said *Live in the moment.* Jackson tried not to scowl.

"Detective Jackson, this is Joel Greer." Rice gestured at the young man. "He sold the Ford Explorer to your suspect."

They both nodded but didn't shake hands. "Thanks for coming in."

Rice held out a piece of white drawing paper. "It's the best I could do under the circumstances."

The suspect was older than most of the criminals Jackson dealt with, but still an attractive person with a narrow face and a strong chin. Rice had drawn him with sunglasses and a hat, because that's how Greer had seen him. Jackson's heart sank. Without the eyes or hair, there just wasn't enough to identify him.

He caught Greer's attention. "Do you feel confident this is a good likeness?"

The witness cocked his head. "There's something still not right about it."

Jackson visualized Bekker. "Are his cheeks fuller here?" He pointed to the area under the eyes.

"No. I think the mouth is wrong in this sketch, but I don't know how to fix it."

"Did you see his teeth? Jackson asked. "Anything noteworthy?"

Greer sat up a little straighter. "Now that you mention it, he had perfect teeth. Like someone with caps or dentures."

Officer Rice grabbed the sketch and erased the bottom half of the suspect's face. She was an artist and preferred to work by hand, rather than use software. She drew it again, this time with more fullness, especially around the mouth. Rice held the drawing for Greer to see. "This is how he looks with dentures."

"That's much better," Greer said.

Jackson smiled. "Good work. Thanks, both of you." He shook Greer's hand, feeling better about the young man. He turned to Officer Rice. "Can I take this?"

"Of course."

Jackson took the image to the department's spokesperson and media liaison. She made several copies for him to take with him, then said she would send the sketch to all three TV stations and the local paper.

When he arrived back at his desk, he discovered a stack of faxed newspaper clippings on his chair. The top one was dated September 2, 2000. Sophie had done the favor he'd asked and sent him significant stories from the weeks before his parents' murders. Jackson set them on his desk, started to read the top story, then pushed the stack off to the side. Lammers had instructed him to focus on Gina's shooting. His parents' case would have to wait.

He opened a Word document and began to key in his handwritten notes, starting with the evidence: *.38 copper bullet casing* *and ski mask (both at crime lab).* He checked his watch: 12:05. Probably too soon to call the lab and ask for anything. Next, he made notes about the vehicle used in the shooting: *1996 dark green Ford Explorer, purchased at noon the day of the shooting, from a resident on Clark Street.*

Was the location significant? When Evans had asked Greer if the buyer had called first, he said he hadn't advertised the vehicle in the paper, only put a sign in the window and parked it on the street. That meant the shooter had seen the vehicle for sale while passing by. Did he live in the neighborhood? A little hum of adrenaline thrummed in his spine. If someone recognized the man in the sketch and his address was nearby, that would be enough to get a subpoena for his DNA. Juries loved circumstantial evidence that added up and made their decision easier.

As Jackson finished keying in his notes, Evans strode up. "You should have come with me to the Stahls." Vibrating with excitement, she grabbed his shoulder. "Gina was adopted. I think the blackmail note was written to her biological parent."

Jackson tried to remember what the note said. "That seems like a leap."

Evans pulled up a chair the way Lammers had earlier, set her shoulder bag on it, and dug out Gina's practice letter. She shoved the paper at him. "Read it again, then let's meet in the conference room. I'll be right back." She headed off in the direction of the restroom.

Jackson reread the note. *I've known who you are for years but I've never contacted you. I'm writing now because I need your help. My health has been poor and I've run up a lot of medical bills. I was also unable to work for a while. If you could loan me $20,000, I would be deeply grateful and keep your secret forever.*

He tried to decipher the scratched-out salutation. It may have originally been two words. *Dear Mother?* Jackson pulled a magnifying glass from his drawer and looked more closely. The first letter in the second word was an *F*: *Dear Father?* The signature had been crossed out as well. He held the magnifier over it and decided it had once said *Your daughter, Gina.* Jackson now thought Evans' theory was probably correct. Gina had contacted her biological father for money. Had that been the trigger?

He ordered sandwiches from a nearby deli and headed for the conference room. On the way, he called Schak and left a message: "I'm working yesterday's shooting, and Lammers said to round up some help. If you've got time, check in with me. Evans and I are meeting now."

He set his file and notebook on the table, grateful for the new furnishings. Still, the conference room was too small for comfort and he couldn't wait to move into their new headquarters on Country Club Road. A year of remodeling had to take place first.

Evans hurried in behind him. "It's strange having a meeting with just us," she said. "Should I take the board?"

"Please do." Jackson slid into a chair, suddenly feeling bone tired after three nights of little sleep. "Lammers said to get help on the case, so I called Schak. I think we'll use him to put up pictures of the perp in the neighborhood where he bought the vehicle."

"You think someone might have seen him around?"

"I think he might live or work in the neighborhood. Greer said he didn't advertise the Explorer, so our shooter must have seen the *For Sale* sign while passing by."

"Good thinking. Clark is not exactly a main street." Evans drew a line down the middle of the five-foot dry-erase board. On one side, she wrote *2008 assault/overdose*, and on the other side she wrote *2010 shooting*.

"Do you think we have two perpetrators?"

"Not really, but we do have two assaults and two sets of evidence. I think it makes sense to keep them separate, even though it's the same victim." She looked at him for approval.

"Makes sense." He watched Evans list everything she knew about both assaults. She had a methodical mind, nice penmanship, and a great ass. He could do a lot worse for a partner. He noticed *camera footage* in the first column. "What film do you have?"

She turned to face him. "Gina's apartment complex had a security camera at the gate. I tracked down the footage and dropped it off with Joe."

"What's he looking for?"

"A red Chevy truck. That's what Bekker drives. Or a man in a ski mask."

"We need to get this sketch over to the lab right away." Jackson slid the oversize paper out of his folder.

Evans came around the table and stood next to him, scrutinizing the suspect's face. Her hip brushed against his arm, and Jackson lost his train of thought.

The desk officer knocked on the door and stepped in with two white bags. "You ordered sandwiches?" He set down their lunch, gave a mock salute, and turned to leave.

"Thanks," Jackson called after him. He grabbed a Diet Pepsi, popped the top, and took a long pull.

Evans kept studying the sketch. "How old would you say the perp is?"

"Fifty-five or so. Maybe older."

"It's kind of unusual, isn't it?"

"Somewhat. Remember the Waddling Bandit? He was in his sixties." Jackson pointed to the blackmail note. "I think Gina wrote this to her biological father. Look at the first letter." He handed Evans the magnifier, wishing she'd move one step away.

Evans looked at the salutation and closing line. "You're right. Shit." She tapped the magnifier in her palm. "So Gina tried to squeeze money out of her biological father by promising to keep his secret." Evans began to pace. "But what secret? The fact that he had a daughter no one knew about?"

"It must be bigger than that if he killed her over it." Jackson could not imagine anyone killing their own child for any reason.

"How did she find out his secret? When and how did she discover he was her father?" Evans paced in front of the board as she talked. "Gina's parents say she wasn't interested in knowing her biological parents. They said she never looked for her mother."

"She may have told them that to spare their feelings." Jackson gestured at the lunch bags. "Why don't you sit down and have a sandwich?"

Evans ignored him. "We have to find Gina's mother, the young woman who gave her up for adoption."

"What do you know about her?

Evans turned to the board and wrote, *Underage? Family knew lawyer, Michael Walburg.*

"Have you contacted the lawyer?" Jackson asked between bites.

"He's dead. The adoption took place in 1965."

"Who's dead?" Schak sauntered in, a little grin playing on his face.

"An old lawyer," Jackson said. "I'm glad you're here." He would tell him about putting up posters a little later.

"We've got a pool going on whether Bekker shot his ex-wife," Schak said. "I bet against the trend and said he didn't do it, so you'd better tell me you have a new suspect."

"We do." Jackson slid the sketch over as Schak sat down.

"Sweet deal." Schak snapped his fingers. "I'm long overdue for a win." He studied the image. "This nose and mouth looks kind of familiar, but the name isn't coming to me." Schak glanced at Evans. "Are you going to eat that sandwich?"

"I'll split it with you."

Jackson studied the sketch again and didn't get a feel for the man at all. He spent five minutes bringing Schak up to date while they ate their turkey on whole wheat.

"Boy, this dude really wanted her dead," Schak said. "What's the plan?"

"We're trying to figure out how to track down a private adoption from forty-six years ago."

"I'll contact the lawyer's family and see if they still have any of his paperwork," Evans offered.

"Are private adoptions registered with the state?" Schak asked. "Can we get a court order to look at old records?"

"Why don't you find out?" Jackson said. "That would be a great help."

"What's the lawyer's name and what was the year?" Schak made notes as Evans gave him the information.

Jackson's phone rang, and he looked at the ID: Jasmine Parker. "It's the lab." He clicked on the speaker button and set the cell on the table. "Parker. I'm in a meeting with Schak and Evans and I've got you on speakerphone."

"Can you hear me all right?" She came though well, despite the static.

"You're fine. What have you got for us?"

"I checked the trace evidence in the Jackson murders against the database. Still nothing. The perp has no fingerprints or DNA in the system."

"I appreciate that," Jackson said. "But I had to put that case on hold. Do you have anything on the shooting yesterday?"

"I do." They heard her shuffle some papers. "The ski mask had a hair clinging to the fabric. The hair is 3.2 centimeters long and gray at the base, fading to dark blond. The perpetrator uses artificial color on his hair. I said 'his' because the hair is more consistent with the texture and thickness of male hair than with female hair."

"Did either hair have a follicle? Did you get a DNA sample?"

"Yes. I sent it over to the lab this morning." Parker paused. "There's more. The structure of the hair I examined from the ski mask in the Gina Stahl murder seemed so familiar I thought I might have confused it with the trace evidence from the Jackson murders. But of course, I don't make mistakes like that. So I compared the two hair samples. The color has changed some, but the composition of the medulla and the pattern of the cuticle are the same."

"What exactly does that mean?" Jackson asked.

"They're from the same person."

CHAPTER 27

"Holy shit." Evans jumped up. "This means we have the same killer. Our cases are connected."

"How in the hell is that possible?" Jackson now had a sharp pain between his eyes. "The murders were nine years apart and had completely unrelated victims."

Parker said, "I'll let you figure that out," and hung up.

After a long silence, Evans said, "The victims have some kind of connection. We just have to find it. I think it must be related to the adoption and the identity of the biological father."

"What about the loan shark?" Schak offered. "Durkin had dealings with the Jackson family, and Gina was in financial trouble. Maybe she borrowed money from him too."

"It's possible," Jackson said, "But Durkin was on parole in 2008. I hate to point this out, but Bekker investigated my parents' case and is closely connected to Gina. He's still a possibility."

"Damn. I thought I was gonna win this bet." Schak stood. "Should I get going? I can start with a call to a friend over in the courthouse."

"I'll try to track down the adoption lawyer's files," Evans said. They both looked at Jackson.

"I'll drop off a copy of this sketch to Joe, then go home and finish reading my parents' personal mail, which has been sitting in a box all these years. I've been slowly going through it when I had time. Now it suddenly seems critical." He gathered up his things, needing to get out and be alone for a moment. "We'll meet back here at five unless someone catches a break before then. Keep me posted."

On the drive to the crime lab, Jackson's brain bounced from one thought to another, and none made sense. He kept coming back to the idea that his parents were strangers to him. They'd had a whole dimension to their lives he'd never known about. Something they were involved in, or someone they knew, had led to their deaths and he had no idea who or what. Was Ray Durkin still a suspect? Jackson debated whether he should bring Durkin in again and question him about Gina and his whereabouts yesterday afternoon. A surge of guilt twisted in his gut. If he had arrested Durkin yesterday, would Gina still be alive?

It occurred to Jackson that Derrick knew more than he was willing to admit. He waited for a break in the traffic on Sixth Avenue, then checked his earpiece and called Derrick. His brother didn't answer, and Jackson didn't bother leaving a message. He glanced at the time on his phone: 2:55. Katie was still in school and then she had drill-team practice until five thirty. He pressed the gas, thinking he had time to make a quick stop at the lab and get some work done at home before picking her up.

Jackson pulled through the security gate and drove to the lab's back parking lot. The overhead door on the big bay was open, and Joe was using a powerful hand vacuum on the front seat of the Explorer. Jackson parked and climbed out. "Hey, Joe. Are you finding anything?"

The technician backed out of the vehicle. "The door handle and the steering column have been wiped clean. We got a couple of decent prints off the inside door latch, but they didn't match anyone in the system." Joe brightened. "Still, if you find the guy, they could be one more piece of the puzzle."

"Any trace evidence? Or something personal left behind?"

Joe shook his head. "I would have told you already." He nodded at the paper in Jackson's hand. "Is that the perp?"

"It's a likeness of the guy who bought the vehicle used in the crime. With the hat and glasses, it's not a lot to work with." Jackson put the sketch in Joe's outstretched hand. "I understand you're looking at video footage of the security gate at Gina Stahl's old apartment. You might as well keep an eye out for our shooter."

"Emily is looking at the footage now. Let's take this up."

Joe stepped out of the bay and used a remote to close the overhead door. They headed for the exterior entry, then went inside the main building and up the stairs. The video-viewing equipment was in a ten-by-ten windowless room in the back of the building. A young woman with a long ponytail stared at a monitor. The footage was speeded up, so the occasional car appeared to be flying though.

Emily pressed Pause and looked up. "No red Chevy truck or man in a mask yet." She smiled at Jackson. "Hi again." He'd met her once at a crime scene but wouldn't have remembered her name if Joe hadn't said it.

"Hello, Emily." He handed her the sketch. "We have a new suspect. Have you seen anyone resembling this guy?"

"The hat and glasses make it hard to say." She attached the sketch to a holder that extended from her monitor. "I'll have to start at the beginning and watch for this face."

"I appreciate your help," Jackson said.

"No problem." Another dazzling grin.

Was she flirting with him?

"Anything else I should know or look for?"

An idea struck him. "Watch for a city-issued sedan."

Emily raised her penciled brows. "You think he's a cop?"

"Maybe. Either way, he might be driving a similar type car."

Jackson wanted to get moving. "Thanks again." He hurried from the small dark room, thinking he would go crazy if he had to sit in there all day like Emily did.

They walked toward Joe's office, and Jackson said, "What about the bullets? Anything significant?"

"Not really. They're .38 slugs consistent with those made by Smith and Wesson, but I still need a weapon to compare them to."

"Will you compare the slugs from yesterday's shooting to the Jackson homicides in 2000?"

"I already did. Jasmine reported her findings on the trace evidence, so I checked the slugs. The Jackson case had .22 caliber bullets. It's not the same gun, but we'll work late and look at everything else, side by side."

"Thanks, Joe. If you come up with anything, call me. I don't care how late it is. I'm sure I'll still be working too."

On the drive home, he called Kera, needing to hear her warm, supportive voice.

She picked up right away. "Hey, Jackson. I'm with Isaac, one of my veteran patients."

"Sorry. We can talk later."

"I have a minute and I can tell something is bothering you. What is it?"

Jackson hesitated. The case details were confidential, but Kera was the most trustworthy woman he'd ever known. "Gina Stahl, the woman who was shot yesterday? The same man killed my parents. The trace evidence proves it."

"That is bizarre. Any idea how they're connected?"

"Not yet." Jackson let out a soft laugh. "But I'm open to ideas."

"All the victims either had something the killer wanted or knew something he needed to keep quiet."

"You've got a good mind. I wish I could brainstorm with you." Jackson knew she had to get off the phone. "I know I don't have to say this, but that information is confidential."

"I know. When will I see you?"

"I don't know, sweetheart. I'll be working late tonight, for sure."

"Take care of yourself."

At home, Jackson brewed a small pot of coffee, knowing he might be up late again. He would rather take one of Evans' little narcolepsy pills, but that wasn't an option at the moment. He wished he were the kind of guy who could ask his doctor for the prescription, but that would never happen.

He brought the second box in from the garage and set it on the kitchen floor. He poured a cup of coffee, took off his jacket and weapon, and dumped half of the contents on the table.

A thick manila envelope caught his eye. Jackson opened it to discover a trove of black-and-white photos. He flipped through the images, sometimes recognizing relatives, but mostly he had no idea who the people were. Many shots were of his mother and her siblings when they were teenagers. The clothing and the cars indicated the pictures had been taken in the early sixties. *Could the killer be someone in these photos?* Their perp was an older man, so it was certainly possible.

Jackson shuffled through another stack, looking for a blond young man with a small nose and a strong chin. He came up with nothing and set all the snapshots aside. He started on a bundle of letters he quickly learned were from his grandmother to his mother while she was in college. His mother had saved letters from her youth and Derrick, in turn, had saved all his mother's correspondence. Jackson was glad he hadn't inherited the packrat gene.

He reached for another stack of letters and began to scan. Most were from his Aunt Irene to his mother. A few were from a cousin in California, also to his mother. He skimmed through news of weddings, babies, and new jobs. At the end of one letter from Irene, Jackson stopped and reread: *As to your question about whether you should contact both of them, I think you should. I don't know why you waited this long.* He checked the date: September 15, 2000. Eight days before the murders. *Contact who?* Had his mother followed this advice? Had contacting these people triggered his parents' death?

Jackson remembered Derrick saying his mother had been upset about something in the news right before the murders. *Damn!* He'd left the news stories Sophie had faxed him on his desk. Pain flared behind his eyeballs again. Jackson looked for some aspirin, attributing his headache to lack of sleep. He made a trip to the medicine cabinet and took prednisone as well.

Back in the living room, he opened drawers and searched the bookcase. Where in heck was his address book? After ten minutes, he found the booklet…with the family numbers he never contacted.

He called the listing for David and Irene Schultz. An older male voice answered.

"Uncle David? It's Wade Jackson, your nephew."

"Wade! You sounded just like your dad. About gave me a heart attack."

"Sorry. How are you?"

"Not bad for an old guy with a gimpy leg and a weak heart. What about you? What's on your mind?"

"It's a long story, but I'm looking into my parents' murders. I've been going through their papers that Derrick saved. I found a letter from Irene, and I wanted to ask her about something."

"I'm not sure how Irene can help you, but even if she could, she can't come to the phone."

"Is she okay?"

"Not really. Irene has congestive heart failure and she's fading fast. I'm going to be a widower soon." His uncle sounded resigned.

"I'm sorry to hear that. How long does she have?"

"Maybe a week."

"That soon? I didn't know she was sick."

"You haven't been in touch."

Guilt jabbed him in the chest with an angry finger, and he didn't know what to say. Everything sounded so lame. "It's not too late to come see her."

Jackson struggled to come up with a reasonable response. Something that didn't make him seem like an asshole. "Is she coherent? Would she even know I was there?"

"She sleeps a lot, but when she's awake she's lucid. Irene would love to see you and Katie."

"Let me talk to Katie and see what she has going on. Maybe we'll drive down this weekend."

"I understand." His uncle's voice judged him for not making a commitment.

Jackson hated himself for asking, but he had to. "About the letter Irene wrote to Evelyn. Can I read you a couple lines and see if you know what it means?"

"Sure."

Jackson grabbed the stationery and read the last line of Irene's letter. "Do you have any idea what it means?"

"None."

"Will you ask Irene for me and call back?"

"I'll try."

"Thanks, Uncle David. I'll call you soon and let you know our plans."

"Good to hear from you, Wade."

Jackson hung up and looked at his watch: 5:15. He had just enough time to pick up Katie.

On the trip to her school, he made up his mind. When Katie climbed in the car, he said, "How would you like to drive to Canyonville tonight and visit my aunt and uncle?"

CHAPTER 28

Thursday, September 9, 3:05 p.m.

Trying to find information about the lawyer Michael Walburg quickly tested Evans' patience. The name didn't come up in the citizen database, nor did a Google search produce anything. He had likely quit practicing law long before everyone had their own internet page, but she hoped to find his wife or family. Evans searched the internet yellow pages for just the name Walburg, thinking he might have a son who practiced law. No Walburg lawyers. On a whim, she keyed Walburg into a citizen directory and came up with Donald Walburg. She noted his Springfield address, but no phone number was listed.

Evans jogged down to the closet where they kept newspapers and old phone books for about ten years before tossing them in the recycling. It was meant as a pre-internet resource, but she wondered if anyone ever used it. Standing in the crowded ten-foot space, she flipped open a thick directory from 2000, but didn't find Michael Walburg listed among lawyers. Not having the patience to wade though ink-covered newspapers, Evans jogged back to her desk and called Sophie Speranza. Until meeting her the day before, Evans had considered media people to be mostly a liability. But Sophie's interest in making sure Bekker's victims had a voice and a lawyer had changed Evans' mind about the reporter. She also felt desperate to solve this one—for Gina, whom she had failed, and for Jackson, who needed closure. More than anything, she wanted to make Jackson happy and proud of her.

Relieved when Sophie answered the phone, Evans blurted out, "I need a favor."

"Is this Detective Evans?"

"Yes. I'm trying to track down a man named Michael Walburg. He's dead, but he used to have a law practice here in Eugene. I need to find his relatives."

"Is this connected to Gina Stahl's shooting yesterday?"

"Yes, but you can't print it yet."

"What can I print? You have to give me something in exchange."

"We have a break in the case. In fact, our PR person faxed the sketch of the suspect this afternoon."

"I saw the image and it will run with my story tomorrow, but it's not exclusive."

Evans hesitated. What could she give her? "You can't quote me personally, just say 'someone familiar with the case.' But here's the statement: we believe Gina's Stahl's murder is more complex than a domestic grudge."

"You're saying the ex-husband didn't do it?"

"That's all I can give you."

Sophie paused and Evans visualized her frantically scribbling notes. "Will you see what you can locate on Michael Walburg and his family? I need the info ASAP."

"Give me twenty minutes."

Evans stood, her energy near a bursting point. She rushed out of the violent-crimes area and walked briskly through the U-shaped hall. A memory of running in the halls with Jackson the night before made her smile, but she quickly suppressed it. She was missing something critical in these cases, and she hoped the cardio would stimulate her brain.

On her second loop, it hit her. *Bekker!* He had been married to Gina and might know who her biological parents were. Spouses usually shared stuff like that. Evans ran back to her desk. On the way, someone called out, "Lay off the coffee, would ya? You're making us all jumpy."

Evans kept moving. Had Bekker already been released? If so, she would find him at home. Evans thought he could still be at the jail. Even a straightforward release could take hours. A monitored release with a house arrest could take days to process, depending on how busy the jail was. She called and learned Bekker was still an inmate. She asked them to hold him until she got there. Evans grabbed her things and trotted down the stairs. On her way to her car, she changed her mind and decided to power walk over to the jail instead. It was only six blocks, and the exercise would help dissipate some energy.

Inside the facility, Evans took the stairs two at a time. On a Thursday afternoon, the waiting area at the jail reception was empty, save for an older woman trying to put cash on the books for her incarcerated loved one. Evans wanted to tell her to not waste her money, but resisted butting in.

When the woman walked away, Evans stepped up and introduced herself. "I need to see Gary Bekker."

"Weren't you here this morning?" The female deputy used a tone Evans couldn't quite figure.

"Yep. Now I'm here again. This is important."

"Our inmates have schedules. Showing up without calling first is highly disruptive."

Evans visualized slapping the fat bitch. The thought blew off just enough steam to keep her from shouting obscenities. "First, I did call just a few minutes ago. Second, homicide is highly disruptive, especially for the victims. Gary Bekker has information that could solve three murders. Let me see him."

The deputy gave her a hostile look, then keyed in Bekker's name. "He's in his cell, just waiting for his ankle bracelet. I'll bring him up to the interview room."

The deputy closed and locked the door behind Evans, leaving her alone with Bekker in the pale-green room. Her chest tightened and her heart skipped a beat. Not only was she locked in, but the last time she'd been alone with Bekker he'd smashed her head. Evans suppressed the urge to touch her still-tender scalp. Even though Bekker was cuffed, she wished like hell she had her weapon, which was inside a locker down the hall.

Show no fear! Evans sat across from Bekker, keeping her face deadpan.

"Detective Evans. You're looking good."

"Let's cut to the bone. I need some information about Gina. If you help me, the DA will drop the charges related to your ex-wife."

"You finally figured out I didn't do it, and now you want my help." Bekker chuckled. "The DA will drop those charges anyway, because there is no case. If you want to bargain, you'll have to do better."

Evans regretted her direct approach. She should have tried to con the information out of him. "I'm sure we can work something out. Do you know who Gina's biological parents are?"

"What are you talking about?"

"You knew Gina was adopted, correct?"

"It came up once. Why?"

"Did she mention knowing who her biological parents were?"

Bekker's eyes calculated his position and he smiled. "Are you willing to drop *your* case against me to find out?"

Evans had prepared for this moment, yet her heart hammered and blood rushed into her ears. She forced herself to keep from moving a single muscle in her body. After a long moment, she said, "No." She leaned forward an inch. "Are you willing to spend the rest of your life in prison, leaving your son to fend for himself, just to spite me?"

"You bitch!" Bekker lunged forward in his chair.

Evans leaped to her feet and shouted, "Help yourself, you jackass! Give me their names."

Bekker glanced at the door, and Evans realized he didn't have the information. He sat back. "Bring the DA in here with a written plea deal, and I'll tell you who they are."

Evans slammed the buzzer and waited for a deputy to open the door.

"Go fuck yourself," she said, walking out.

* * *

Sophie spent ten minutes perusing the newspaper archives for Michael Walburg, finally finding an obituary that listed his relatives. The news item also mentioned that Walburg had once been a lawyer. *How was an eighty-year-old (now dead) lawyer connected to Gina Stahl's murder?* Sophie wrote *call the Walburgs* on her list of things to do. First, she had to give the information to the police. She dug out the business card Evans had given her, then copied and pasted the relatives' names into an e-mail. After sending it, she called Detective Evans and left her a message, telling her to check for the information.

More complex than a domestic grudge.

What exactly did that mean? Gina had convinced Sophie her ex-husband tried to kill her, and Sophie had assumed Gary Bekker had been the shooter yesterday. Was he still the prime suspect? And if not, who was?

Sophie was torn. She still intended to interview the women Bekker had victimized, but her instincts told her it was a back-burner story. The shooting was front-page news, and she needed an eyewitness account. Sophie suspected Gina's parents had been with her when she died. Cringing at her own insensitivity, Sophie called the Stahls, feeling almost relieved when they didn't answer. Who else could she talk to about the shooting? The spokesperson at the police department had already given her a canned statement.

Sophie snapped her fingers. *Jasmine Parker.* Her lover sometimes provided little tidbits of crime information Sophie couldn't get anywhere else. No one knew they dated, and they liked to keep it that way.

She called Jasmine, who rang back moments later. "Hi, Sophie. I had a great time last night. Of course, I'm tired today, but you're worth it." Jasmine kept her voice low.

"Keep that in mind when I ask this favor, one I intend to pay for in the currency of your choice."

"You're wicked. What do you want?"

"I need to know about the complexities of Gina Stahl's murder. I have good information that says Gary Bekker didn't kill her."

Jasmine let out a startled noise. "How did you learn that?"

"Someone in the department told me."

"I want to know who."

"Give me something significant and I'll buy you dinner and tell you my source."

Jasmine hesitated. "I'll tell you something, but you can't print it yet.

"Fine."

Jasmine whispered, "Trace evidence links Gina Stahl's killer to murders in the past."

"A serial killer?" Sophie tried not to sound too eager.

"No. Just let it go for now. I think they'll break this case soon."

"Let me know if they do, so I can ask the right questions and get this story into print."

"Where are you taking me to dinner?"

"Your choice, lover. That was a very sweet scoop." She gave Jasmine a kiss through the phone and hung up. Her cube neighbor, an older guy who covered the finance beat, popped up and glared at her over the short cubicle wall. Sophie blew him a kiss too and got to work on her story.

CHAPTER 29

Thursday, September 9, 5:35 p.m.

"Are you serious?" Katie acted like he'd just asked her to shave her head.

"My aunt is dying, and she wants to see both of us. This is important."

"Just like that, we're supposed to drop everything and drive to Canyonville?" Katie shoved her backpack to the floor of the car. "I don't even know your aunt and uncle. I haven't seen them since they visited us way back, like when I was in the second grade."

Jackson put the car in gear and merged into the traffic leaving the school's parking lot. He wanted to give Katie a minute to process her fate. He also wanted to get moving so she couldn't bail out on him. "I know this is not what you had in mind for this evening, but please make the best of it. We'll buy our favorite snacks and bring some music we both like. A road trip with Dad."

"Can we take the GTO?"

"Of course."

"Okay, but I want Salsa Verde Doritos and Peanut Butter M&M's."

When they were on Amazon Parkway, Katie turned to him and asked. "How did you find out your aunt was dying?"

"I called and Uncle David told me." He knew where she was going with this, but he wouldn't lie to her.

"Why did you call them?"

"There's something in one of my mother's letters I want to ask Irene about."

"I knew it." Katie poked his shoulder. "This is work. You're investigating your parents' murders and need to question Irene about something."

"You got me." He reached over and tousled her hair. "Still, we're going to make a dying woman happy."

"You owe me."

"You can miss your first class tomorrow morning."

She rolled her eyes, pulled out her cell, and started texting.

He hoped she wouldn't spend the whole drive south in that mode, but he'd wait to mention it.

While Katie changed her clothes and got ready to leave, Jackson called Derrick again. His brother, as usual, didn't answer. Jackson left an impatient message: "Aunt Irene is dying, and Katie and I are driving down to see her tonight. You should come with us. Either way, call me. I have something important I want to talk about."

Katie came into the living room as he was hanging up. "You sound mad at your brother."

"He knows I'm investigating this case, yet he never answers his phone."

"Maybe it's hard for him to talk about your parents."

"Maybe. Are you ready?"

"As I'm ever gonna be."

Canyonville was ninety-five miles south on I-5. Forests bordered the highway for most of the route, so the drive was easy and beautiful. The sun had started to slide down the horizon, but they still had fading pink daylight for most of the trip.

Katie wanted to know what it had been like growing up with his parents, and Jackson was content to talk about it. He remembered his childhood as mostly happy, with a lot of time spent riding his bike with his friends and playing baseball with Derrick at the nearby ball fields. His mother had been loving, but not particularly talkative, and his father had been quick to laugh. The four of them had sat around the table, playing Monopoly, Uno, or Yahtzee on weekend nights. The only real conflict he recalled had been over homework and poor grades. He hadn't been a good student until junior high. Yet Jackson knew memory was selective, and he wondered if Derrick would have the same perceptions.

After an hour, Katie got bored with his stories and started texting her friends, so Jackson put on his new iPod Shuffle and listened to Led Zeppelin and Van Halen.

They arrived in Canyonville around seven thirty. Katie commented on the giant casino overshadowing the just-off-the-freeway town. Jackson mumbled something about tribal land and tried to remember the directions. He hadn't been to his aunt and uncle's home since he was in his early twenties, and he felt nervous about seeing them. He'd driven by on the freeway a few times over the years, but had never stopped.

His Uncle David came out on the porch and gave them both a long hug. His big belly pressed into Jackson, and the old man smelled of corned beef and beer. "Come in the house. Relax a bit. Would you like a brew?"

"No thanks." Jackson never drank around Katie. "I'll take a diet soda if you have one." He wasn't thirsty, just trying to be polite.

"I'll see what we've got." Uncle David went to the kitchen, while Jackson and Katie took a seat on the couch.

"This house smells weird," Katie whispered.

"I know." *It smells like sickness and death*, Jackson thought. "We won't stay long." He was already feeling jumpy. He told himself he was working a case, and that helped get him into a zone.

His uncle came into the room and handed them both a can of diet cream soda. "Irene is sleeping, but I'll see if I can wake her." He winked and left the room again.

Please let Irene be coherent enough to talk to me, Jackson pleaded with the universe. He wondered if he would have made the trip just as a family obligation. He was ashamed to admit he probably wouldn't have. Dragging Katie along had been selfish. He held her hand for moment. "I love you."

"I love you too." Her sweet face frowned. "Are you okay?"

"I'm fine."

Jackson barely recognized his aunt. Her skin was yellow and puffy from retaining water, and her hair had gone silver-white. She sat up against a stack of pillows, but it was obvious she hadn't left the bed in a long time.

"Little Wade," she called out in a weak voice.

Jackson willed himself forward and sat in one of the chairs his uncle had brought in. His daughter hung back.

"And Katie. You're so tall and pretty."

"Thanks." Katie slipped up next to Jackson's chair. "I remembered you liked peppermint patties when you visited us, so I brought some." Katie held out a small bag of the candies.

Irene took the bag and laughed out loud. "I haven't had these in years. My doctor made me quit sugar. I guess it doesn't matter now." She held out a blue-veined hand to Katie. "Thanks, sweetie."

Katie gave her a quick squeeze and stepped back. Jackson was proud of his daughter for making this effort.

After ten minutes of catching up on family news, Irene started to sound weary. Jackson turned to Katie. "Would you excuse us for a moment?"

"Of course." Katie was on the move before the words were out of her mouth.

Jackson didn't know what his aunt would say, but he wanted her to speak freely, and Katie's presence might have inhibited her. "Irene, I need to ask what you meant in a letter you sent my mother. The letter is dated a week before they were killed."

"David told me what you called about. I don't think your mother would want you to know."

"The man who went to jail is not the killer. I'm trying to find the real murderer and get justice for my parents after all these years."

"Evelyn swore me to secrecy."

Jackson grabbed his aunt's hand. "She's dead. And a murderer is going free. You have to tell me what you know," he pleaded.

Irene closed her eyes. After a moment, she said, "Your mother had written me a letter asking my advice. She wanted to know if I thought she should finally contact her daughter."

The words hit Jackson like a blow to the chest. "Her daughter?"

"Evelyn had a baby girl when she was eighteen. Our family lawyer arranged an adoption with a young married couple." Irene stopped to cough. She held a tissue to her mouth and spit. Jackson was too stunned to be bothered by it. Irene continued. "Evelyn didn't know the couple personally, but she insisted on knowing who they were. She also stipulated that the baby be named Gina."

Another shock wave pummeled him. Gina Stahl was his sister. She'd been murdered just like his parents had been. He'd never even met her. Evans had handled the case and he'd never spoken to his sister. A rush of emotions overwhelmed him. Loss, rage, confusion. It hurt to breathe.

Jackson stood and pulled in long gulps of air.

"Your mother was a good woman. She kept track of Gina but never contacted her." Irene struggled to speak, drawing in weak breaths between sentences. "She said if her daughter wanted to find her, she could. She left it up to Gina. Until that fateful year. I don't know what made her change her mind."

"Who is the father?" That was all that mattered now. Because as heinous as it seemed, he was likely the killer. He had murdered them all for his own selfish gain, whatever the hell it was.

"I don't know. Evelyn wouldn't tell me."

The news was too crushing to believe. "You can't protect your sister any longer. You're only protecting her killer. Tell me."

"I don't know." Irene tried to be forceful, but ended up with a coughing spasm.

"Who was she dating at the time?"

"No one. Our parents were very religious and strict. Neither of us dated until we left home. They kicked Evelyn out when they realized she was pregnant."

"Why wouldn't she tell you who the father was?" Jackson could hear the anguish in his voice and was powerless to control it.

"Evie was ashamed. She told me she'd been raped and that it was her own fault. That's why she never reported it."

"She was raped?" Jackson had to sit again. "How could that be her fault?"

"I don't know." A tear rolled down Irene's face.

He felt guilty for pressing the old woman so hard, but he couldn't stop. "Do you have any idea who the father could be?"

"I thought it might be someone where she worked."

"Where was that?"

"Emerson Oats, only it's not called that anymore."

Jackson had never heard of it. No surprise. His mother had worked there forty-six years earlier. It had probably gone out of business by now. "Is there anyone else who might know who the father is?"

Irene shook her head. "Your mother and I were best friends. She came to live with me after she was kicked out. If she didn't tell me, she didn't tell anyone."

Except possibly the father. Jackson had learned all he could from Irene. "Thank you for telling me. I know it wasn't easy."

"It feels good to get that off my chest. I wanted Evie to tell you boys long ago, but she said it had to wait until Gina was ready."

But his half-sister had never been ready to know her other family. She'd been raised by wonderful people and had never sought out her biological mother. Yet Evelyn had finally contacted her. Why?

CHAPTER 30

Friday, September 10, 5:30 a.m.

After another short night of sleep, Jackson woke from a bizarre dream in which his mother gave birth to twins and turned them over to him to raise. In the dream, he was twelve and Derrick was not around.

Shaking off the weird images and feelings, Jackson dragged himself out of bed and stood in the shower until his brain kicked in. He and Katie had arrived home from their trip south around one that morning. Katie had slept most of the way, and he'd kept the window wide open to help stay awake.

Still groggy, he grabbed the newspaper from the front porch, poured a cup of coffee, and sat at the table. More engrossed in the coffee than the paper, Jackson flipped mindlessly through the pages. He reached the city section and stared. A photo of the Stahls' home took up a good chunk of the page, while the sketch artist's image of the perpetrator was only three inches wide. The story that went with the photos had Sophie Speranza's byline.

Jackson skimmed through it, then stopped short when he read: *A police department official familiar with the two attacks on Stahl says her murder "is more complex than a domestic grudge." Another source says some of the evidence indicates the shooting could have links to crimes in the past.*

What the hell? Who was Sophie quoting? He didn't believe Schak or Evans would tell the reporter something so sensitive. *Crap.* This was exactly the kind of information they didn't want a suspect to know.

Pissed off and physically stiff from days of inactivity, Jackson went out for a run. He tried to focus on the details of the case, but his thoughts kept coming back to his mother and the secret she'd kept from him all these years. Had his father known about his wife's first child? How painful it must have been for her to give up her baby girl. Jackson was disappointed his mother had never told him about Gina, even after he became a parent. Yet he was proud of his mother for insisting she know who the adoptive parents were. He assumed she had kept track of Gina as she grew up to make sure she was in a good home, and she had been. He hadn't met the Stahls, but Evans had commented on how sweet they were and how they'd taken such good care of Gina while she was in a coma. Jackson was grateful his sister's life had been good…up to a point. He wished he'd had the chance to know her.

The warmth of the early morning sun made him take off his windbreaker as he turned up Twenty-Third Avenue. His legs felt heavy and sore from inactivity, and his lower abdomen ached. Jackson's mind came back around to the case. How could he figure out who Gina's father was? The rape and conception had occurred forty-six years ago. His only real hope was that someone would recognize the man in the sketch. He also had to keep an open mind. Gina's biological father might not be the killer. A whole other element to this case might surface yet.

After a few minutes, Jackson looked up to realize he was on Emerald Street and coming up on his parents' house. His subconscious had brought him here to confront Derrick.

He jogged up to the door and pounded loudly. Derrick would not appreciate the early wake-up, but he'd get over it. Jackson didn't have time to circle back here today. He pounded again, and Derrick yanked open the door.

"What the hell is your problem? It's not even seven yet." Derrick wore a bathrobe and had the puffy-eyed look of someone not yet awake.

"I know. I'm sorry. I was out running and decided to stop and ask you something. It's important."

Derrick groaned. "Of course it is. Come in so I can make coffee."

Jackson followed him into the house. "This won't take long." In the kitchen, Jackson blurted out, "Did you know Mom had a baby girl when she was eighteen and gave her up for adoption?"

Derrick turned slowly to face him. "How did you find out?"

Jealousy burned like a hot flame around his heart. "I went to see Aunt Irene, but that's not what's important here. When did you find out?"

"When I was nineteen."

"Why did Mom tell you and not me? I don't understand."

Derrick sighed. "Don't be upset, Wade. Mom didn't plan to tell me. I walked in on her crying one day. She was holding a picture of a baby, so I asked her about it. She tried to make up some cover story, but I knew her too well, and I finally got the truth out of her."

"Why didn't *you* tell me? We were still close then."

"Mom made me promise to never tell anyone."

Jackson was too hurt to think straight. His family had kept a secret from him his whole life. "Did she tell you the baby's name?"

Derrick pushed his coffee cup away. "Of course not."

"I think you just lied to me. Why?"

"I didn't, Wade. You're just worked up."

"Do you know who the father is?"

"No. She wouldn't tell me." Derrick's brow creased. "Why did you go see Aunt Irene? What's going on that this is coming up now?"

Under typical circumstances, Jackson wouldn't give details about a case he was working, but the victims were Derrick's family too and Sophie's news story this morning had already hinted at the connection. "Aunt Irene is dying, which is why I went to see her. I've also learned that the person who killed our parents likely killed our sister, Gina Stahl."

"Good god." Derrick looked stunned.

Jackson was still struggling with the idea that his mother had bonded with Derrick in a way that she'd never bonded with him. "I have to go." He bolted for the door.

"I got that job I interviewed for," Derrick called after him. Jackson turned, gave a silent thumbs-up and went out the front door.

Driving to the department, Jackson called Evans and Schak and asked them to meet him in the conference room at eight thirty. They had to stop wasting time looking for the adoption lawyer and start brainstorming Gina's biological father. First, he would find out which one of them had talked to Sophie Speranza.

Evans was already in the conference room when Jackson walked in. She looked bright-eyed and pretty in a turquoise jacket, and the abrasion near her hairline was healing quickly.

"Good morning. I have a major piece of information, but we'll wait for Schak."

"I'm glad you've got something, because the Walburgs were a dead end." Evans made a face. "The old man was in a nursing home when he died, and his files were tossed long before."

Jackson caught himself staring at Evans. Why was he suddenly noticing that she was pretty? Was it simply because they were spending more time together? He hoped that was all it amounted to. "Did you talk to Sophie Speranza yesterday?" he asked, wanting to get the unpleasantness out of the way.

"I did. I asked her to look for Michael Walburg in the newspaper archives."

"Did you tell her Gina's murder was more complex than a domestic grudge?" Jackson laid the newspaper on the table and pointed to the second phrase. "Or that the evidence indicated the crime had links to the past?"

Evans blanched. "I gave her that first piece about the complexity, but I did not mention crimes of the past."

Jackson scrutinized her face and saw no duplicity.

"I needed her help, so I gave Sophie a small vague quote. I thought it would be okay."

Jackson had never heard Evans sound chastised before. It made him feel guilty, which also pissed him off. "The second piece of information is more damaging than the one you offered, but you still should have cleared it with me."

"I'm sorry."

Schak burst in, jacket open and coffee in hand. "I know I'm not late, but you two always make me feel late. Do you ever sleep in? Or have a bad morning?"

"We just fake it better," Evans said, with a pained smile.

"I have to get this question out of the way," Jackson said, pointing to the newspaper. "Did you talk to Sophie Speranza?"

"Hell, no. Never have, never will."

"Then it had to be someone in the lab." Jackson still didn't understand who or why.

"Do you think it was Parker?" Schak looked skeptical.

"No. She's the last person I'd suspect. She's like a vault."

Schak plopped down and spilled a little coffee. Evans handed him a tissue but didn't make one of her amusing comments.

"I drove to Canyonville last night to see my mother's sister."

Both his partners snapped to attention.

Jackson continued, "I discovered my mother had a baby girl in 1965 that she gave up for adoption. She named her Gina."

"Gina's your sister?" Evans' mouth hung open.

"Presumably. Now we need to figure out who the father is." Jackson wanted to avoid as much personal discussion as possible.

"You know what?" Evans said. "Gina looks like you. I thought I recognized her the first time I saw her."

Jackson refused to be pulled in. "Gina was born in 1965. The first murders were committed in 2000."

"Nineteen sixty-five?" Schak interrupted, doing the math in his head. "The perp must be at least sixty. Probably older."

"Do you think the dates are important?" Evans asked.

"It's all we have to work with." He abruptly realized that wasn't true. Jackson bolted out of his chair. "I'll be right back."

He ran to his desk and looked for the stack of newspaper clippings Sophie had faxed him. He'd shoved them aside when Lammers made him put the case on hold. He found the stories in his file holder and hurried back to the conference room.

"What have you got?" Schak asked.

"Newspaper stories from September 2000. My mother was upset about something in the news right before her death. Something she didn't want to happen again."

He handed half of the clippings to Schak, then turned to Evans. "Let's get a timeline on the board, starting with Gina's birth and including all the crimes."

While Evans mapped out the events, he and Schak skimmed through the news of 2000. He set aside the Longo murders and the couple who'd won the lottery. Neither story seemed like it would have affected his mother personally, unless she'd known the people.

Jackson read through the next clipping, holding his breath. Roger Norquist, a candidate for the Senate, had been accused of rape. One of his young female staff members had claimed Norquist had sexually assaulted her after a staff party when they'd both been drinking. Norquist had held a news conference and, in return, accused the woman of being a political saboteur, a drug addict, and a liar. The district attorney had asked Lisa Caldwell to submit to a lie detector test and a urine analysis. She'd refused both, and the DA failed to file charges. Norquist claimed his political opponent had paid Caldwell to sabotage his campaign. Jackson remembered that Norquist had gone on to win and serve in the Senate, then lost his bid for reelection.

He looked up at the timeline, and a surge of adrenaline ran through his chest. "I think we've got him. My aunt said my mother was raped, but she never reported it." He stood, unable to stay in his chair. "In 2000, Roger Norquist was accused of rape during his campaign for the Senate. What if Norquist is the father? What if my mother saw this news story about the rape and contacted him?"

Schak added, "If she threatened to expose his earlier rape, it would have ruined his career."

"She must have contacted Gina then too," Evans speculated. "Maybe she told her everything."

"Why did Norquist wait nine years to go after Gina?" Schak was still trying to get caught up on the developments.

"Gina got into financial trouble and contacted him," Jackson theorized. "She offered to keep his secret in exchange for twenty thousand. By then, he was planning another run for the Senate and had even more to lose."

"Doesn't Norquist own Valley Fresh Bakery?" Evans asked.

Jackson spun toward her. "Did it used to be called Emerson Oats?"

"I don't know, but Valley Fresh is five blocks from where the shooter bought the Explorer."

"Emerson Oats is where my mother was working when she was raped, and someone from Valley Fresh called my parents the night before the murders." Jackson grabbed his notes and shoved them into his folder. "We need a subpoena for Norquist's DNA." Jackson started to tell Evans to go see the judge, then realized it wouldn't be fair to her. This was her case as much as it was his. "Schak, I need you to get the subpoena. Don't take no for an answer. Evans, we're going out to find this bastard."

CHAPTER 31

Norquist's home address proved difficult to locate. As a well-off businessman and an ex-senator, he apparently tried to maintain some privacy and wasn't in any of the databases Jackson had tried. Evans was at her desk phoning prominent locals who might have his address, so Jackson called his contact at the department of motor vehicles.

"Stacy, it's Jackson. I need an important favor."

"If I can." She sounded weary, a Friday morning at the DMV.

"I need everything you've got on Roger Norquist."

In a muffled voice, she whispered, "The ex-senator?"

"I wouldn't ask without good reason, and I need to find Norquist today."

"Give me ten minutes and I'll call you back. I have to get this hothead out of here first."

Jackson went to the break room for a Diet Pepsi while he waited. He wanted coffee, but the stuff the department provided was undrinkable. He bought a soda for Evans too and pulled up a chair at her desk when he saw she was still on the phone.

"I've got nothing." Evans said, after hanging up.

"We'll start with his office at Valley Fresh." Jackson was on his feet. "Stacy will call soon with his home address."

"Do you think Norquist saw the story in the paper this morning? It implied we had linked all his murders."

"I don't know. He's a politician. Probably."

"Should we split up and cover more ground, in case he's on the move?"

"I want us both there when we bring him in. He's likely to either attempt to blow us off, because he thinks he's untouchable, or he may run. Either way, we need a show of force."

* * *

Evans loved that Jackson wanted her as a backup. She'd expected him to send her for the subpoena and to bring Schak along for the takedown. He was treating her like a real partner even though she'd screwed up by giving the reporter too much information.

Jackson started for the stairs to the parking lot.

"Should we update Lammers?" she asked.

"We'll do it by phone." Jackson kept moving, so Evans followed.

In the car, his phone rang, so he put in his earpiece and took the call. Evans grabbed her notepad, hoping it was the DMV contact.

Jackson listened, then repeated the information for Evans to write down: *34680 Bloomberg Road, 2009 blue Lexus, 871 CTZ.*

"Thanks, Stacy. You're a godsend." Jackson hung up and started the car. He turned to her, grinned, and said, "You get to call Lammers and tell her we're picking up Roger Norquist for questioning and a cheek swab."

"You weasel." Evans was glad for the chance to make up for her error and damn happy she didn't have to tell the boss in person. She called Lammers and prayed she wouldn't pick up.

The sergeant did. "Where the hell is everyone this morning?" Lammers yelled. "And why do I have to find out in the newspaper about a break in this case?"

"We learned late yesterday afternoon that trace evidence links the Jackson murders to Gina Stahl's shooting. We think it's the same killer. We spent last night trying to find a connection."

"And? Did you find one?"

"Gina is Jackson's half-sister. We think her biological father killed Jackson's parents to protect himself from exposure as a rapist and the father of an illegitimate child."

"Oh, for fuck's sake. Break that down for me."

Jackson started the car and pulled into the street. Evans said, "I don't have time. We're on our way to pick up Roger Norquist. We think he's our man."

"The ex-senator who's gearing up to run again?"

Evans decided to lay it all out and see if it still made sense. "We believe he raped and impregnated Evelyn Jackson in 1965. He probably raped a campaign staffer in 2000, then killed Jackson's parents when they threatened to expose the earlier unreported rape. He tried to kill Gina in 2008 when she asked him for money in exchange for keeping his secret. He finished the job Wednesday after hearing she'd come out of her coma."

"Jesus. A full-blown sociopath. What can I do to help?"

"Put out an attempt-to-locate on Norquist. He's driving a 2009 blue Lexus, license plate 871 CTZ. Schak is working on the DNA subpoena."

"Good work, all of you. Tell Jackson too, and keep me posted." Lammers hung up.

Evans laughed and patted Jackson on the head. "Good work." Her moment of levity quickly disappeared as she mentally recounted Norquist's crimes. "Lammers just called Norquist a sociopath. I wonder how many other women he raped or assaulted over the years."

"How does he get away with it? Why didn't my mother report him?" Jackson's voice couldn't hide his anguish.

"It was 1965. He was her boss. She was probably afraid of him."

"She lived with that assault all these years."

"A lot of women live with degradation."

Jackson gave her a questioning look, but Evans held up her hand. "It doesn't matter now. We have a job to do."

Valley Fresh Bakery took up a huge tract of land near the corner of West First and Chambers. Evans had never set foot on the property or given it much thought until yesterday, when she'd noticed it on her way to find the owner of the Explorer. She'd known the Norquists owned it only because she followed politics and paid attention to where campaign money came from.

An office building had been added to the main factory, and they headed toward it. Inside, a middle-aged woman sat behind a large desk and two younger women had workspaces along the back wall. The three looked up, startled, as they entered.

Jackson nodded at her to take the lead, so Evans stepped up and showed her badge, something she rarely did. She wasn't in a mood for civility. "We're here to see Roger Norquist."

"He's not in today. He called this morning and canceled all his meetings."

Oh fuck. Evans visualized Norquist reading Sophie's story in the paper and wondering how much time he had before they came after him "Where would he go if he wanted to be alone for a while?"

The woman, clearly flustered, said, "I'm not sure. I'm his administrative assistant, not his wife."

"Where can we find his wife?"

"Most likely at home. She's not well." The administrator signaled for the younger women to carry on with their jobs. "We all have to get back to work."

Evans handed the woman her business card. "If you hear from him, call me immediately. We'd prefer you didn't tell him we were here."

As they walked outside, Evans muttered, "Fat fricking chance." Norquist's assistant was probably on the phone to him already.

"Let's head for his home and hope he's still packing," Jackson said.

CHAPTER 32

Norquist grabbed his large travel suitcase and stuffed it with jeans and pullovers. He might not need to wear a business suit again for a long time. Breathing deeply, he tried to slow his heart. His pulse had been racing since he'd seen the story in the paper this morning, and now he worried he'd have a heart attack. The news article indicated they had evidence linking the shooting with *crimes of the past*. That little phrase had scared the hell out of him.

A moment later, sitting across from him at the breakfast table, his wife had joked that the man in the sketch looked strangely like him. Norquist had laughed politely, left the table, and made two important calls. Plan B was now in motion.

He was leaving it all behind—his dream of another six years in the Senate, his boring job as CEO of his family's cereal company, and his rich but sickly wife. Giving up his political ambitions was the hardest, but thank god he had a little place on the beach near Cabo San Lucas. He'd bought it years ago when he'd had an affair with a congresswoman and they needed a place to be alone. He had money stashed in a bank in the Cayman Islands too. All he needed was a new ID, and in Mexico that would be easy.

Damn. He'd planned the shooting so meticulously, then he'd dropped the goddamn ski mask and didn't even realize it until he'd ridden too far down the path. He'd considered going back for it, but the risk had seemed too great.

Norquist grabbed his shaving kit, his favorite jewelry, and most of the cash in the bedroom safe. If he could go back in time and change the outcome of that fateful day at Evelyn's, he would. If only she'd taken the money and kept quiet. Causing Evie's death had nearly broken him, but he'd made up for it by doing a lot of good work with his time in office. Then out of nowhere, Gina Stahl had contacted him, claiming to be his daughter and looking for money. After a lot of thought and a little research, he'd decided to squelch that problem once and for all. But the damn woman hadn't died and he refused to let her derail his plan to return to the Senate. Now he had to let the dream go. Norquist shook his head. How fragile a person's fate could be.

* * *

Their suspect lived in a million-dollar home on the hill across from Lane Community College. The property didn't have much acreage, but the panoramic view was stunning. As Jackson and Evans walked up the cobblestone path, he said, "I expect this to be civil, but if it gets squirrelly, call for backup while I try to handle it."

Jackson pounded on the double front doors with the etched glass, thinking that criminals came in all tax brackets. Last month, he'd arrested a homeless man for killing an acquaintance over a shopping cart. Now he was about to arrest a millionaire for three murders rooted in lust, greed, and selfishness.

The woman who opened the door was heavyset, with gray hair pulled into a bun, and Jackson knew instinctively she was not the wife.

"We need to talk to Roger Norquist."

"He's not here." The woman started to close the door.

Jackson stuck his foot in to block it. "Then I'd like to see Mrs. Norquist. I'm Detective Jackson, Eugene Police, and this is Detective Evans."

"Wait here. I'll get her." The woman, likely a housekeeper, closed the door and walked away.

Five long minutes later, she came back and gestured for them to follow. The maid led them into a large corner office with tinted windows. An older woman sat in front of a computer, playing online chess. The oversize office chair dwarfed her frail body. Her gray hair was thinning and her cheekbones protruded in an unhealthy way. She spun her chair around as they came in. "Have a seat, detectives. I can give you a few minutes, then I have to get back to my chess game. I'm Theresa Norquist, by the way."

"Thank you for your time." Jackson masked his irritation as they sat on a small couch. "We need to ask your husband, Roger Norquist, some questions. Where is he?"

"What is this about?"

"We can't discuss it just yet, but your cooperation is essential."

Mrs. Norquist stared at Jackson, weighing her priorities. "Portland," she said finally. "He packed his suitcase a while ago and said he had to attend an unexpected meeting to raise campaign money."

"Where in Portland? Who is he meeting?"

"Can't this wait until he gets back?"

"No. We need the information now."

Theresa's emaciated face collapsed in grief. "I really don't know. He was vague and upset when he left. Roger has been acting so strangely lately. I think he's having an affair."

It's considerably worse than that, Jackson thought. "Where was he Wednesday afternoon?"

"He spent the morning at our bakery, then went to look at some rentals for his campaign office."

"You think he's driving to Portland now?"

"He probably flew." She let out a bitter laugh. "Roger is too impatient to drive that far."

Damn. Norquist could be on his way to the airport. Jackson started to speak, but Evans cut in.

"Are you sure he flew? It's pretty difficult to get a last-minute ticket out of Eugene these days."

"Oh, he doesn't fly commercial. Roger has his own plane. He bought it when he was a senator so he could commute back and forth without having to deal with the airlines."

"He's a pilot?"

"Yes. He flies me to Portland for my vitamin treatments too."

Evans spoke up again. "Do you have chronic pain?"

"I have fibromyalgia and lupus, so yes, I live with pain."

"Do you take Demerol for it?" Evans asked.

"Sometimes. Why?"

"It's one of the things we want to ask your husband about."

Jackson was anxious to get moving. "Did your husband say anything else this morning? Anything that seemed odd or ominous?"

Theresa looked alarmed. "What is this about?"

"How long ago did Mr. Norquist leave?"

"About twenty minutes."

"Where does he keep his plane?"

She hesitated. "You're starting to scare me, and I don't think I should tell you."

"This is important," Jackson nearly shouted.

"At the Creswell airport."

Jackson stood. "If you hear from your husband, please call me." He bolted from the room with Evans right behind.

Four minutes later they were on the freeway, barreling south. Jackson hit the siren only when he needed to move parallel drivers out of his way. In another five minutes, Hobby Field appeared on the left.

"I've lived in Eugene all my life and I've never been to this airport," Jackson said, as he changed lanes. "I don't see an exit."

"You have to take the Creswell exit, then turn on Cloverdale."

"You've been to Hobby Field?"

"I go skydiving sometimes," Evans said, not looking at him.

"That's a little crazy."

"That's why I've never told you."

As they approached the long row of metal buildings, Jackson slowed down. The runway off to the right extended beyond the hangars, but only another five hundred yards. "This is not much of an airport."

"That's why it's called Hobby Field." Evans gestured toward the runway. "Turn right on that little exit road. We'll drive right up to the hangars."

Jackson followed her direction. He didn't see a blue Lexus in the parking lot, but it could have been tucked in among the SUVs, sports cars, and trucks. Norquist was either in one of the hangars prepping his plane or in the air making his escape. Or somewhere else entirely and they were wasting their time.

He drove slowly past closed metal doors, grateful it was Friday and the airport was not hopping with weekend warriors. Farther down the tarmac, two people practiced skydiving moves between the building and the runway. In the distance, the roar of an engine caught his attention.

Jackson glanced over, but didn't see any planes on the runway. The third hangar's door was open, so Jackson stopped at the edge of the opening. "Let's check this one."

They climbed out and Jackson touched his Sig Sauer out of habit. He didn't want to draw the weapon unless it was necessary. This might not be Norquist's hangar, and he didn't want to frighten an innocent. Would Norquist be armed? He'd shot his daughter in broad daylight, so he was unpredictable and dangerous. A smart man would have tossed the weapon. A killer may have acquired another one.

As they moved toward the opening, he heard male voices. Jackson's pulse quickened and he drew his weapon, leaving it at his side. Evans followed his lead. At an angle, they crossed the threshold into the hangar. A silver-and-blue plane took up most of the space. Its engine rumbled, filling the air with exhaust. Jackson thought it looked like a Cessna, the kind with the wings near the top, but he was no expert. They moved past the nose of the plane, and the voices grew louder. Two men stood near the plane's open door, and the presence of the second man unnerved him. Jackson pulled his weapon up into firing position.

"Put your hands in the air," he called out. Out of the corner of his eye, he saw Evans raise her weapon too.

The men turned. Roger Norquist and Derrick faced him, both looking startled.

What the hell was his brother doing here? It took every ounce of control Jackson possessed to keep from crying out Derrick's name. "Hands up," he yelled again.

Derrick raised his arms. "Wade, I'm glad you're here."

Norquist was silent, unmoving. From his position twenty feet away, Jackson didn't see a weapon.

An engine roared to life in the hangar next to them. Momentarily startled, Jackson glanced over and back. In that instant, Norquist grabbed Derrick and yanked him in front of his body. Norquist locked one arm around Derrick's throat and the other held a gun to his head. A weapon Jackson hadn't seen.

"Back off or I'll kill him."

Nobody moved.

"It's over, Norquist," Jackson said, just loudly enough to be heard. "We have your DNA at both crime scenes. Put your weapon down and your hands in the air."

"I'm getting out of here, and if I have to take a hostage, I will." Norquist's voice sounded oddly familiar. "Put your guns down and back off."

Jackson had never been in a hostage situation before and he refused to let his brother's presence influence him. Norquist would not kill his hostage. If he did, he no longer had protection. Jackson kept his Sig Sauer aimed at the suspect.

Yet his big brother was in the way. If he lowered his weapon, would Norquist shoot him? Would he shoot Evans too? How else could this play out?

Jackson said to Evans in a low voice, "Keep your weapon on Norquist, no matter what."

She nodded.

Jackson raised his voice. "I'm going to put down my gun and you're going to let the hostage go. My partner will keep her weapon to make sure you don't kill us. After you've released the hostage, I suggest you surrender. If you want to make a run for it, that's your call."

Jackson slowly squatted to the ground. He set his Sig Sauer on the oily concrete and said a silent prayer. He stood and stepped forward. Evans followed, weapon still held straight out like she'd been trained. They'd been in a similar situation that spring and she'd handled it great for a rookie.

Norquist stepped toward the door of the plane, dragging Derrick with him. Jackson watched, empty-handed and feeling helpless.

Without taking his eyes off Evans' weapon, Norquist slammed his gun down on the back of Derrick's head. Letting go of his hostage, Norquist leaped into the plane's interior. Derrick fell toward the plane, his body half inside the door. Norquist shouted an obscenity and climbed into the pilot's chair.

Jackson recovered his weapon and instinctively ran toward Derrick. The plane lurched forward and his brother fell to the cement. Blood ran from a gash in his head. As Jackson reached Derrick and knelt next to him, the plane rolled out the opening of the hangar.

CHAPTER 33

Evans saw the hostage fall and Jackson run toward him. After a split second of indecision, she bolted after the plane. As she ran, it cleared the hangar and rolled across the tarmac toward the runway. In the open, she fired at the plane's small wheels, but it kept gaining momentum.

Evans pumped her arms and sprinted as if her life depended on it. The plane slowly picked up speed. Lungs burning, sensible shoes pounding, Evans gained ground. Norquist had heard her shots and kept looking over his shoulder. She knew he still had his weapon, but he couldn't shoot at her and pilot the plane at the same time.

Sucking wind yet bursting with adrenaline, Evans was soon parallel with the open door. She tried to form a plan but couldn't think and sprint at the same time. Without making a conscious decision, Evans threw herself through the open door, landing on her hands and knees in the cargo space. She recovered her bearings, crawled forward, and aimed her weapon at Norquist.

"Stop the plane! Don't make me shoot you."

Norquist jerked to face her. "Get out, goddamnit."

He eased the plane to the left and onto the runway. He gunned the engine and the Cessna picked up more speed.

Evans' heart pounded in her ears and the roar of the wind through the open door was deafening. "Stop this plane, you motherfucker, or I will shoot you." *Where was his weapon?*

They continued to pick up speed, and Evans started to panic. Would the fucker lift off with her in the back? Would he pull a crazy stunt and dump her out from five thousand feet? Her heart missed a beat thinking about it. She decided to shoot him in the leg.

Just as she pulled the trigger, Norquist jerked the steering column and the plane lurched to the left. Evans fell sideways as her weapon fired. Ears ringing from the blast, she struggled into a squatting position and took in the scenario. The plane had shot off the runway and was heading straight into an open field. Norquist slumped against the wall of the cockpit, blood running from his neck.

Oh fuck! Evans inched toward the controls. She needed to shut down the engine before they crashed into a farmhouse. Did the damn thing have an ignition? A kill switch? Evans scanned the dashboard, panic rising in her throat. Finally, she grabbed the throttle and pulled it toward her. The engine sputtered and a few moments later died.

The plane slowed, but was still bumping wildly over an uneven field. A large farmhouse loomed ahead. Did planes have brakes? She couldn't climb into the pilot's seat, because Norquist's body was in the way, so Evans crawled forward and pressed the brake with one hand, her weapon still in the other.

The plane rolled into a shallow drainage ditch and jerked to a stop. Evans' head slammed into the steering wheel as it did. The farmhouse was a hundred yards away. Fighting her emotional instinct, which told her to get the hell out, Evans reached for Norquist's wrist and held it for a moment. He still had a pulse.

She leaned over and examined his neck where the blood was coming from. The bullet had missed his main artery and had torn through his trachea. His blood loss was minor for a gunshot wound, yet his face was turning blue and he struggled to breathe. Evans recalled her paramedic training. His damaged windpipe wasn't letting enough air into his lungs. She needed to clear his airway. She reached two fingers down his trachea and felt a chunk of tissue. With a tentative grip on the blood-slick tissue, she tried to pull it free, but it didn't budge.

The sound of a car engine made her look up. Jackson was barreling toward them across the field, his cruiser bouncing with every dip in the grass. He was such a good man. Evans looked back at Norquist. Why should she even try to save the bastard? He'd killed Jackson's parents and his own daughter. He was a repeat rapist as well. The world was a better place without him.

Evans froze, undecided.

Jackson called out, "Are you okay?"

She turned as he climbed into the plane. "I'm fine. I accidentally shot Norquist in the neck. He's not bleeding much, but I think he needs a tracheotomy."

Jackson looked at her for a long moment but didn't say anything.

* * *

Norquist deserved to die, Jackson thought. *It was for the best. No trial. No lifelong prison expense for taxpayers.* It would just be over and he wouldn't have to think about him again. He surprised himself by saying, "Can you do a tracheotomy?"

"I think so." Evans met his eyes. "Are you sure?"

"Death is too good for him. Life in prison is a far worse punishment."

"You're right." Evans grabbed a rag from the floor of the plane and held it to Norquist's neck to stem the blood flow. "I've got a utility knife and a pen in my bag. It's in your car. Go grab them."

Jackson ran to the vehicle, grabbed Evans' carryall, and hustled back inside the plane. With Evans' direction, he located the little sliding blade in the pocket, then dug for a pen.

"Pull the guts out and hand me the hollow tube."

As Jackson dismantled the cheap, department-issue pen, Evans said, "Here goes."

She stuck the tip of the blade into the hollow of Norquist's throat and made a twisting motion. Blood oozed from the puncture. Evans turned to Jackson and held out her hand, like a doctor asking for the next instrument.

Jackson passed her the skeleton of the ink pen, and Evans pressed the makeshift straw into the small bloody hole. Norquist made a sucking sound as air entered his lungs. His chest began to move in a rhythmic pattern and color flowed into his face.

"You called for backup, right?" Evans asked.

"I think I hear the sirens."

"Will you watch this guy? I need to get out of this plane for a second."

Evans crawled past him and out the door. She let out a little squeal as she stood on the ground. Jackson took her place near Norquist and pressed his hand on the wound above his tracheotomy.

"You should let me die." Norquist's voice was whispery and weird because of the pen in his esophagus.

Jackson stared at the man who had destroyed his family. He had so many things he wanted to ask. First, he grabbed cuffs from his jacket pocket and secured his suspect's hands. "Why did you kill my parents?"

"You're Wade Jackson?"

"Yes. I need to know what happened." Jackson worried Norquist might not live. He needed to hear an admission of guilt.

"It was an accident. I went there to talk to Evelyn, to offer her money to keep quiet about our affair and our child."

Jackson wanted to hit him for calling the rape an *affair*. But he'd learned to let suspects talk and reveal their crimes from their own perspective. "What went wrong?"

"She got upset and came at me. Then your fool of a father charged in with his gun. I didn't even know he was home." Norquist's every word was a laborious effort. "I tried to take the gun away and calm him down. I accidentally shot him instead."

"What about my mother?"

"She wouldn't stop screaming."

"So you shot her in the head?"

"It just happened." Norquist closed his eyes. "I loved her, you know."

Jackson burned with hatred. "You raped her, you sick bastard. Don't call it love."

"It wasn't rape. She only felt that way because she was mad at me for a while. She was my lover."

"Don't say that, you pervert." A siren wailed near the airport and Jackson breathed a sigh of relief. "What was Derrick doing in the hangar? How do you know him?" Jackson had left his brother cuffed and semiconscious on the floor, not understanding his involvement with Norquist.

"He came to confront me," Norquist said. "He had just figured out who I was."

"What do you mean?"

"I'm Derrick's father."

CHAPTER 34

Saturday, September 11, 9:50 a.m.

Jackson and Derrick attended Gina's memorial service together. Both Katie and Kera had offered to come with him for support, but he'd declined. Evans was also there, but sat alone in the back. Sitting next to his brother at a funeral service kept pulling Jackson back to the days following their parents' deaths. His grief for his half-sister, whom he'd never known, mingled with grief for his parents and felt more intense than he'd anticipated. Gina's adoptive parents cried openly during the service, and Jackson struggled not to absorb their pain.

Afterward, he drove Derrick back to his house, riding in silence for the first part of the trip. Jackson had so much he wanted to ask and so much more he wanted to say. Knowing Derrick's biological father was a substandard human being had given Jackson a new patience with his brother.

"You must have been shocked to learn Norquist was your father," Jackson said finally. "How did you deduce that?"

"I wanted to help you solve the murders, so I was trying to figure out who Gina's biological father was. Then I remembered Mom had worked for Norquist's bakery when she was young. I googled Norquist, and when I stared at his picture and realized we had the same cobalt-blue eyes, I just knew." Derrick glanced at Jackson and shifted in his seat. "I'd always suspected Clark wasn't my father. I was so different from the two of you. I never measured up."

Jackson turned on Emerald Street. "I wish you had called me instead of tailing him and confronting him. You almost got killed."

"I'm sorry. I wanted to look him in the eyes and demand the truth. I was afraid I'd never get the chance again."

"Are you okay with knowing what he is?" Jackson knew he wouldn't be.

His brother let out a soft laugh. "Nobody wants to be related to a killer, but in some ways, it takes the pressure off. If you know what I mean."

"I think I do." Jackson struggled for the right words. "You're a good man, Derrick. Don't ever think otherwise."

"I'm going to try harder. I want your respect." Derrick was quiet for a moment. "What do you think will happen to Norquist?"

"He's already recanted everything he said to me, but we'll get a conviction. His DNA is connected to both crime scenes and they spotted him on the security video at Gina's old apartment."

"Will he get the death penalty?"

"It's hard to say. Do you plan to go see him once he's transferred to jail?"

"Hell, no. I hate the son of a bitch. The genetics mean nothing to me."

Jackson didn't tell Derrick what Norquist had said about their mother being a lover rather than a rape victim. It was possible she had been both, but he preferred not to think about the complexities of it.

He pulled into the driveway and they sat looking at the childhood home they'd shared. "We had a lot of good times here."

"We did." Derrick turned in his seat to face him. "I'm sorry I never paid you for your half of the equity. If you want to sell the house we can, but I have another idea."

"I'm listening."

"I got a job as a long-haul truck driver. I'll be on the road for weeks at a time and won't need this place for a while. You and Katie can move in here when your house sells. The mortgage is paid, and it's your turn to get some benefit."

Too surprised to respond, Jackson pondered the possible ramifications. Kera would be disappointed, but he suspected she already knew he wasn't ready to move in with her and Danette and the baby. This situation would likely be temporary, but it would buy him some time. "Thanks for the offer. It sure is tempting. I'll discuss it with Kera and Katie."

"I'll move Mom and Dad's boxes back out to the garage, but you can't throw them away."

Jackson patted his shoulder. "Never, brother."

* * *

Monday, September 13, 10:15 a.m.

The door to Lammers' office was open, so Evans walked in, feeling nervous. The boss had called her earlier and requested a meeting. Evans speculated about all the things she could be in trouble for—visiting Bekker at the jail, giving a reporter too much information, jumping into a taxiing airplane to apprehend a suspect, or maybe all of the above.

"Close the door and have a seat, Evans." Lammers didn't even look up from her paperwork.

Evans did as requested and braced herself. She bit her tongue to keep from blurting out apologies and making the situation worse.

"Do you know why you're here?"

"I may have made some mistakes on Gina Stahl's case, but I did my best."

"I wasn't aware you'd made mistakes." Lammers sounded amused. "Jackson tells me you ran an excellent investigation, and in reading your report, I'd have to add that you showed remarkable persistence and ingenuity."

"Thank you." Evans suppressed a yelp of joy. "I appreciate the opportunity you gave me."

Lammers held up the paperwork she'd been reading. "This is a recommendation that you be made a permanent member of the Violent Crimes Unit when your training is over."

Evans wanted to jump up and shout, *Hot damn!* Instead, she said, "Thank you, sergeant. You won't regret it."

Things were looking up all over. Ben Stricklyn, the gorgeous IA detective, had called her the night before and asked her out, and she'd accepted. *Why not?* If she was destined to have the hots for a man who carried a gun, it might as well be someone available.

As she left the office, Evans jumped in the air and gave a little kick.

* * *

Wednesday, September 15, 10:45 p.m.

Jackson was in bed at Kera's when his cell phone rang. He fumbled in the dark and found it on the floor. "Jackson here."

"This is Sergeant Lammers. We've had a homicide, and I need you at the scene."

He sat up and swung his legs to the floor. "What's the situation and where am I heading?" Kera woke and laid a gentle hand on his back.

"The Courtyard Apartments, 623 West Fourth, apartment five. A man has been stabbed, and his assailant claims it was self-defense. She called 911 and she's still in the apartment."

"Anything else I need to know?" Jackson stood and reached for his pants.

"A patrol officer is on the scene and he says the victim is wearing a monitoring ankle bracelet. I think it's Gary Bekker."

ABOUT THE AUTHOR

L.J. Sellers is a native of Eugene, Oregon, the setting of her thrillers. She's an award-winning journalist and bestselling novelist, as well as a cyclist, social networker, and thrill-seeking fanatic. A long-standing fan of police procedurals, she counts John Sandford, Michael Connelly, Ridley Pearson, and Lawrence Sanders among her favorites. Her own novels, featuring Detective Jackson, include *The Sex Club*, *Secrets to Die For*, *Thrilled to Death*, *Passions of the Dead*, *Dying for Justice*, *Liars, Cheaters & Thieves*, and *Rules of Crime*. In addition, she's penned three standalone thrillers: *The Baby Thief*, *The Gauntlet Assassin*, and *The Lethal Effect*. When not plotting crime, she's also been known to perform standup comedy and occasionally jump out of airplanes.

Printed in Germany
by Amazon Distribution
GmbH, Leipzig